Dreamchasers

Entrepreneurs from the South of the Vindhyas

Shobha Warrier

Vitasta

Let Knowledge Spread

Published by
Renu Kaul Verma
Vitasta Publishing Pvt Ltd
2/15 Ansari Road, Daryaganj
New Delhi - 110 002
info@vitastapublishing.com

ISBN 978-93-82711-61-2

First Edition 2017
3rd Reprint 2019
MRP ₹ 495

Cover and Layout: Vitasta Publishing Pvt Ltd
Photographs: Sreeram Selvaraj
Printed by Vits Press, New Delhi

Dedicated to the indefatigable human spirit!

Acknowledgements

Thanks to all the wonderful entrepreneurs who spoke to me about their amazing journeys.

Thanks to rediff.com, for giving me the opportunity to meet all these extraordinary people.

Thank you Renu, for being a supportive publisher.

Thank you Papri, for being my friend and the editor of the book.

Thank you Sreeram Selvaraj, for taking pictures for the book.

Thank you Prabhu, for your help in facilitating some of the interviews.

Thank you Saraswathi and Siddhu for going through the manuscript.

Finally, thank you, my dearest Som, for being my invisible guiding force from somewhere out there in the universe.

Foreword

Shobha Warrier is a great listener. She writes beautiful stories, especially 'people stories'.

I noticed it when she first interviewed me some twenty years back, while I was driving the development and adoption of Wireless in Local Loop (WLL) technology. We were in great difficulty at the time, and I spoke my heart out when I met her. What came out was a fascinating interview next week on Rediff.com. This interview was read all over the world, and a lot of people came to us with offers to help, appreciating our work and determination. It was a great confidence booster, and we were ready to fight yet again.

The feeling was no different when I began reading this book of hers, *Dreamchasers: Entrepreneurs from the South of the Vindhyas*. I expected heart-rending stories, and they are all such stories.

But I was in for a surprise. I had not expected such thoughtful assemblage of the stories, which can be so enriching an experience for anyone who wants to be an entrepreneur tomorrow. It stands out amongst the plethora of books on startups that appear today. It gives entrepreneurship a context and a new meaning.

The book is thoughtfully divided into three sections. The first is the 'Trendsetters'; stories of those who had started in the late 1970s and '80s when 'the words entrepreneur and startup were not in vogue.' There was no support system. Society was not yet ready to respect and encourage entrepreneurs. Most businesses were inherited. The License Raj limited opportunities and defined what could be done and what could not be. Business was not known to be very honest, and 'making money' had an evil tinge to it.

From such times, Shobha picks up some jewels from the south of the Vindhyas, and weaves their stories together—stories of Dilip Kapur, CK Ranganathan, Patricia Thomas, Arun Jain, Kalpathi S Suresh, Dr K Srinivasan and M Mahadevan. Most of them are men and women from modest beginnings, and several of them from small towns.

Many are from large families; for instance, Arun Jain, the ninth among ten children with poor health as a child. He learnt organisational skills by arranging the marriages of his five sisters.

Suresh was the brightest spark among all the children in their large joint family of 15-20 people.

Ranganathan was not good in academics and fared the worst amongst his siblings. But like Dilip Kapur, they all thought they would be able to change the world. Some of them, like Mahadevan, wanted to be rich and thought they could become rich by becoming businessmen. Their lessons in entrepreneurship started as children by 'binding books' and selling Bhel Puri (and making Rs 30 in a day). They started small and went up step by step; for instance Dilip Kapur was overjoyed to sell a leather bag for Rs 300 after he returned from the USA with a PhD in International Relations.

But they had their own struggles too. For example, Patricia started her kiosk when she was in her thirties and 'to her disappointment', on the first day, she could sell only one cup of coffee for just fifty paise!

And they had their share of embarrassment too; Mahadevan was told by his mother 'Are you mad? You are a teacher, and then you are going and cleaning tables?' But he was able to convince her that soon he would own a hotel, and so he did. One thing in common amongst them is that all of them were determined. They 'braved red tape, an unfriendly bureaucracy, and a complete lack of infrastructure to build their businesses up, and were successful only because of the passion they brought to their jobs.'

Unlike the businessmen of those days, they were a new generation of clean businessmen, paying taxes, working within the law. While this placed a considerable burden upon them at times, it gave them an advantage too; for instance, Ranganthan recollects, 'Do you know what the bank manager wrote on our loan application? He wrote—the applicant does not have any collateral to offer but there is something interesting about this Small Scale Industry [SSI] unit; unlike many others, his company pays income tax!'

There is a mistaken belief today that those who started their businesses in India in the eighties and succeeded were all from the IT industry. There is also a mistaken notion that only the IT industry in India, where there were no government controls, provided opportunities in entrepreneurship. There is a mistaken impression that it is only in this industry that people are honest and paid taxes. The stories in this Trendsetters section break these myths. Only one of the seven stories is from the software industry and one more is about training for the IT industry. Other stories are about successes in other fields. As Shobha puts it, 'their stories are inspirational and can be treated as study material for upcoming young entrepreneurs.'

The next section, titled 'The Next Wave' has stories of people who started at the turn of the century. The year 1991 had changed India and its industries. The turn of the century made entrepreneurship more acceptable and welcome. The stories in this section are of people who have not made it as big as those covered in Section 1. They are, however, equally fascinating. Perhaps the most successful among these is Phanindra Sama, who introduced e-services and e-commerce in India with redBus, India's largest online bus ticketing system.

Ajit Narayanan is perhaps the most innovative with Invention Labs. His giving voice (Awaz) to autistic children is a great example of technology doing social good. His more recent Free Speech has been the best-selling app on Apple platform. The story of Sarathbabu is the most fascinating. He was brought up by a mother who sold idlis in the mornings, before she went to the mid-day meal centre from where she was able to get food for Sarathbabu and his siblings. From such a background, he went to BITS Pilani and then to IIM Ahmedabad. His story tells us how even after the IIM degree, he had to sleep on a platform one night to get his first big order. From there, he went on to become the food-court king, employing a thousand people.

Mustafa is another person who came from a highly underprivileged background. He failed in the 6th standard but went on to join an REC and then IIM-B. Today, fresh idli and dosa batter made from his company, ID Fresh, reaches the homes of Bangalore, Chennai, Pune, Mumbai, Mysore, Hyderabad, Mangalore and Dubai.

As a young boy, Karthikeyan Vijayakumar felt that he would be a failure if he did not become an entrepreneur. Today he connects job-seekers and job-providers.

Saundarya Rajesh is attempting to help women find a career after a break.

Kalyan Manyam is a serial entrepreneur, having created four startups.

Suresh Sambandam believes that India should become a home for software products and leads OrangeScape.

Each story illustrates that success comes after multiple failures and that entrepreneurship is as much about failures as it is about successes. According to Shobha, 'Each story epitomises the power and potential of the human spirit and the impact their efforts have on society.'

The final section titled 'The New Generation' is about those young entrepreneurs who started their journeys after 2010. Shobha considers them lucky because 'by the time they began to hatch their plans, an ecosystem to help and encourage entrepreneurs was in place, society was knowledgeable enough to accept and applaud their entrepreneurial spirit, and venture capitalists, angel investors and mentors abounded to help them.' But that does not make their journey easy by any means, as illustrated by the stories in this section. There are people like Arun Krishnamurthy whose purpose in life is to save the environment, animals, wildlife, and lakes.

Then there are youngsters like AG Padmanabhan who goes around the city collecting food and serving it to the hungry, while also teaching children not to waste food. The story of Arul Murugan and Arun Prakash who studied Agriculture, is one about snacking healthy and how they founded 'Snackexperts'. It is the same struggle, 'We had so many plans then but things did not go as we had planned. We got only 150 online orders per month and when we spent Rs 4-5 lakh, we generated only Rs1 lakh!' after spending a significant part of a large prize money.

Koushik, Piyush and Shankar founded 'SustainEarth Energy Solutions' to provide Biogas plants to rural households.

Karthik and Swathi founded Skcript which has become the Pied Piper of India.

Eshwar has stuck to his passion of making a dosa machine. Though he started off with a deal with a street-side vendor selling idlis, he is reasonably successful today.

And then there is the story of Tibin Parakal, a networking professional in Delhi, who went back to Kerala to take to organic farming. His biggest success was to persuade his father to cultivate kuruvai on his entire one-acre plot following zero budget natural farming. His dream is to attract as many youngsters as possible to farming. There are also these two studious young women, Diana Jue and Jackie Stenson, from MIT, founders of Essmart Global, a company that believes in rural India and creates essential technologies which rural people can afford.

The stories are beautiful and inspirational. Most entrepreneurs believe that R&D is nothing but trial and error, and lots of trials are required before one succeeds in achieving one's ambition and building one's products. They believe that everything is achievable, however difficult it may appear in the beginning. They also faced the same questions the Trendsetters faced, 'Do we want to be businessmen? Do we want to do social good? Can the two be integrated?'

But all these people believe that 'an entrepreneurial journey is worth taking just for the experience. Entrepreneurship has completely changed [our] perspective on society', and they recognise, 'In an entrepreneur's life, tough times come suddenly and leave you with the feeling that your business is going to vanish into the ether. But you come back through sheer resilience.' As is evident, it is not all about the IT industry but about the diverse and large Indian market.

Yes, India is on the roll. Thanks to Shobha Warrier for bringing this out in this fascinating book.

—Padmashri Professor Ashok Jhunjhunwala, IIT Madras

Author's Note

There isn't a human alive that doesn't dream. Dream of making it big, dream of accomplishing something tangible.

But some people dream bigger than others. They then chase those dreams with courage and determination, even when they get the feeling that their dreams may be unachievable.

And they chase. And chase.

Until they see their dreams turn into reality.

This book is about people like these: entrepreneurs who never stopped dreaming, not even when parts of their journey to realising the dream turned into veritable nightmares.

They are the Dreamchasers!

The Dreamchasers

Entrepreneurs from the South of the Vindhyas

Contents

THE NEW GENERATION

The Trendsetters

In the late 1970s and '80s, the words entrepreneur and startup were not in vogue. But it was in this climate that passionate entrepreneurs like Dilip Kapur, CK Ranganathan, Dr P Srinivasan, Patricia Thomas, Arun Jain, Kalpathi S Suresh and M Mahadevan chose to undertake their journeys into the unknown.

They braved red tape, an unfriendly bureaucracy and a complete lack of infrastructure to build their businesses up, and were successful only because of the passion they brought to their jobs.

Their stories are inspirational and can be treated as study material for upcoming young entrepreneurs.

The Reluctant Businessman

The story of Dilip Kapur as a reluctant businessman is an incredibly crucial and interesting one that has passion, rectitude, conscience and sensitivity to the environment we live in.

Thirty eight years ago, this man came back to India from America as a hippie and started designing leather bags for creative pleasure. When someone bought one of these off him, he decided to start Hidesign with just Rs 25,000 and a cobbler to assist him. Today, it is an international brand with a business worth over Rs 150 crore (Rs 1.5 billion), with 76 exclusive showrooms and a distribution network in 23 countries of over 2,000 stores, and has 3,000 people working for him.

But he still is a reluctant businessman and feels the conflict between the businessman in him and the person in him. Yet he continues to build the business so that it has a story to tell to the future generation.

Here I bring you the story of Hidesign and that of Dilip Kapur the founder-president of Hidesign, an inspiring one for the present and the future.

Dilip Kapur is the founder of Hidesign that creates internationally known leather hand bags and accessories for men and women

HIDESIGN
Handcrafted. Since 1978.

'ALL THROUGH the years, I had this conflict, whether I want to be a businessman or go and live in Auroville. That conflict continues. For many years, it upset me that I was a businessman. I wondered what mistakes I had made in my life to be one. Deep down, I still have doubts about it. I am not sure I firmly believed in it. Business is not something I wanted to do. There are a lot of things I question about doing business. It is very strange.'

It is very strange for a person who runs a billion rupee business to say so. And that may be because...

Having lived in America from the age of 15 through to when he was 30, he was a part of the Counterculture movement that swept through the United States in the 1960s, the hippie movement and had participated in the anti-Vietnam protests and the radical movement there. 'Yes, there is a contradiction in what I do now. But what drives me is the creative satisfaction and responsibility to the environment than selling more bags and expanding my brand reach.'

This contradiction is what Aurobindo also spoke to his followers about; on how to connect the material world with the spiritual world, though connecting the two is difficult. His own life was an example: from fiery revolutionary and freedom fighter to a savant.

In the first ten years after he built his business, Dilip never let it be a major part of his life; he just loved designing bags and selling them as a hobby. What started off as spending 90% of his time for something else and 10% for business has become the other way round now! His is the story of how someone transformed a hobby into a passion and a successful business.

There are many interesting twists and turns in his life which ultimately made him what he is today, a hippie turned capitalist. He feels there is a role for capitalists in a society. 'Wealth creation is the job of individuals and not the job of the government. Wealth distribution is the government's job. I would say you need both the creator and the distributor.'

It all began in 1954 when Dilip Kapur's parents decided to leave Delhi and join the Aurobindo Ashram in Pondicherry though his father was a rich businessman with his own manufacturing factory in Agra. Dilip was just four then. 'What I still remember, even at that age, was the presence of the beautiful sea. Coming from Delhi, that was something I saw for the first time. Also, everybody needed a passport to come to Pondicherry as it was a French colony then. And we had to go through the Customs at the airport. That is why I have a French passport!'

What he and his sister liked the most was the kind of freedom the Ashram offered. 'Coming from a conservative society in north India to the ashram was like setting us free. The Punjabi boy from Delhi suddenly became a free spirited human being at the Ashram. Even in school, we could just wander around in shorts. I loved the freedom in education, I also loved the freedom I could enjoy even in my thoughts.'

The freedom children enjoyed at the Ashram kindled the creativity in them which later helped Dilip become a free spirited entrepreneur and design out of the box bags. 'Creativity comes from free education as the ashram didn't have a rigid education system. It allowed us to do what we wanted to. I was the first among the 30 students who were given free system of education at the Ashram. I enjoyed it. It was great to be studying in the Ashram school after the scary and regimented atmosphere I had in the convent school I went to in Delhi. It was a close, warm atmosphere and was liberating even for such a small child. I had the freedom to study whenever and whatever I wanted, and there were no exams.'

And of course, Mother's[1] insistence on aesthetics, cleanliness, simplicity and anything that is natural helped him develop a different kind of aesthetics. 'If you look at all the ashram houses, you will see that they are all simple, whitewashed either grey or yellow and never made complicated. All the old colonial French houses are maintained so well. Her emphasis on simplicity helped me a lot in my life as a human being and also a designer. Everything we did, we discussed with her.'

Mother was such a tolerant lady that he could be an atheist and still stay at the Ashram, though a lot of people at the Ashram argued with him for what he believed in. But Mother never did! 'She said, great! She was very anti-religion and never agreed with the rigidity of religion. She questioned anything rigid and broke down anything that was rigid, and encouraged us also to do that. That made me dislike rigidity and encouraged me to question even as a child.'

The cosmopolitan nature of the Ashram helped him develop into a free-thinking person even at that young age. His own mother who was always in saris changed to short pants and started doing athletics, swimming and gymnastics every day, something she had never done before in her life.

Though his father was a rich businessman in Delhi, when he chose to join the Ashram, the job Mother gave him was that of a watchman. He was shocked initially, but he did the job till the end. It taught him the dignity in all jobs and also humility. There was no difference between anyone in the Ashram. 'That was the way Mother broke down rigidity and made all equal. He later said, fulfilling the duties of a watchman taught him humility.' Having lived and studied in the Ashram, by the time he finished school at the age of 15, he felt confined and was totally out of touch with the outside world. 'The Ashram was very liberating but it seemed too closed and small for a 15-year-old who wanted to see the world. I wanted to go to America, as to me it was the centre of the world at the time.'

---

1. Mirra Alfassa (21 February 1878 – 17 November 1973), known to her followers as The Mother, was the spiritual collaborator of Sri Aurobindo.

From the list of best schools in the world in *Time* magazine, he chose Phillips Academy, Andover, and wrote to the Head Master that he wanted to study there.

'Those were the days when there was no Internet and I wrote a handwritten letter to the Head Master and posted it. They not only replied to my letter but gave me admission at the Academy with a scholarship, as well. I think they must have liked the way I wrote the letter. That was because of the life I had led at the Ashram and the kind of liberating education I had there. I am sure my letter impressed them. Otherwise, they would not have written back; Andover was the most elitist school in the US at that time.'

So, he packed his bags and off he went to America from the small world of the Aurobindo Ashram to study and explore the 'outside' world.

The time was 1964, and at that time, there was not much foreign exchange that a person could get. The Reserve Bank of India gave him $8 when he went to study! 'The level of education at the Ashram school was so good that I had no difficulty competing with the Andover students who were the toppers in some school before they got in at Andover. At 15, when you are abroad and on your own, you overcome problems and find solutions on your own.'

And he did extremely well in many subjects like English and American History.

After the Phillips Academy, he joined Princeton to study liberal arts and International Affairs. 'After Andover, Princeton was easy. By then, I had found my feet in the American society. There were not many Indians at that time; I was the only Indian at Andover and one of the other two Indians at Princeton. I did my PhD also in International Affairs at Princeton.'

When he was at the University, the Vietnam war had started and along with that, the hippie movement too. He became a hippie with long hair; not a poor hippie but an elitist one! 'We thought we would be able to change the world. I was in no danger as they couldn't send me to Vietnam to fight the war, as I was not an American. But I was clearly a part of the anti-Vietnam war movement. The only danger I was in was, I could have been thrown out of America. The movement took over buildings and started the Third World Liberation Front, and stopped the marines from recruiting. It was a close shave but somehow I escaped them sending me back to India. I really believed Vietnam was American imperialism. Maybe, because I was an Indian, I felt connected to Vietnam. The arrogance of America worried and upset me a lot; they thought they could do anything to any country. I admired Vietnam for the way they fought America.'

An idealist hippie and an anti-business person. 'As I was not terribly mainstream, I didn't want a job and be very successful. I was more interested in doing something more experimental and challenging.'

That was why he chose to work in a leather goods company for nine months and that changed his life. He loved the feel and smell of leather. He also learnt then that India used to be a big centre of vegetable tanned leather other than Italy and Brazil. But with the arrival of chemical tanning, vegetable tanning, which is slow, had vanished from India.

But the more he got to know America, the less he liked the country. Vietnam War was only one of the reasons why he decided to come back to India as he always knew one day he was going to be back. So, after his studies and working there for nine months, he packed his bags. 'I wanted to come back because I had this pride that I was an Indian and wanted to live in India. No Indian who went to America at that time came back. Even though I had an American wife at that time, I was clear that I was going to come back.'

It was when he was planning to come back to India that Auroville was started as an experimental place for human unity. When he arrived in Pondicherry from America, it was a desert; but he saw the residents planting trees in their hundreds. Soon, Auroville was transformed from a desert to a beautiful ashram with three million trees.

But for him, the question was, what would he do there? There was nothing to do in Auroville except plant trees and plan the affairs of Auroville—not quite the challenge for a man with a PhD in International Affairs.

That was when he started getting the smell of leather in his nostrils once again. Off he went to then Madras, the centre of the

Indian leather tanning industry, to buy leather. He used the leather he purchased to design bags, thereby entertaining himself and getting the creative juices flowing.

Having grown up 'very close to nature' in Auroville, he could not think of polluting nature with chemicals. So, he chose to use only vegetable tanned leather for his bags; a decision he continues to abide by.

When a very rich friend of his paid him Rs 300 and bought a bag he had designed, he was taken aback! 'I never expected someone to pay money and buy what I had made with my own hands! My friend knew I was making bags. When the first bag was finished, she said, "It's so beautiful!" and bought it. My first feeling was whether she bought it just to make me feel good.'

What she liked about the bag was its natural look. Most leather bags at that time were plasticky and unnatural. But 'us hippies, the generation that came out of the counter-revolution, liked more natural leather; certainly not what was in the leather market then. As I had lived in America till I was 30 during the hippie movement, my design sensibilities were American.'

In 1978, with a capital investment of Rs 25,000, he continued his hobby. Half the money went into buying leather and cloth linings for his bags. With the rest, he bought a sewing machine, some tools, and created a small space on the terrace of his flat with just one cobbler, Murugan (whose son still works for Dilip!), to assist him. The two of them sat on the floor with Dilip designing the bag and Murugan cutting the leather later and stitching it up on the sewing machine.

The next turning point on his journey was when a German friend of his saw his creations and was bowled over by them. He was then the head of the German World Hunger Organisation, and they were looking for items to fill his charity sales catalogue, the profits of which went to reducing hunger in the developing world. So impressed was he that he ordered not just 1 or 2, but 1,400 bags. 'Just imagine, I was making one bag a day and had only one cobbler working for me. The realisation that someone would place such a huge order was simply amazing!'

But there was a problem; in spite of working hard for six months, he could supply only 200 bags.

The 1,400 orders gave Dilip the confidence to expand his hiring plans, though it took some time for him to supply the full order.

Murugan brought his nephew Mani over. The third person to join them was Pramila, a young girl of 16. An interesting aside here is that Mani fell in love with and married Pramila, and they continue to work for Dilip!

A little later, in 1979, they moved to a proper factory, and hired even more people!

Today, 38 years after Hidesign was born, it has 3,000 people working for them. 'It was just a hobby for me at the time. If I knew it would grow into a business, I would have closed it down at that time itself. I am not a socialist or a communist. I am not even a capitalist; I am a liberalist. I am happy that 3,000 people work for Hidesign, but that is not why I run this business. I don't derive satisfaction from creating jobs. It is great that I've had the opportunity to create jobs but that is not the only reason why we are there.'

The next step in the journey came when a friend of his from Auroville who was working in a car factory in Australia broke his back and received $12,000 as compensation from his employers. He came back to Auroville, saw Dilip's bags, was impressed and bought some with his compensation money to sell in Australia. He discovered that there was a market for the bags down under; thereby taking Hidesign all the way to the antipodes.

As the business grew, Dilip Kapur moved out of Auroville into Pondicherry. But in 1986, he decided to move back. 'I remember saying in the Auroville General Body that one day I would sell Hidesign and work in Auroville. But that's not happened yet, though I continue to live in Auroville.'

After Germany and Australia, the next country where Hidesign reached was the United Kingdom, and again, it was thanks to another friend of his. He had bought a bag from Dilip for his own personal use. But when he got a job with John Lewis, a major department store chain in the UK, he felt there might be more people like him out there in the UK who might appreciate Hidesign bags just as much. He therefore got John Lewis's London shops to stock Hidesign bags.

Until Hidesign hit the shelves of John Lewis in London in 1988, their customers were primarily rebels who were once involved in the counterculture movement of the 1960s. While success at getting stocked by a stores chain as prestigious as John Lewis was exciting for Dilip, they came under increasing pressure to go mainstream.

'By then, attitudes in the west had changed and people became less conservative and more casual. Yes, I felt a little bad when we moved from the rebel camp to the mainstream camp. Our leather was hand dyed, and so was uneven and rough. But they [John Lewis] wanted us to make it a little more even for the European market that was used to Italian bags.'

Ten years after he started Hidesign, he accepted the fact that it had become a business and not a hobby anymore. By then, he had a factory with more than 300 people working for him. He describes starting of the factory as the 'end of [his] innocence.'

The next market they penetrated was America, and once again, it happened by chance. Somebody who visited Auroville from California saw Hidesign bags, bought them, and started selling them there. 'All of the commercialisation [of Hidesign] happened without even me realising what was happening.'

The next turning point was in 1992 when Hidesign's Boxy Bag won the Accessory of the Year award from *Accessory* magazine. It was a little suitcase that looked like a box with a long strap. Princess Diana gave out the award to Dilip, and even took one with her!

It was only after twenty years that Hidesign opened its first store in India; in Pondicherry, where it all began.

Just as the liberalisation of the Indian economy and society after 1991 resulted in young Indians becoming more global in their outlook and likely consumers of Hidesign products, Dilip found he began to feel even more Indian as the time he spent in India grew. 'Having lived in America from the age of 15 and having then lived a secluded life in Auroville designing bags for an international customer, I was more an American than an Indian. But all of that changed with us opening stores all over India. It was only after that that I began to discover India and my Indianness. It [opening stores in India] was the first time that we came directly in contact with our customers. That was a big change for me.'

In the years since the first Hidesign store opened in India, Dilip's biggest surprise has been how quickly India has become one of his largest markets. The man who once thought he would never be able to sell anything in India now sees it as Hidesign's quickest growing market after China, Malaysia, Vietnam and Sri Lanka.

'In 2000, we sold only 6% of our products here. We couldn't find a distributor here in India who understood our products. Today, half of our sales are in India. After liberalisation [in 1991], the world came to India and Indians went to the world. Suddenly you see many Indians who have the same lifestyle as that of a person in San Francisco or London. They see the soul behind a creation, and those made by hands have more soul than those made by machines. Natural and non-plasticky leather has become more acceptable and mainstream today.'

There were other exciting moments in Dilip's long journey with Hidesign. Things like the time Steven Spielberg purchased a Hidesign bag from a shop in California and used it in one of his movies, or the moment he found out that both Bob Hawke (then Prime Minister of Australia) and Nelson Mandela (the father of modern South Africa) carried Hidesign bags with them wherever they travelled.

'The most interesting experience of all, however, was when the Malaysian Prime Minister visited our factory with an entourage of 60 people. They bought all the bags that were in stock at the factory on the day. He told me that he had twenty three Hidesign bags in his collection; a collection he had started when he was a student in Cambridge. And he always thought Hidesign was a UK brand and when he saw the bag at the hotel in Delhi, he was surprised. When he was told that it was an Indian brand, he wanted to visit us!'

He admits the contradiction in what he does now; after all he started out as a rebel only to find himself selling his products to the upper crust of global society. 'Yes, there is a contradiction. Many of us who thought we could change the world back then did not succeed.

Finally, we ended up joining the world. But I have kept my values intact: things like being against racism and environmental pollution. It is perhaps because we started out as rebels that we were able to create more innovative things. Whether it is in music, literature or even in business, rebels have innovated. Look at Steve Jobs. He was a hippie. So was Richard Branson. They all started off as rebels and hippies but went on to become successful entrepreneurs. It was not the turnover that helped me move forward. What gave me satisfaction was designing bags and not the profit I made or the number of countries we conquered. I didn't know how to read my profit and loss account in the first ten years.'

And there was no guilt in making money too. 'I don't feel guilty about making money as my connection to money is not that strong. I am not too bothered whether I am making money or not making money. My needs are few. I live in Auroville. My house doesn't belong to me; it belongs to Auroville. Within Auroville, I still use my 1977 Bullet. I like very simple food and my food is largely vegetarian. I like wine, and that's about it.'

What gave him pleasure in the initial days was fiddling with leather and designing something new. Even today, that is exactly what continues to give him the greatest pleasure.

The reluctant businessman also has dreams; that of continuing to grow the Hidesign brand globally. 'But I don't think in terms of numbers and rupees. I want people to relate to it; I want them to want it. I want our brand to be relevant; one that improves the lives of those who use our products. We want to stay natural and ecological.'

But Dilip Kapur, the person, dreams of getting more involved in his local community. 'If Hidesign is not there tomorrow, it would not affect me too badly. Hidesign remaining alive and doing well is fine but that is not the be-all and end-all for me. We should have a reason to be there and a story to tell.'

A Social Entrepreneur

There are hundreds and thousands of successful doctors in India but here is a doctor who prefers to be known as a social entrepreneur and a wild life photographer more than a successful medical practitioner. Here is a doctor who recharges his batteries by retreating into the deep jungles in Africa and the hidden depths of the Himalayas to silently take pictures of the wild animals.

Though his journey as an entrepreneur started at the age of 11, he became a social entrepreneur in 1995, twenty years after he became a medical doctor. He started Jeevan Blood Bank with the sole intention of providing blood components of the highest quality to those in dire need. He is Dr Srinivasan Periathiruvadi, the Co-Founder and Chairman of Jeevan Blood Bank and Research Centre, Jeevan Public Cord Blood Bank and Jeevan Stem Cell Registry.

He is a doctor who believes in the goodness of people and miracles as every time he and his team have felt helpless and clueless about the future of Jeevan, some angels have come forward to help him tide over all the difficulties.

'Now that all our units are well in place, I am happy, satisfied and ready to go!' says he.

I don't think anyone who has benefitted from Jeevan will let him go that easily!

Dr P Srinivasan, a social entrepreneur, is the founder of Jeevan Blood Bank

WAY BACK in the fifties when Srinivasan grew up in Thuthookudi (Tuticorin), a small town in Tamil Nadu, his father, a professor in the Teacher's Training College could not afford to give pocket money to his children. Rather, pocket money was a term unheard of for the children who grew up in those days but they also needed some money to indulge themselves with toffee once in a while.

'My father had a salary for Rs 200 and he had to take care of the needs of five children and two adults. I don't remember any financial difficulty at home as all of us had learnt to live with whatever we had. One advice my father used to give us all the time was, do whatever you want but don't ever cheat anyone. He also used to say that even if you do the lowliest job, do it well and ask for the money you deserve. It was this advice of his that encouraged me to do certain things which I liked and take care of my needs even when I was in school.'

Perhaps his father's advice kindled the entrepreneur in him when he was just 11. He bought vegetables in bulk from the market and distributed to his neighbourhood households.

'What I did then was what Big Basket is doing today by delivering vegetables and provisions at home when you book online! As I was the person who was buying all the vegetables and groceries for the family, I thought why not collect orders from our neighbours too? I went to the market at 4.30 in the morning and bought vegetables and fruits at wholesale price, and I could make a 100% profit because I was buying in bulk. I used to make at least a profit of Rs 5 a day—it was very big money for an 11 year old in 1964!'

Other than buying vegetables for the neighbourhood mamis, another work also came his way. His grandfather, a Physics Professor had written a book on Physics and he used to frequent the press to see the progress of the printing and binding. While in the press, he learnt the art of book-binding. He made use of this skill when the school reopened, binding books of his friends for a charge.

Other than buying vegetables and book-binding, he also made kites during the kite flying season and made some money.

All these, he did between the age of 11 and 17 but the little boy didn't spend a single paisa to indulge himself in small pleasures but saved the entire money in his post office savings account. Every time he got some money, he went to the post office and deposited it. 'By the time I got admission in the Government Kilpauk Medical College in Chennai which was Madras then, I had more than a thousand rupees, a substantial amount in those days, saved in my account. My father used to be very proud of my achievement.'

In 1970 when he got admission in the medical college in Chennai, his family also decided to move to the city. His father, DS Periathiruvadi became the Principal of the Padma Seshadri Bala Bhavan, and later on, he was instrumental in setting up startup educational institutions like the Jaigopal Garodia School, AVM Matriculation School and Venkateshwara Matriculation School in Chennai.

The fees to study Medicine then was just Rs 240 a year and it was Rs 1,200 for his entire medical education. 'That was when I decided that I would work only in India, as I felt I had used public money to study Medicine and hence I had a responsibility to the public. I wanted to give something back to society.'

Doctor turns entrepreneur

On the 1st of January 1981, soon after he finished his MD in Medicine, he started working in a 100-bed hospital in Chennai. While working in the hospital, under the compulsion to have reliable test results to treat his patients, he started spending time in the laboratory to learn the processes.

In 1985, he decided to quit his job and was contemplating the next move when some of the young people with whom he was working, asked him, 'Doctor, why don't you start a laboratory? As a physician, you know the importance of a good lab.'

They also assured him that they were willing to be a part of the venture, and also ready to wait to be paid till he made money.

That was the beginning of his second entrepreneurial journey, this time as a Doctor. 'Medicine and technology were not married in the early and late '80s. Perhaps it happened only in the '90s. So, there was a huge need to fill the gap and we decided to do that.'

On the 6th of June 1985, he started Lister Laboratory with a capital of Rs 2 lakh, most of which was borrowed.

'Any entrepreneur can have a dream but for the dream to be a reality, you need a good partner in the venture to walk with you and the right team to help you visualise the dream. And I fortunately had both.'

The partner was a young microbiologist, Dr Saranya Narayan, who had just completed her postgraduation and joined him. In no time, she took over the operational part while he was in charge of the administration. Saranya was to be a part of his entrepreneurial journey from then on.

Lister Laboratory grew rapidly by 10-15% a year, and in the next ten years, it became a brand trusted by the people of Chennai.

Idea of a blood bank

Then something unexpected happened.

In 1992, Dr Saranya showed him some statistics from their lab. It showed the number of tests done month-wise for HIV, Hepatitis B and Cancer. The number of people tested positive was unbelievably high, and most of them were over 55.

Then, she showed him another set of statistics; 80% of them had had a major surgery in the last one year, and had blood transfusion. Every time they needed blood transfusion, it was a struggle to get blood.

She then told him that they needed to find an answer to the problem, and according to her the answer lay in setting up a blood bank.

So, it was Dr Saranya who planted the seed of the idea of starting a public blood bank.

They needed at least Rs 75 lakh for the venture and it was big money for a non-profit venture in 1992. Inability to find funds delayed the ambitious project till 1995.

However, a few incidents took place in 1994.

One evening, he got a call saying that a freedom fighter, after an operation was bleeding and needed A Positive blood. He being a regular blood donor, rushed there with a friend of his to donate blood. He didn't disclose his identity as a doctor while donating blood but felt unhappy with the way the hospital treated a blood donor.

There was another incident when a two-year-old was brought to his laboratory for testing HIV. The girl child was a precious baby, born after seven years of marriage. Before the mother became pregnant, she had a kidney problem and had undergone blood transfusion. It so happened that she contracted HIV virus through blood transfusion and died at childbirth. Unfortunately, the child was born HIV+.

The third incident happened on the 31st of December 1994. Dr Saranya asked him on New Year eve, 'if you were hit by a bus on your way home today, where do you want your blood to come from? Perhaps you may not be able to tell them then. Think about it and tell me.'

That question hit him hard. It was then that he decided to go ahead with the project of starting a blood bank, come what may.

New Year 1995

On the 1st of January, at 6 am in the morning , he called Dr Saranya and said, 'We are going to start a public blood bank, a not-for-profit organisation. I always say, social entrepreneurship is all about being hit on the pain spot and that what affects others is also going to affect you.'

It took nine months and 24 days for Jeevan Blood Bank to come to life; like a baby. They had to borrow around Rs 25 lakh to start with.

'I must say getting donations from the people of Chennai was a big task. But what touched me was, when I mentioned what we were going to do to the carpenters, plumbers and electricians, all of them said they would work for free as it was for a social cause. I think if you believe strongly about something, you should take the plunge and make it real.'

The team wanted Jeevan Blood Bank to provide the safest blood components to people. 'Our motto was, blood should be free or affordable, and blood donation should be 100% voluntary. Nobody needs blood in totality, so we store blood collected as components in our blood bank; as plasma, platelets and red cells. When we separate blood into its components, its shelf life increases. Soon Jeevan became India's first blood bank with an ISO ranking. That shows our commitment to quality though ours is a non-profit organisation.'

People who cannot afford to pay still have access to the safest blood components as those who are able to reimburse the cost of processing.

In 2000, they were responsible for the Government of Tamil Nadu issuing a GO to set up satellite blood storage centres in hospitals, and the first one was established in India, at the Sundaram Medical Foundation in Chennai. Jeevan made the blood component available to them so that a lot of time was saved when someone needed blood.

In December 2011, the Government of India issued a gazette notification and made it a national policy.

Jeevan so far has collected around 147,000 blood donations and given away 322,000 units of blood components to people.

Dr Srinivasan is proud that Jeevan has set several milestones in India.

Time for the next venture

When Jeevan Blood Bank celebrated its 10th anniversary, a larger problem that affected Indians globally came to his notice. A young Indian in the US who had blood cancer could have been cured if he had got a suitable bone marrow donor on time. Unfortunately, he died when they could not find a donor on time.

Another shocking statistic that hit him was, more than 120,000 Indians were diagnosed with blood cancer every year and another

10,000 born with Thalassemia. Over 60% of children with Thalassemia and over 80% of patients with blood cancer could be cured with bone marrow transplant. This is not confined to India alone but has been happening across the world for over twenty five years.

A public cord blood bank in 2008

After a baby is born, the umbilical cord is cut but it takes another 10 minutes for the placenta to come out. At that time, with the same needle and bag used for blood donation, the hospital can collect the left-over blood in the placenta and umbilical cord. That is one of the richest sources of stem cells called cord blood cells and it has a shelf life of twenty four years.

When he and his team found that Indians found it difficult to get matching donors in international registries, as the match is ethnicity dependent, they decided to set up a public cord blood bank for Indians living globally. The idea was to accept cord blood as donation, harvest the stem cells, HLA type them and store them till someone needed it.

The initial investment required was around Rs 2 crore.

The public cord blood bank became live in November 2008.

Crisis looms large

But in 2012, they were on the verge of closing the cord blood bank down.

'It costs us Rs 30,000 to process each cord blood donation. We thought we would easily find 30,000 Indians who would give us Rs 30,000 each to create an inventory to serve Indians globally. Unfortunately, it did not happen the way in which we envisaged because people did not understand what we were talking about. There were no funds coming as what we had planned was a Rs 90 crore project.'

He and Dr Saranya were thinking of shutting Jeevan Public Cord Blood Bank in December 2012 if no funds came by then. As it was a painful decision to take, somehow, Dr Srinivasan made the trustees agree to wait till March 2013.

'Some angel was listening to our woes on 24 September 2012, which was Jeevan's anniversary. We got a call from ICICI Bank which was managing a Technology Services Revolving Fund of the Government of India, and said that the bank wanted to give us a loan. We told them that we were in the process of winding up and were not definitely interested in a loan. But they insisted on meeting us and helping us in our project. They wanted to give us a loan of Rs15.5 crores with 1% service charge repayable by 2023!'

Within a week of grabbing the Rs 15.5 crores from ICICI Bank, they got a call from the Secretary of Health and Family Welfare department of the Tamil Nadu Government. They had sent an appeal to the Chief Minister in 2010 for a Rs 9 crore loan for three years to collect and process cord blood donations from Tamil Nadu, and had totally forgotten about it.

'By March, we got that fund too and suddenly there was a flurry of activities. I have to say it again and again, I do believe in miracles.'

Because of those miracles, the journey of the Public Cord Blood bank continues even today and so far, they have collected over 10,000 cord blood donations and processed and stored 5,000 stem cell units ready for transplant. Jeevan has facilitated five transplants till date and a few more are in the pipeline.

Today, Jeevan is the largest active, public stem cell bank in the entire SAARC region. 'Our target is 30,000 stem cell units by 2020 and then seven out ten Indians can find a match. Though the matching stem cells are ready, the cost of a transplant is around Rs 25 lakh in India which not many can afford. This is one challenge we are working on, we have to somehow find a solution to reduce the cost.'

Jeevan Bone Marrow Donor Registry in 2015

In 2015, they started a Jeevan Bone Marrow Donor Registry with a seed funding of Rs 5 crore from Tata Trust, Sundaram Finance Ltd and Consulate General of Australia. In September 2013, they decided to start a High Resolution HLA Typing Laboratory which is essential for bone marrow and other transplants. Human leukocyte antigen (HLA) is a protein—or marker—found on most cells in a human being's body and is used to match the person with a donor for the bone marrow or cord blood transplant. The best transplant outcome happens only when a patient's HLA and the donor's HLA closely match.

'At the beginning of the cord blood bank (2008), Jeevan started performing low resolution HLA typing. This method is good enough for initial registry data base. Once, if there is a low resolution match, that particular sample can be re-typed on high resolution technology through outsourcing. Unfortunately, this outsourcing had to be done to USA or Germany as there was no laboratory in India capable of doing this. And this involved huge costs.'

By starting a High Resolution HLA Typing Laboratory, they could see to it that all cord blood donations and bone marrow donors were tested to the high resolution standards in India itself, thus eliminating a second round of testing. This also cut down the waiting time to know whether there is a perfect match or not.

'Most importantly, we added India to the global map of High resolution HLA typing labs and in the long run, this will bring in the sustainability component to the project. Today, we have done over 7,000 HLA Typing as a not-for-profit service. We do the testing for free for poor people.'

What Dr Srinivasan started as a small blood bank is today operating four verticals. 'We have come a long way from the time we started thirty years ago. If not for a great team, we would not have achieved this. We have thirty six members and seven trustees. We have reached a stage that even without me, this will continue as everything is in place now.'

Wildlife photographer

The doctor turned social entrepreneur has another face too; that of an award-winning wildlife photographer. By holding exhibitions of the wild life pictures taken by him, he collects funds for Jeevan.

It all started with a Kodak Click 3 camera, which he got from a relative when he was just 11. Initially, he used to go to a studio in Tuticorin to learn all about developing and processing. After his medical studies, he set up his own dark room and printing room.

But when he became a social entrepreneur in 1985, the cameras disappeared and the photographer in him took a back seat. For twenty years, he did not take even a single photo. In 2005, when he was diagnosed with a brain tumour, which fortunately turned out to be a benign one, it became a turning point in his life and after the surgery, he took out his camera once again.

'In 2006, I came back to wild life photography with a vengeance. Whenever I disappear into the jungles of Africa and to the Himalayas, I get a lot of time to reflect on my personal life and the projects. Those trips help me recharge my batteries. When one watches animals, one can learn a lot of lessons from them. One thing is, they don't hurt another animal unless they are hungry or provoked. My wife says I communicate better with animals!'

From Kodak Click 3, today he has moved on to the Phase One professional camera!

Looking back

He has faced one question quite frequently; why did he become a struggling social entrepreneur when doctors in this country make a lot of money through medical practice?

'First, I get a lot of joy doing this. Beyond a point, money doesn't play any role in my life. In 2007, when a big businessman told me, if I made Jeevan a private enterprise, he would invest Rs 25 crore, I said, no thanks. My journey as a social entrepreneur would not have happened if I had not been an entrepreneur for ten years. Definitely the journey of Jeevan is more satisfying than the first ten years of my journey as an entrepreneur.

'Looking back, I feel I am one of those blessed people who could do so much for society. Yes, I am happy and satisfied with life!'

Bringing Lifestyle to Rural India

The story of CK Ranganathan, the Chairman and Managing Director of CavinKare, is that of an entrepreneur from small-town India who showed the world that it is possible to beat the multinationals on their turf. That he did this way back in the 1980s and in the extremely difficult market of fast moving consumer goods makes it only more laudable.

Ranganathan's journey, which started from the small town of Cuddalore in Tamil Nadu, has been an amazing and inspiring one. He started his business with just Rs 15,000 as capital. It is now worth Rs 1,300 crores and employs 5,000 people. He started off selling shampoo sachets, and now owns an entire gamut of cosmetic products under the brand CavinKare: a brand sold not just in India but also in many South East Asian countries.

Being an innovator constantly on the lookout for new ideas, he has diversified his business into various fields. For instance, his dairy products unit (turnover: Rs. 250 crores) sells its products in countries like Singapore, Indonesia, Malaysia, Bangladesh and Nepal. To take another example, there is the chain of saloons he owns under the brand name Green Trends.

The story of Ranganathan's journey as an entrepreneur is a textbook that budding entrepreneurs would do well to follow and try to emulate.

CK Ranganathan, founder of CavinKare Pvt Ltd that produces beauty cosmetics, dairy products, foods and snacks

CavinKare
Making Lives Happier

KOODALUR, AS Cuddalore was Known before the British anglicised the name, means 'confluence' in Tamil. It was in this small place in Tamil Nadu that CK Ranganathan was born and grew up. It was here that he took his first steps as an entrepreneur. His father, Chinni Krishnan, was a school teacher, and his mother Hemalatha ran her own school; one that quite impressively started as a nursery for toddlers and grew into a Higher Secondary school over the years.

His mother's success as an entrepreneur proved to be inspiring to young Ranganathan. 'If I have succeeded today as an entrepreneur, it is because of what I learnt from my mother and the values she inculcated in her children. Her story as an entrepreneur shows that if you have the passion and desire to learn, you can build anything from scratch. Without any experience of running a school, she started one and grew it to the size she did. She learnt all of the skills she needed to on her own. The way she made her school grow was very inspirational to all of us, her children. One thing my mother always used to tell us was to look ahead and not back.'

Ranganathan admits quite frankly that, unlike his siblings who were very good academically, he was just an average student. While they went to English medium schools, he had to be moved to a Tamil medium school when one of his teachers at his English language school found him 'blinking blindly' in class. While his older brother and sister grew up to become doctors and a third brother became a lawyer, Ranganathan even failed years in school. Naturally, all through his youth, he suffered from an inferiority complex because of his poor academic performance.

Academic study never interested him the way rearing pets did. Again, it was his mother who made him interested in pets. 'Our house was in the middle of a large farm and there were lots and lots of coconut and palm trees all around. My mother had dogs and birds as pets. Even as a child, I had my own pets. From dogs to chickens to rabbits to birds, the number and variety of my pets increased, the older I grew as a child. But it was pigeons that became my abiding passion! At one time, I had 500 pigeons and I spent all of my time dreaming of pigeons of different colours. Even at that age, I started dabbling in the world of business; I sold a few of the pigeons to my friend to earn my pocket money.'

Perhaps, those were the first signs of the entrepreneur he would grow up to become. His obsession with animals resulted in him spending less and less time on his education. His worried mother then sent him to a private tuition master.

'While all my siblings studied on their own, I had to go to extra tuition classes after school; I never enjoyed them much. In spite of all the extra tuition, I only managed to just about scrape through most exams. But it was when I failed an exam that my mother told me, "You are going to sell off all the pigeons". Though it broke my heart, being an obedient son, I sold off all of my pigeons for Rs 10,000.'

After the pigeons were gone, it was not his studies that took up his time; instead, he started spending his time climbing trees, swimming in the ponds, and playing with the children of the local fishermen. The way he whiled his time away made his mother angry. She used to admonish him saying, 'You are only fit to rear buffaloes'. Because of his poor academic record, his father encouraged him to either start a business or become a farmer.

It was somewhere around this time that his father quit his teaching job and started running a small-scale pharmaceutical packaging unit before moving on to manufacture of pharmaceutical products and cosmetics. His father's justification for switching from teaching to running a business was this: 'As a teacher, I can impart knowledge to children but as a businessman, I can provide people with a livelihood!' His advice to all his children was to be job creators rather than job seekers.

His father was more of an innovator than an entrepreneur and struggled to market his ideas. It was he, who came up with the idea of selling things in small sachets at a time when the Indian market had not seen them at all.

Ranganathan says, 'He described sachets as the product of the future. When talcum powder was sold only in tin containers, he introduced 100gm, 50gm and 20gm packs. When Epsom salt came in 100gm packets, my father brought out salt sachets as small as 5gm. He told me, "Whatever I make, I want the poor and the downtrodden; people like rickshaw pullers to be able to afford". He tried selling things like shampoos and honey in sachets but he just could not market the concept well enough to make it a success. He was also restless, and constantly moved from one innovation to the next. He was a great innovator, but a poor marketer.'

A couple of years after he introduced the idea of things in small sachets to the Indian market, he passed away. It was sudden and unexpected. Ranganathan had just started college then. 'One day, as I was coming back from college, my friends came up to me and told me to rush as my father was unwell. When I reached home, I found that he had already died of a heart attack.'

His father's death was a 'big defining moment' in his life. 'Till then, all the decisions in my life were taken by him. I did whatever he asked me to. Suddenly I found there was nobody to direct my life and I decided to choose a path for myself.'

After his father's death in 1979, the family found that he had left behind large debts, including a bank loan of Rs 200,000, a huge amount at the time. But his mother was a fighter. She fought against the odds to repay all of the money.

'She stood up and faced all the people who came for money. She taught us not to run away but face problems with courage, all very important values. She also taught us to dream and think of what we could achieve in the future. Whenever I am faced with a challenge, I think of what my mother taught me; that allows me to deal with any problem easily. The way she conducted herself when we were in difficulties has had a great impact on me to this day.'

It was when they had no means to repay the Rs 200,000 bank loan that his mother decided to close down her husband's business. But the bank wanted them to repay the money first and then close the business down. So, his older brothers, who worked as a doctor and a lawyer, decided to discontinue their practice and take charge of the family business.

Their first decision as businessmen was to re-launch their father's idea of selling shampoo in sachets. Branded Velvette Shampoo, it was a very successful product. They took the brand to even greater heights by tying up with the Godrej industrial conglomerate and advertising aggressively on TV.

Joining the family business in 1981—and leaving

After finishing college, Ranganathan also joined them and was in charge of the production floor and formulating the product. But the stint lasted only nine months. When he found that his idea of running a business clashed with that of his brothers', he decided to quit.

'Naturally, there were clashes. As I was in the manufacturing unit, I did not know anything about marketing or finance. But by then I had sufficiently overcome my inferiority complex from being a poor student. I gained the confidence to try and implement my ideas of running the business better.'

But he was sure that he did not want any share in the family business before moving out. 'I didn't want the family business or land to be split up or sold. So, without taking a single paisa from anyone, I walked out. My mother and grandmother were in tears when I left; but it was one of those things that just had to be done.'

Starting his own business with Rs 15,000

He had saved Rs 15,000 from the salary he was paid for his work in the now-thriving family business. That was all the seed capital he had! Yet, he was confident of achieving success.

The first thing he did was to rent a small 200 sq ft home-office just a few meters away from his large family home for Rs 250 a month against an advance of Rs 1,000. The man who drove around in cars until then began to use a bicycle. This decision to stay close to the family home while still staying apart was met with a lot of protests. But he pressed on with his plans nevertheless.

'I was confident that I would succeed. I thought of how I succeeded rearing pigeons as a young boy. But I knew only production and research, and nothing about management or accounting—that was my brothers' forte.'

For a week, he could not make up his mind as to what business to get into. 'I knew only two things—making shampoo and rearing pets. Initially, I didn't want to venture into the shampoo business, as I was worried it would increase the friction with my brothers. However, I ultimately decided to do that anyway as manufacturing shampoo was my most marketable skill.'

He then rented a small factory space for Rs 300 a month against an advance of Rs 900, purchased a shampoo-packing machine for Rs 3,500, and appointed four people. After all of these expenses, all that was left of his Rs 15,000 was a mere Rs 1,500. He had to purchase the raw materials he needed to get the factory going, on credit.

How Chik Shampoo was born

After the factory was ready to roll, he decided that he too would sell his shampoo exclusively in sachets. He named it Chik shampoo, after his father Chinni Krishnan.

In the first month alone, he sold 20,000 sachets! And within the short span of 2-3 months, he was turning over Rs 50,000 a month. What helped him conquer the market was the new and bewitching fragrance they used.

Initially he only looked at the state of Tamil Nadu as his market. His plan was to expand out of Tamil Nadu slowly, as his business grew and stabilised.

To fund his expansion plans, Ranganathan needed a loan. But all of the banks he approached asked for collateral that he did not have. Finally, three years into the first sachet of Chik shampoo rolling off the factory floor, Vijaya Bank [a public sector bank] gave him a loan of

Rs 25,000. Through the years, as he paid his loans back, the bank lent him even more; first Rs 400,000, and then Rs 1,500,000, and so on.

Ranganthan recollects, 'Do you know what the bank manager wrote on our loan application? He wrote, "the applicant does not have any collateral to offer but there is something interesting about this Small Scale Industry [SSI] unit. Unlike many others, his company pays income tax!" I must say my business never looked back from that point, and I am glad I was very particular about paying my taxes.'

Looking back at his days of struggle, Ranganathan says, 'If you have talent and the desire to succeed, you can achieve anything. I never looked at money as a problem that prevented me from growing my business; having an idea and the desire to do something is more important than money. The desire to succeed was so strong in my mind that I knew I could not fail. I didn't want to go back to my brothers and admit that I had failed. That was the last thing I wanted to do. I had burnt all the bridges and I had only one option in front of me, and that was to succeed. And I succeeded!'

It was the desire to succeed that got him reading books. 'Both my written and conversational English was poor, but I didn't want to confine my business area to Tamil Nadu alone. So, what I did first was to start reading books in order to improve my English. I started by learning five new words everyday and constructing at least 25 sentences with those words. I allocated one and a half hours every morning for this activity. I continued this for two years. It was a desire to succeed beyond the confines of Tamil Nadu that made me work so hard.'

Moving to Chennai

The first step to spreading his wings was to move his company to Chennai. 'In 1990, when our turnover was around Rs 4-5 crores, I decided to move to Chennai, mainly because I felt quite restricted in Cuddalore.'

He knew he would be able to conquer the entire Indian market only from a city like Chennai, with its abundance of talent and strong connectivity and accessibility to markets. But his manufacturing unit continued to be in Cuddalore and Pondicherry.

The move to Chennai proved lucky for Ranganathan as his company grew several fold every year. He recruited quality professionals and it made a lot of difference in the way the company planned its strategies. Ultimately, these new strategies paid dividends.

By 1992, their market share grew to the point that they became numero uno in South India. After he started out, it took him nine years to overtake his brothers' Velvette shampoo business that had Godrej's marketing muscle behind it. But the idea that allowed Chik to conquer the market was quite a simple scheme; they exchanged five used sachets of any shampoo for a free Chik Shampoo sachet.

Later, they altered the scheme by giving one free Chik Shampoo sachet in lieu of five used Chik Shampoo sachets. Soon, with this scheme, consumers began demanding Chik sachets exclusively. With this scheme, the sales of the shampoo went up from Rs 35,000 to Rs 1,000,000 in just a single month.

Another idea that worked was the variety of strong fragrance used. 'When we introduced jasmine and rose fragrances, our sales went up to Rs 30 lakh (Rs 3 million) per month, and when we got a Tamil actress to model our shampoo, our sales rose to Rs 1 crore (Rs 10 million) a month! Each idea of ours was rewarded by our customers. There has been no looking back since then.'

Beating multinationals through rural Indian market

Ranganathan realised that the multinational companies sold products in big bottles and not in sachets, and they sold only from fancy shops and did not sell their shampoo in rural India at all!

He recalls, 'That is the reason we chose the hitherto untapped huge rural market; but they were not used to shampoo at all. So, first we went to rural South India. We started by sending our vans to villages and showing them how to use a shampoo by demonstrating its effectiveness on a young boy picked at random from the crowd. Once our demonstration was done, we then asked those assembled to feel and smell the boy's hair.'

The first target was the Tamil Nadu market. They also planned Chik Shampoo- sponsored shows of the Tamil superstar Rajniknath's films in villages across Tamil Nadu. 'During the interval, we screened our advertisements and then demonstrated our product live. We also distributed free sachets among the audience after the shows. This worked wonders in rural Tamil Nadu, and later in Andhra Pradesh too. After every show, our shampoo sales went up by a factor of 3 or 4.'

After conquering the Tamil Nadu, Andhra Pradesh, Karnataka and Kerala markets, Ranganathan and his team moved to the north and the east of India. One fourth of the Rs 1,500 crore market in the north and east was theirs in no time. He says that, even today, the Indian rural market is growing at a pace double that of the urban market.

Starting Beauty Cosmetics

In 1990, when they were a company with a turnover of Rs 5 crores, he also invested Rs15 lakh to start a lamination and packing company called Packaging India in Pondicherry. He thought the investment might come in handy to pack his core product, Chik Shampoo. Soon, however, he found that Packaging India could not meet Chik Shampoo's requirements, and so he instead started doing work for companies like Britannia. In 2006, when Packaging India grew to become a Rs 125 crore company, he sold it to the Zee group.

In 1991, with his mother and grandmother as his partners, he started the private limited company, Beauty Cosmetics Pvt Ltd. They continued with Chik Shampoo for seven years before slowly venturing into more products like Shikakai powder shampoo, talcum powder, deodorant and hair dyes.

'We introduced Meera Herbal powder first but it was actually not our idea. Shaw Wallace [a now-defunct Indian manufacturing conglomerate] already had a herbal product but it was marketed very poorly. We felt there was a demand for herbal products and that we could make a good product. And guess what? In the third month itself, we topped the market. In six months, we had a 95% market share, while Shaw Wallace had only 4-5%.'

'Similarly, we wanted to cater to those who could not afford high priced perfumes and deodorants. Good perfumes came at a huge price that was beyond the means of ordinary people. That is why we came out with a Rs 10 pack of Spinz deodorant. We were successful in that market segment too.'

On the decision to launch a fairness cream

Research states that when a product is good, consumers do not shift to a new brand and that was exactly what Ranganathan's team told him when he decided to venture into the fairness cream market. But he went ahead and launched Fairever in 1997, a product made with saffron, an ingredient traditionally used in India to lighten one's skin. In six months, the sale of the product galloped and in no time, they became the second largest player in the market.

'Many people asked me, why a fairness cream? But it is meeting a basic human need: people always go after what they are not. Fair people tan their bodies to have a wheatish complexion. It is like grass is greener on the other side. I disagree with allegations that we are exploiting people's sentiments; we are just fulfilling their needs.'

How Beauty Cosmetics became CavinKare

When they planned to diversify to new products, they thought the name Beauty Cosmetics would be restrictive. In 1998, they ran a contest among the employees for a name and the company offered a reward of Rs 5,000. Two employees came up with the name CavinKare; with the letters C and K spelt in capital letters: as C and K were the letters Ranganathan used in his initials (his father's name abbreviated) while Cavin in Tamil means beauty and grace.

From beauty care to pickles

Again in 2002, it was sachets that got CavinKare into the food market. 'Pickles were not available in sachets until then as it was an inconsistent mass to pack into something as small as a sachet. The pickles that were sold in plastic packets were packed unhygenically. We thought that if we came out with attractive clean packaging, here was a huge market. We developed a machine to pack pickles in sachets. We started with the Chinni's brand name and then went on to acquire Ruchi pickles. It was a big success in Tamil Nadu where it was introduced first. We then moved on to other states.'

CavinKare became number one in this field too and sells close to 5,000 tonnes of pickles every year!

Entering the saloon market

As they had all the cosmetic products, Ranganathan thought of starting a network of beauty saloons that he called Green Trends in 2000. The plan was to have a channel whereby CavinKare could introduce their cosmetic products directly to customers and get their first-hand opinions. Today, they have 335 saloons all over India and the business is worth Rs 150 crores.

Then the Dairy market

Always on the lookout for opportunities to diversify, CavinKare entered the dairy market in 2009 by acquiring a sick company that supplied milk to Tamil Nadu and Kerala. They then began to market milk shakes of various flavours. Within a year, they became number one in the milkshake market with a share of 24% in the south of the country.

Reasons behind Ranganathan's success

Ranganathan considers teamwork as the main reason behind his success. 'We have good professionals who work really hard. If you can motivate your team very well, you can create miracles. Another reason for my success is that I took just average people like me; but every one of them was highly spirited and motivated. All of us have discussions and debates before we take a final decision.

'The second reason for our success is innovation. We have executed innovative ideas very well. Apart from my initial seed of Rs 15,000 until last year when we received a private equity capital injection of Rs 250 crores, I haven't invested a single paisa into CavinKare. I believe that if you have powerful ideas, money will follow you.'

Ranganathan also doesn't believe in blind risk taking. 'I take each step upwards very carefully. It is only after I consolidate on a step that I try to go up to the next step.'

Giving back to society

Ranganathan says, 'CEOs of global companies in the US including Microsoft, Apple, and Facebook make lots of money. But the culture of the country is such that they donate most of their wealth.

'This is how a country and its business should function. Society should not criticise a businessman for making money. On the other hand, the government must bring societal pressure on them to uplift the downtrodden by way of charity. India is not a communist country. Entrepreneurs will work hard to create wealth.

'If you don't want businessmen to make more money, you should run a communist country. Yet, the government must encourage the rich to take care of the have-nots. Every successful businessman in India should help the poor. You derive much greater pleasure from giving back to society. So, there is nothing wrong in making money but you should learn to take care of those who are struggling to make ends meet. And society must applaud those who do it.

'And that is the rationale behind the CavinKare Ability Awards for physically disabled achievers. I once was a tenant of Jayashree Ravindran, the woman who started the Ability Foundation. One day, she said she wanted to start a magazine for the disabled. Though she did not ask for sponsorship, I gave her a cheque of Rs 25,000. I also became one of the Foundation's founder members. Once we came to know about the disabled who have climbed the ladder of success, we, Ability Foundation and CavinKare decided to institute an award for them. When I started my career, I only faced a shortage of funds. But these people fight hurdles that are far higher. We must applaud their fighting spirit. I feel each of us has to give something back to the society. I have great admiration for those who fight against all odds and attain success.'

A Software Startup

Arun Jain built his first startup in 1983 when nobody had heard of what a startup was. He had just graduated from Delhi Engineering College with no background in entrepreneurship. But Arun had the passion to start something of his own and that was the reason behind his success as an entrepreneur. In fact, the seeds of entrepreneurship were sown even as he was a school student.

His father was a government employee working for the Post and Telegraph department.

Jain founded International Information Systems in 1983 (along with two other Partners, Vishnu Dusad and Yogesh Andlay) with absolutely no capital. This later became Nucleus, and finally grew into Polaris Consulting Services Ltd, a Rs 2,400 crore IT behemoth. In 2016, he sold his shares to Virtusa to focus his energies on Intellect, his software product development company.

Arun Jain is a fearless entrepreneur, never scared to take risks, experiment, change the name of a well known brand, or set 'unachievable' targets for himself. For instance, he had set himself a 'Lakshya' of hitting Rs 100 crore revenue in a mere 7 years at a point when Polaris was merely a Rs 2 crore company.

Here is the story of how Arun Jain built his Rs 2,400 crore company.

Arun Jain, founder of the Rs 2,400 crore IT behemoth,
Polaris Consulting Services Ltd

intellect™
Design for Digital

IT WAS only when he turned 8 that Arun Jain, the 9th child among ten, first went to school, after years spent at home due to his poor health. He was then admitted straight into the Third standard. But from the Third to the Eleventh standard, he changed five schools as his father, an employee of the Post and Telegraph department, got transferred around Delhi.

'I had to cope with health issues, and also with the challenges involved first in skipping the First and Second standards, going straight to Third standard and then in switching between six different schools. If I look at my childhood with a little bit of humour, I would call it diversity at home and also in school! To live among nine siblings was a great learning experience in understanding human beings and I feel it helped me a lot later on in life in dealing with people as an entrepreneur. Also, my father was the only earning member and naturally, there were financial constraints but you learn to live with all the constraints. That's why I call my childhood a great learning experience.'

Later, as a young man, he learnt organisational skills while arranging the marriages of his five sisters.

As school children, he and 25 others in their residential colony used to participate in acts of social service. But the entrepreneur in him had its first outing when the 15-year-old Arun and three of his friends organised a food stall for an event. 'We had to make some money for sustaining our activities. We had seen many stalls by street hawkers on Janmashtami festival, opposite to Birla Mandir in Delhi, and they used to do very good business. We thought to ourselves, "Why not put up a food stall on Janmashtami day when many people visit the Mandir"?'

And they decided to run a Bhel Puri stall. His mother supplied them with all the sauces they needed. But at the stall, it was the kids themselves who made Bhel Puri and sold to the visitors. 'Our stall was a huge hit. People were first amused to see children selling Bhel Puri amongst street hawkers. Perhaps our Bhel Puri was tasty too, as we had sold all our stock in no time at all.'

Having spent just Rs10, they made a cool profit of Rs 30—a large amount in 1975. 'Rs 30 then is probably the equivalent of Rs 10,000 today. Our first success as entrepreneurs gave us a lot of confidence. We ventured into unknown territory, selling food in an area dominated by street hawkers and rubbing shoulders with them. Everything went right for us, all the way from the identification of the product to selling it in the right marketplace.'

His second experiment as an entrepreneur happened when he was a 2nd year student of Engineering. His plan was to do something on a larger scale so that more people were targeted. After many hours of brainstorming, he decided on a charity film show. 'It was a long process; we had to get a theatre for the show, get a movie from a distributor, get an entertainment tax exemption and then sell tickets. The final thing we had to do after all that was to print souvenirs for our customers.'

They managed the entire process in a span of 10 months and each one was like jumping a huge hurdle. 'When we went to the distributor and asked for a film print, he didn't take us 19 year olds seriously. The same was the case when we went out to get tax exemption for the show.'

They were not ready to accept defeat and persistence paid off, and they finally got a theatre for rent, the Dharmendra film *Satyakam* to show, and tax exemption from the authorities. The show was full and they made a profit of Rs 3,000, which they used to arrange health camps in the rural areas outside Delhi.

He believes it was the middle class values inculcated into his life by his parents and elder sisters that inspired him to serve society, even when he was just a teenager.

Though he'd always wanted to be an engineer, his father asked him to study medicine as in his brother the family already had an engineer in the family. But just one year into his pre-medical studies, he found that Medicine was not his cup of tea. He decided to drop out and study Engineering the next year.

'That's the problem with middle class families. They always look at only the employability of your degree and not what you are interested in. When I did better than expected in my final school examinations, my father suggested that I take up the study of medicine. At that time, I didn't think it through either. When my father assured me that it was a good profession with excellent prospects, I agreed and went ahead. Six months into the course, I knew I was not interested in it.'

So, he joined Delhi College of Engineering next year and studied Electrical and Electronics Engineering. When he graduated in 1983, he had two mainstream options in front of him: moving to the United States, since he had a Green Card in his hand or joining the Tata Engineering and Locomotive Company (TELCO, now known as Tata Motors).

But his mind was on a third option; an option that came to his mind following his final year project for which he'd built a BASIC interpreter with more than 2,000 bytes of RAM using a microprocessor kit. 'It was a very interesting project and we knew our interpreter could come in quite handy for college labs and the wider tech industry.'

As a result, he knew what he was going to do even before he'd graduated. By then, he'd designed a logo and letterhead for the company he christened International Information Systems. Once he'd printed 50 copies of the letterhead, he knew he was ready to go!

Though his father was a salaried government employee, he was very open and supportive of his son starting an enterprise of his own instead of taking up a well-paid job. 'He told me to follow my passion!' Another person who wholeheartedly supported him was his brother, who was already working in the US.

'He used to send me long letters giving me the confidence that I could do it. He was like a mentor to me in many ways. Having studied in a government school, I always had this inherent fear of speaking in English. When I was studying Engineering, I felt shy talking in English to those who were very fluent in the language. I always felt that though I was good in technology, I was not good at English. Many entrepreneurs who come from such a background have this unnecessary fear and [inferiority] complex. I feel that even today, many young entrepreneurs fear to come to the forefront because of their fear of speaking English.'

Thus it came to be that, without accepting any of the jobs offered, Arun decided to launch International Information Systems in July 1983 with no backing capital. Joining him were two of his friends from IIT Delhi, Vishnu Dusad and Yogesh Andlay. Arun's house was designated International Information Systems' first office, principally because his father's work at the Post and Telegraph department had ensured they had a telephone there—procuring a telephone connection was extremely difficult in the India of 1983.

The first thing they did was to send twelve letters to those who they thought would be their first 'prospective clients'—people who manufactured microprocessor kits for colleges! Three out of the 12 responded to their letters, and they started working on their first assignment.

They worked on implementing the product, but their first experience turned out to be a disaster. They hadn't signed a proper contract and the company they designed the product for refused to buy it after it had been designed.

While they were worrying about the first failure, they got a programming assignment from the Thapar Group, an industrial conglomerate. And just six months into the start of the company in January 1984, they received their first payment of Rs 15,000. They could manage without any money until then as they didn't have to spend any money on office or telephone.

The first asset they made was to buy a second-hand electronic typewriter from the World Health Organisation (WHO) at an auction. They paid Rs 7,500, ie. 50% of the first payment. Arun Jain has, for sentimental reasons, preserved the electronic typewriter, which now takes pride of place in his office at Intellect.

When asked why he'd purchased an electronic typewriter, Arun Jain recalls, 'We didn't have the money to buy a computer or printer. But we still wanted our proposals to look different from what our competitors produced on normal typewriters. What was written on an electronic typewriter had more sophistication and glamour. We thought that if the proposal from a company is written using an electronic typewriter, the brand value of the company might appear to be higher: it worked, and we learnt that what an entrepreneur needs first is brand positioning. Even in the startup phase, the value of a brand is very important. I tell every young entrepreneur to invest in things that add value to their brand. But nobody taught us this; we were just aware of it.'

It was only much later that they purchased their own computer; until then, they worked out of the client's office. By 1985, having mentored IIS to a turnover of Rs 5 lakh per annum, they moved to an office space and had 20 people working for them. More and more programming assignments kept coming their way.

Not going to US in spite of being a Green Card holder

Though his brother was already in America and Arun held a green card, Arun Jain had decided that he would stay on in India as an entrepreneur. His resolve was reaffirmed following an incident during his student days in Delhi. One of his brothers-in-law who worked in America was visiting, and began to criticise everything that was wrong with India. This riled the rebel in the young Arun, who began to argue.

'I said to him, "you were educated in this country. You went to America from this country. How can you be so pessimistic as to say that nothing can be done in India and nothing will work? You are what you are today because what the country gave you when you were young." He was trying to sell me the idea of moving to America, but it didn't work! I told him about my father who started off as a clerk in the P&T department and retired as an officer, while supporting a family of 12 and educating ten children on one salary. "Doesn't that show what can be achieved in this country?", I asked him. And just one generation on, I would be starting my career as an engineer, a class-1 officer. "Everything is possible, and in India too!", I told him.'

Over the years, IIS began to do better and better. It was then that his brother asked him to pay a visit to the US in order to see how things work there. 'He told me that there was no harm in visiting the US and that the experience would help me as an entrepreneur. That was when I decided to go and see why it is such a developed country and how business is done there.'

Off he went on a Green Card to the US for a month. As he went exploring the city of Boston, he saw a job fair and was suddenly filled with the urge to find out whether they would find him employable. He told them that he was an engineer from India, and they immediately interviewed him—and voila, he was offered a job as a senior programmer!

'I wanted to know how they conduct interviews. I was also testing my skills. When Wang Laboratories offered me the job, I was in a dilemma as I was a tourist there and had not come to work.'

Back at his brother's house, he spoke about his dilemma. His brother was of the opinion that he should take it as the job was offered to him not on the basis of his qualifications but on the basis of his knowledge and understanding of Computer Science. As the money Wang Laboratories offered Arun was quite huge, he decided to work for them for a few months and make some money. He didn't want to work for any longer for the fear of ending up stuck in the United States out of habit.

The biggest learning opportunity for him came from the opportunity to understand the workings of the software industry. 'Although our company was in the technology space, I realised that until then, we didn't understand the software industry at all. We were programmers only because that was the easiest way to make money without any capital. I understood that the software market was huge and it was a huge industry. Software hadn't quite become an industry in India, and was viewed merely as an opportunity to make quick money. At the time, India's biggest company TCS had only 400-500 people working for them, while Wang Laboratories had hundreds of engineers coding on each floor.'

Back in India after his short stint Stateside, he used the US dollars he had saved to buy himself a Maruṭi 800 car (which was available for purchase in dollars at the time). He then convinced his partners that software development was fast becoming a big industry, and that they should try and focus on exploiting the growing market. The first change they made was to divide up responsibilities—so, while Vishnu Dusad took charge of marketing, Arun became the Chief Operating Officer and Yogesh Andlay the Chief Technologist.

Citibank Contract

In 1986, they decided to start a new company Nucleus Software focusing on Banking Software applications. The same year, they pitched for a small Citibank contract. Beating back bids from giants like TCS, Infosys and Mastek, Nucleus Software won the contract. 'Perhaps Citibank's CEO felt that we youngsters, with our enthusiasm, were better suited for the contract than the other well-known companies. While the contract itself was worth a mere Rs 2-3 lakh, it marked the start of our long association with Citibank.'

They launched the Nucleus Software Workshop division to do all of the Citibank work. 'We devised loan products and deposit products for them. We became the first company to create an automatic teller machine for Citibank in India. In 1987, Citibank launched India's first ATM. It was we who programmed all of the systems necessary for the launch!'

To Madras from Delhi

It was in 1989 that Arun Jain came to Madras (now known as Chennai). Citibank had just acquired the Diner's Club franchise and awarded Nucleus Software the contract for developing the software required for their credit card business. One of the stipulations of the contract was that all of the work had to be done from Madras, as those involved in credit card operations were all based out of there.

The project, which resulted in Citibank becoming the first company to launch credit cards in India, was a success. Arun's original plan was to move back to Delhi on the completion of the project, but he changed his mind and relocated permanently to Chennai in 1990.

He recollects, 'My wife and I liked Madras so much that we decided to stay back here. It was a better place to live in as it was smaller. I also felt we could do honest business here. My first office space here was bought with white money, something you can't even think of in Delhi. It was such a huge surprise for me that I could buy real estate space using a cheque!' Amusingly, twenty six years on from when he first moved to Chennai, Arun still can't speak Tamil. However, that hasn't stopped him from running a business that is now headquartered in Chennai!

At this point, Nucleus Software's business had hit an annual turnover of Rs 1 crore. It was expanding rapidly and employed 150-200 people in Delhi and Chennai.

Other changes were afoot too. Vishnu moved to Singapore to look to expand Nucleus Software in the Far East. This, combined with Arun's move southward to Chennai in 1990, were strategic moves for the company. 'We were bold enough to experiment, which was why Vishnu moved to Singapore to work in the Singaporean and Malaysian market.'

The biggest learning experience for them was from Citibank, Arun recalls. 'As we worked so closely with them, we imbibed many of their best practices, such as the practice of including employees in all of the company's activities. This was something Indian companies did not often do at the time. In 1987, we celebrated our first Nucleus Day at a 5-star hotel. This helped build a lot of pride within the company. Most of the time, startups do not spend any money on their employees. But I think it is very important to involve all the employees and make them feel proud of the company.'

1993: Re-launching Nucleus

It is often believed that the split of Nucleus Software into four companies under a single umbrella was the result of a rift between the three friends and co-founders. Arun Jain disagrees.

'We [Vishnu, Yogesh, and I] were operating from three different locations. I was in Chennai, Vishnu in Singapore and Yogesh in Delhi and we found it extremely difficult to take decisions for Nucleus. As we had always taken consensus decisions, our locations slowed the decision-making process down, and it had begun to affect the operation of the company. Those were not the days of fast connectivity and concalls, and phone lines were very expensive! A phone call from Chennai to Delhi cost us Rs 32 a minute!'

That was when they decided to make each company independent. In Arun's words, 'We just restructured or reorganised the company.'

Arun Jain took a 51% equity share in Nucleus Software Workshop, Vishnu a 51% of Nucleus Software Exports, and Yogesh 51% equity in Nucleus Software Engineers. Additionally, a fourth person, Arun Shekhar had joined with a 51% equity in Nucsoft Offshore in Mumbai. While all four companies stayed under the Nucleus umbrella, the person who held the controlling stake in each company became its CEO. All four companies committed to 1% of revenue going to charity.

What was unique about Nucleus at the time was that unlike most companies, especially at the time, Arun Jain did not appoint family members to the company's board and instead filled it with professionals. 'It was to make everything transparent. I am of the opinion that all entrepreneurs should remember this.'

Polaris journey starts in 1996

In 1996, Arun Jain decided to create a new brand that he christened Polaris Software Labs, as he felt there could be a Brand conflict in future with Nucleus. Nucleus Software Workshop was subsumed into the new brand, and thus began Arun's Polaris journey.

Though he knew it was a risk to create a whole new brand while discarding a well-known brand, he went ahead with the plan as he liked to take risks in business.

'I feel these are the sort of strategic decisions entrepreneurs have to take in the course of their journey. I am of the opinion that your brand has to have a personality. By starting Polaris, I was trying to give it a new face. This kind of rebranding is very essential in an entrepreneur's journey. Your brand will become your persona and consumers will see you through your product alone. I was not scared of building a new brand. After all, what is entrepreneurship but a journey without fear!'

Arun Jain is of the opinion that organisations, like humans, are possessed of a subconscious, and believes that the subconscious exerts a much stronger influence than the conscious. To him, the subconscious power of an organisation lies in the shared vision of its associates (employees are referred as associates).

A lakshya—goal—is also just as important in an entrepreneur's journey, Arun Jain feels. When Nucleus had its annual Lakshya meeting with its employees in December 1993, the company had a turnover of Rs 2 crore. The lakshya they set for seven years was Rs100 crore—a goal that may have sounded unachievable to many around the table at that time. But in spite of that, that was the goal they set for themselves. 'BFSI' (Banking Financial Services & Insurance) was coined during Lakshya 1998, and later became the industry vocabulary, demonstrating 'agenda setter' for the BFSI world.

'It is not possible to calculate business plans mathematically. The business plans many entrepreneurs create today truly don't reflect the real potential, as I think it limits your thinking. If you grow over 40% every year, you may reach Rs 20 crore in seven years. We put the question to groups of our employees, "Where do we want to be in December 2000?". All of them set targets. Out of all of the targets set by our employee groups, we chose the target of Rs100 crore turnover in seven years, though many felt this was unachievable.'

According to Arun, business plans and lakshyas are orthogonal. 'When you have a lakshya in mind, the entire decision-making in the company is done with that particular objective in mind.'

Along with Lakshya, he also started the Konark Trust, Konark being a symbol of commitment and excellence where all those employees who had signed for the goal of achieving Rs100 crore Lakshya became a Konark.

And then, the unachievable was accomplished! In the year 2000, Polaris's revenues stood at Rs 260 crore! The company grew 112% every year. 'It was all because we went all over the world. When an employee offered to go to the Middle East or Australia or New Zealand, I let them go and expand business, albeit on a shoe string budget. It was like a large family spreading all over. Our growth happened because of that alone.'

When Forbes in 2000 listed Polaris as one the top 200 fastest growing companies in the world, Polaris celebrated by taking all of its associates (employees) on an 'International Lakshya' holiday to Bangkok.

Hitting the Rs 260 crore target caused other changes at Polaris. Arun says, 'From 2000 on, we became far more conscious of our brand and success. There was a change in our mindset.'

Going Public

It was in the midst of this rapid growth that Arun Jain decided in 1999 to list Polaris, which then had ten offices around the world, on the Bombay Stock Exchange. This was because he felt that going public was absolutely essential to the process of creating a brand.

In August 1999, when Arun decided to run Polaris's IPO at a price of Rs 210 per share, India was just recovering from the aftermath of the war with Pakistan in Kargil. His managers were shocked and of the opinion that this was too big a risk so soon after the war. But Arun, true to type, refused to alter either the price or the date of the IPO.

His punt was, once again, proved right. Polaris's IPO was oversubscribed 20 times over. The initial list price of Rs 210 per share opened at Rs 600. Over the coming days and weeks, the share price kept rising before settling at Rs 2,000. The company was filled with euphoria.

While Arun had himself given his 10% stock option holding over to the Konark Trust, all of the employees who had taken stock options made a good deal!

The Slowdown

Following the bursting of the Dotcom bubble, Polaris did not continue to grow at the exponential rate it did from 1993 to 2000 and settled down to a 20-30% growth rate which was on par with. India's IT industry as a whole. Many contemporaries of Arun in the tech sector blame the slowdown in their growth to the aftermath of the Dotcom bust and the subsequent global financial crisis in 2008, but Arun himself is unwilling to accept that.

'These are all excuses. I take the blame for what happened to the company. We survived the dotcom bust and many other turbulences, but I do not want to just survive. Though Polaris grew from Rs 260 crore to Rs 2000 crore in the next eleven years, yet something somewhere did not work post-2000. Every company has to occasionally gun for a shift in its orbit to move to the next higher orbit. For that, you need extra centrifugal force; something I think we missed.

'I feel there is a limit to how much a human mind can grow. That is why I feel I still have to unlearn quite a bit. I couldn't take Polaris from being a Rs1,000 crore company to a Rs 5,000 crore company, probably because the unlearning did not work as well as I'd hoped it would. The Rs 5,000 crore landscape is different from a Rs 2,000 crore landscape.'

He looks upon this as a failure and disappointment as an entrepreneur. That was why he decided to sell Polaris to Virtusa when it was a Rs 2,000 crore company with 8,000 people working for it.

Selling Polaris also was a strategic, calculated plan that started in 2007, Arun Jain explains. During the 2007 Lakshya summit, Polaris's leadership team found that the market had room for two different types of software businesses: service providers and product developers. As Arun was personally far more passionate about product development, he wanted to slowly shift focus and concentration on that. As a result, from then on, he began to invest Rs100 crore every year in Polaris Intellect, Polaris's in-house product development centre. Investors did not like this decision and Polaris's share prices began to fall.

In 2013, Arun decided to de-merge the services and products divisions into two different companies called Polaris and Intellect. The market liked the demerger and the share prices began to go back up. Subsequently, in 2015, he felt Virtusa would be the right partner to take Polaris's service division and grow it into a billion dollar business.

Since 2015, Arun Jain has embarked on the next phase of his entrepreneurial journey, this time as the CEO of Intellect, a banking and finance product development company. 'My passion is for the road less travelled, and my dream is to make India a global product development centre. There is nothing wrong with providing IT services, but there lies more pride in developing a product.'

He feels energised in his new quest to take Intellect, currently a Rs 800 crore company, to greater heights. So far, it seems to be working: the company is growing at the rate of 30% per annum. He is delighted that 150 banks are using its products, including international behemoths such as Lloyds Bank in UK, Bank of Montreal in Canada, ANZ in Australia, Citibank in US and Reserve Bank of India in India.

'I wanted to establish our products in developed markets, besides the developing markets. It is only when developed markets buy your product, you are seen as successful. The true success of a product is measured when London, Sydney, Singapore and Wall Street begin to pick up your products.'

The IT industry in India sells services worth $100billion. But Apple alone achieves that with just 50,000 people working for it. Arun Jain believes that the next 100 billion dollars for the Indian IT Industry will have to come from software products. 'What three million people can make in services, 300,000 can make by building products, by the means of patents and copyright.'

In addition, Arun plans to invest his earnings from selling his shares in Polaris to Virtusa in sustainable and scalable social impact institutions in the fields of education and healthcare, thereby striking out on a new path as a social entrepreneur.

Just as in 1983 when he started IIS, and then in 1996 Polaris, Arun is now on his third journey as an entrepreneur, and Intellect is the company and brand that he intends to give a personality to.

Branding Breads, Burgers and Curry Buns

This is the story of a man who wanted to make lots of money when he started off as an entrepreneur but today, as a successful 60 year old, his main interest is to give something back to society.

Today, his motto in life is, to make more to give back more!

This is the story of an entrepreneur who sold bread to the people of India when bread was considered a sick man's food.

M Mahadevan's journey, which started as a professor at the Madras University in 1979, to an entrepreneur in charge of a multi-million-dollar business spanning various countries and to a man more involved in charity, can only be described as amazingly inspiring. Even after tasting success for many decades, the man remains the same: kind hearted and hard working.

The brand he created became so synonymous with him that today he is known not only in India, but overseas too, as 'Hot Breads Mahadevan'. This is the story of 'Hot Breads' Mahadevan.

M Mahadevan, popularly known as Hot Breads Mahadevan, is instrumental in setting up the chain of Hot Breads units in India and abroad

Hot Breads

Chennai
contact@hotbreads.in

Puducherry,
hbpuducherry@gmail.com

France,
hotbreads@hotmail.fr

MAHADEVAN WAS extremely frank when he explained the reason why he became an entrepreneur. 'Let me be very honest. The fire in the belly that one must become an entrepreneur was nothing but earn money. If you ask me today why I became an entrepreneur, I am going to stand on a stage and say, I wanted to make a better India. I wanted to change so many lives. I wanted to provide employment. I wanted to touch lives. But the truth is not that. At that age, I wanted to be a rich man and I thought I could be a rich man by becoming a businessman. It is true I wanted to be in the hotel industry. The drive to be an entrepreneur was only to make money. But I never spent money like the rich I saw in the hotels; my family and I are very stingy about what we spend.

'But over the years, your priorities change as an entrepreneur. When you see poverty around, your priorities change. The change happened when I was around 45. That was when I realised money is only a tool to live and not life itself.'

Early days

Like so many hardworking, successful entrepreneurs, Mahadevan also came from a small town in Tamil Nadu called Udumalpet, 65 km from Coimbatore. Though both his parents were doctors, he didn't want to be a doctor and took his postgraduate degree in Commerce.

'I never saw my father at home; he was more married to the clinic. My mother, though she assisted him in the clinic, was both mother and father to us children. I strongly believe that when you teach a man, you teach a man and when you teach a woman, you teach a whole generation. It was a tough job for my mother to take care of the clinic, house and her six children. I was the last. She saw to it that all of us got very good education.'

While he was doing his postgraduation in Commerce, his interest was in something else, the hotel industry. And the reason for his interest in the hotel industry was because he had read the book *Hotel* by Arthur Hailey. 'I had read his book about hospitals too but it was the book about the hotel industry and hotels that bowled me over. I had just joined college then.'

In hindsight, he realises that what attracted him to the hotel industry was people; he loves meeting people. 'My parents also met people as they are doctors, but only those who were in pain and misery, and I wanted to meet people who are happy. Those who come to a bakery or a restaurant are always in a joyous mood. I enjoy talking to the people who come to restaurants. The other day, I met the third generation of a family in our restaurant. It is always a pleasure meeting people.'

In 1979, he came to Chennai to teach Marketing, Management and Accounts to the students of Madras University and work as an Assistant Professor. But that was during the daytime and he had another job at night.

The passion to be in the hotel industry was so intense that he found work at the Hotel Ambassador Pallava at night for four hours. The intention was to learn more about the hotel industry. 'I was a trainee, a bell boy, a receptionist—everything. So, you can say I was a professor during the daytime and a bellboy in the evening. I saw people splurging money in hotels. Businessmen used to come and spend money like water. But it was this experience that taught me how to handle people.'

Mahadevan's mother was aghast when she came to know about what he was doing after the college hours. She told him, 'Are you mad? You are a teacher, and then you are going and cleaning tables? I can't understand this. You are a Guru during daytime and a cook at night? I will not be able to find a girl to marry you!'

'Those were the days when if you said you were in the hotel industry, people had this image of a guy in veshti with a towel on his shoulders and a pencil in his ear, taking down orders! In those days, no girl from any good family in Tamil Nadu would marry a man who worked in hotels! In short, my mother didn't like what I was doing, a bit. But I told her, "One day, I will become the owner of a hotel and give employment to many people". She was happy to hear that part,' chuckled Mahadevan.

First enterprise with Rs 60,000

In 1986, with Rs 60,000, Mahadevan opened his first venture, a take-out at the Tic-Tac unit in Chennai. He met his business partner while he was working in the hotel.

The unit sold north Indian food and opened at 5 pm and closed at 11.30 pm. Soon he started a Chinese take-away there as that was the time Chinese food was a craze among the people in the city.

One of the persons who came to take food was building a commercial tower and asked him whether he was interested in taking up a place there. So, he opened his first restaurant *Cascade* there and served Chinese, Thai, Malay and Japanese cuisine. 'Those who sold Chinese food had red and green as the interiors, but I wanted something different. I got Parmeshwar Godrej from Mumbai through artist MF Hussain's son who was my neighbour. I told her I wanted all white and blue as I wanted my restaurant to look different. Mind you, the interiors became a selling point. Many came to see the interiors.'

From then on, there was no looking back for Mahadevan, the entrepreneur, as his business soared.

Starting Hot Breads

In those days, he used to go to Singapore to buy ingredients like Chinese sauces for the hotel and that was when he noticed the little bakeries there. He had a conversation with a baker who had gone to Japan to learn all about baking. 'In 300 sq ft, he was baking breads, buns and croissants and making money. That's when I decided that I wanted to run bakeries!'

He came back to India and decided to open a bakery in India and sell bread. People laughed at him. His own partners asked him, 'Are you crazy? The success of Cascade has got to your head! Only in hospitals, they serve bread. People look at bread as something that they take when they are ill. How are you going to sell bread?'

He felt they didn't understand that bread had taken different shapes and forms like cakes, curry buns etc.

With Rs 300,000 which he had as a partner in Cascade, he started his bread unit with another partner. He also got Rs 800,000 as loan. Luckily for him, when he approached the Tamil Nadu Industrial Investment Corporation for the loan, though he didn't have any collateral, they found the idea brilliant. They also felt that as he had run two profitable restaurants before, it was a good bet to give him a loan.

Once he got the loan, he had to import bread-making machines, bakery ovens from Japan and France as they were not made in India then. And it was the license regime then. 'I went to Kualalampur to meet the importer agent. I needed an exchange permit here. For that, I had to meet the Export-Import committee and I needed clearance from the Controller of Imports-Exports. It was worth $30,000 but I had to run around for six months. I gave the project plan and after four months, the committee took a decision though they met every month. Once I got the license, it was mentioned in it what machine I was to import and at what cost. Not even a dollar more was I supposed to bring into the country! It was a nerve-breaking experience. At that time, I was young and I was ready to do anything to start my own bakery. I didn't give up easily. Then, when the machines came, the customs officials wanted to interview me where I had to present my project.'

Now, he had to name the bakery and he wanted a name that was catchy. 'As one walks past a bakery, the smell one gets is of hot bread from there. That was when I decided to name it Hot Breads. I had no plan to bake it somewhere else and bring it to the store. I wanted to serve hot breads to all the customers.'

That is how he started Hot Breads—with Rs 15 lakh in 1989.

There was also another reason behind starting a bakery. He knew if he gave a weighing scale, a machine, the ingredients and a recipe, he could make anyone a baker in three months' time! 'No human judgment is needed as everything is written in the recipe book. They only had to follow the recipe book. I understood this was scalable.'

Finally the bakery was set up. He had decided that he would not be selling just bread alone but curry buns, pastries, pizzas, burgers etc. 'Bread was only a trap for the customer to come inside. We took a bun, filled it with curry and made it a curry bun. We filled chicken tikka inside a Croissant. I got the idea to make these things Indian after I saw what the Japanese did to their bakery items. They were filling sweet things inside the bun but we filled curry and chicken tikka inside. Our curry buns became a big hit from day one.'

The sales on the first day were Rs 9000! Nobody could resist the curry buns and in six hours time, they sold out all the things they had in the bakery. 'I knew my idea would be a success. Though my partner said I was overconfident, I was just confident.'

With each passing day, sales at Hot Breads increased by leaps and bounds and soon it touched Rs 30,000 a day. After that, it stabilised. The success was because the concept was new and the product tasty; it was a perfect cocktail. He broke even in the first year itself and never looked back.

In the third month, people from Kochi and Bangalore came to him to start Hot Breads units there.

In no time, he came to be known as 'Hot Breads Mahadevan'!

First overseas Hot Breads unit in Dubai

In 1994, a Tamil couple who had come to Chennai saw how Hot Breads attracted people in Chennai. They asked him, 'Would you like to come to Dubai?' He instant answer was, 'Yes!'

He had around 12 units in India by then. 'I thought a curry bun which I sold for Rs10 here in India, I could sell for 3 Dirhams. One dirham was Rs 10 then. Moreover, my boys were excited to go to Dubai. Even today, they come and tell me they want to go abroad. To travel itself is exciting for them.'

So Hot Breads went to Dubai, started a unit there and it was also a huge success. But he had to close it down after a year as the area became a no-parking zone. When they were about to wind up, he was a bit sad that his overseas venture did not take off.

At that time itself, however, he got a contract from a union cooperative society in Dubai and from day one, it was a roaring success. 'It was a Godsend. Like they say, when one door closes, ten others open.'

Today, they have many units in Dubai. 'The strangest demand we got was for Arabic bread. A gentleman came to our shop and said, if you don't have Arabic bread when you are here, shut your shop'. The very next day, I hired a Lebanese guy and we started making Arabic bread. Kids might like sandwich bread, but elders still prefer Arabic bread. But what is catching up is the curry-flavoured bread all over.'

Becoming a Non-resident Indian

After he opened his first unit in Dubai, he decided to become an NRI. The rules in India were stringent then. 'If you are investing from India, you have to take permission. In those days, even if one had to cough or sneeze, one had to call the Reserve Bank of India and ask, "Can we sneeze"?'

So to keep his international business away from India, he floated Hot Breads Holding LLC in Dubai which took care of his international operations while his Indian Business comprising three companies was based in Chennai. 'Anyway, I was away for more than 180 days to build my international units. The profits you make internationally are not taxed here. The profits I make are put back to start more units abroad. The rules are different now. But I am happy that I chose the NRI route.'

The second stop was Paris

From Dubai, he moved to Paris and from there to London and New York. He admits that none of the moves were planned; it was the customers who asked him to enter each city. 'A man from Botswana tasted my bread and wanted me to start my operations there. He ran the big super market Woolworth there and in many other cities. He had my bread in Dubai and wanted me to have a franchise in Botswana and he is happy there! Similarly, many units were opened in many cities.'

In the last more than twenty years, he has opened 48 bakeries in sixteen countries with help from others: the United States (New York and San Francisco), Ghana, France (Paris), UAE (Dubai), Botswana, Kuwait, Muscat, Singapore, Malaysia, the United Kingdom (London) etc. Of late, he has cut down the operations in the Middle East and is concentrating on the US as 'the market is big and growing'.

Having done business all over the world, he says India is one of the most toughest places to do business and the most bureaucratic too, where bureaucrats sit on a chair and try to act as hurdles between an entrepreneur and his dreams. 'Things have improved a lot now but at the local level, it has to improve much more. Also, 20-25% tax on a food item just because ours is a brand, is killing. The government thinks branded items are bought only by the rich, they are not. Why do we have a brand? Because we want to give quality food. If I remove the brand Hot Breads from the box, how will the customer know what's inside?'

According to him, the easiest place to do business in is the Middle East and the toughest is the US because they don't allow workers to go there. 'They don't think making sambar is a specialised job. They think everybody can be a cook. No, everybody cannot make dosa or vada or sambar.'

Association with Saravana Bhavan

His association with Saravana Bhavan started when he found that he didn't have a good place in Dubai where he could eat south Indian food. 'My policy is, if somebody is doing good work, join hands with him and not look at him as a competitor. There is no point in trying to be a master of all.'

So he joined hands with Saravana Bhavan and Anjappar Chettinad restaurants and now they have 85 units abroad.

It all started with Rs 60,000, and now, he makes around Rs 250 crore in India and around Rs 1,000 crore internationally. Around 3500 people work in the 80 bakeries and 90 restaurants in India and another 1000 people abroad.

Hand of God

Now that he is 60, he wants to concentrate more on charity work than business. 'I believe in the hand of God. You have to be at the right place at the right time, and God's hands have to be there to help you and guide you. Wherever I went—Dubai, Botswana, San Francisco—a force took me there. My ideas worked because they came at the right time. Instead of 1989, if I had opened Hot Breads in 1980, I would have gone bust. Doing your homework is very important which is studying and understanding the market. I have made many mistakes, but I try to learn from them. My advice to budding entrepreneurs is, innovate and think different. Don't follow anyone's footsteps; leave your own footprints for others to follow. Try to be lean and mean. Don't take your customers for granted. Unless you have passion, you will not be able to carry a smiling face. More than hard work, it is passion that you need to succeed.'

My 'boys'

The change in him happened when he started recruiting young boys in the Middle East. That was when he saw them working so hard to send money home. When he asked them what they would do when they went back home, they replied, 'Sir, we only had a thatched roof till recently. Now I have built a home for my parents.' One boy told him that he spent all the money for his father's illness and when he would go back, his bank balance would be zero.

'That's when I knew life is not about money; life is about caring about people. If my employee is taking care of his parents and sisters and brothers, sacrificing his own life, I realised I should take care of him.'

After he came back to India, he met Paul who ran Little Drops for destitute men and women. 'When I started interacting with him, I understood life was full of miseries. If you are a destitute, you are waiting for your time of death. When I met the destitute men and women at Little Drops, my life took a U turn. I realised then that I had to give back to society. Also, you can give only when you have. You can't give from an empty hand. So, I decided to make more money to give more money.'

Today, Mahadevan tries to make more money from his business so that he can give more to society. 'It is matter of pride for me that God is giving me more so that I can give more to the needy.'

A training institute for bakers

More than a decade ago, he started 'Winners, a Bakers' training institute' in Chennai to teach poor, bright boys to bake and the training is for six months. He felt, when you teach them a skill, you give them a life. At the institute, students were given food, a place to stay and a stipend.

The Corporation of Chennai gave him a space where Winners started training school dropouts first. After that, they started selecting poor students from other areas also.

'It all started when I was expanding my business. I needed people. Then I thought I should take a person who really needed a job. I know we need more bakers. By creating such a school, you are empowering the younger generation. The most important thing is, I have started this for the below the poverty line students. We never tell them to work for us and we don't even keep track of what they are doing. They are free to work for us and also anywhere else they want. That's why there is no bond that says that they have to work for us. At least 300 boys must have trained in our institute so far.'

When he started Eddy's Popcorn, it was as a project designed to provide jobs, training and funds for the Spastics Society of Tamil Nadu (SPASTN).

He decided that he would employ only spastic children there, though there are spastic children employed in other units too.

Looking back

Thirty four years ago, Mahadevan's dream was to make money but today, his dream is to help the needy in society.

'When I started in 1982, my goal was to make money. Half way through, I understood money is not everything. When I was exposed to the misery around, I decided to make money and use it to wipe tears. My mother used to say, if you need only Rs 50 to live and you get Rs 70, you must realise that the extra Rs 20 does not belong to you. Today, I am spending the extra money I make on those who need it. God throws in front of me the people who need help. My mother has taught me that when you are fortunate, you have to help the unfortunate. We are trying to bridge the gap between the haves and have nots. I would like to share what God has given me with those who do not have. I see the Hand of God in whatever I do and whatever I have achieved. God has been kind to give me an opportunity to do what I enjoy; I enjoy my work tremendously. This is what I tell entrepreneurs, MBA students and whoever calls me for lectures—make sure your life is purposeful.'

He also tells budding entrepreneurs that the journey of an entrepreneur is not without falls and injuries. He has also fallen down many times, lost money, closed down units but he made sure that the journey was enjoyable.

'I am happy and my happiness today is not in turning my Rs 60,000 into Rs 250 crore. I am happy because I give employment to 3500 boys in India. India needs not one but 10,000 Mahadevans to give employment to thousands of young people. What I have done, anybody can do. I am an ordinary guy from a small town, but I had big dreams and commitment.'

And he will remain an entrepreneur always, till his last breath. Here is a story Mahadevan narrated, 'I have a French chef in Dubai. His 85-year-old mother still runs a restaurant. She said to me, the day I can't light the stove, I don't want to live. Similarly, the day I can't work, I don't want to live.'

The Man who Built and Sold

When Kalpathi S Suresh, an alumnus of IIT Madras, started SSI in 1990 to train engineering students in IT for the US market, there was no such institute in India. It was like a finishing school in software development.

Eventually, after diversifying into services and tasting huge amount of success with branches all over the world with 4,000 people working for him, he sold everything and became an Angel Investor.

And that's what makes him a trendsetter.

His father was a cashier working for Indian Railways, and his mother had not studied beyond the fifth standard. But Suresh was the brightest spark among all of the children in their large joint family of 15-20 people.

He was the first person from his family to graduate with a degree in Engineering, and that too from an institute no less prestigious than the famed Indian Institute of Technology, Madras. From a family where no one had ever heard of the IITs, he wrote the famously challenging Joint Entrance Examination (JEE) thanks to the encouragement he received from teachers at the school he studied in, and came out with flying colours. He was offered places in the much vaunted Computer Science programmes at both IIT Delhi and IIT Bombay. However, Suresh did not want to leave Chennai, where his family lived, and decided to do a degree in Electronics at IIT Madras.

Kalpathi S Suresh is the founder of SSI Ltd, the high end IT education company which went on to become a global IT provider

SSi
Raising the bar

'I THINK IT was homesickness that might have made me choose Chennai over the CS programmes in Mumbai and Delhi. When you grow up in a joint family, you are so used to having so many people at home, I could not think of staying in a place without my people around', Suresh explains.

But a mere four years on, the self-same homebody who did not wish to leave Chennai for Mumbai or Delhi decided to cross the oceans and go to the United States of America to do a Masters' degree. 'In those days, everybody who graduated from an IIT went to the US for higher studies. But studying in the US was a cultural shock for me. You wake up in the morning and find yourself alone in an apartment.

'Everything was new and different; the people you met were new, the transport system was new, even the education system was new. Those were tough days. Though you could find lots of Indian professionals there, there were not many Indian entrepreneurs in the US at that time. So the moment I finished my studies, I went right back to Chennai.'

As he had specialised in microchip design and was utterly fascinated by them, he looked for a job and ended up working for Siemens. However, his stint with them was short; he quit after a few short months!

His desire then was to go work for HCL, a large Indian outsourcer, in their semiconductors division. But just as he was mulling over applying to them, he heard of opportunities at Philips. 'I interviewed with Philips at their Haddows Road offices in Chennai. I got through multiple rounds on the same day and they asked me to come back in the evening for the final interview. I ate lunch and was wandering about when I saw the HCL R&D office. Suddenly, I thought this was a place I should certainly check out. I had wanted to work there awhile.'

He went inside the office and handed his CV over. They asked him if he'd mind facing an interview board right there, right then. Suresh thought to himself, 'Why not?'. He didn't have to go back to the Philips office until much later.

'I still remember the interview clearly. My answer to all of their questions was "No, I don't know". The interview was over in 4 or 5 minutes. Just as I was leaving, one of the women who interviewed me asked me, "So, when are you joining us?" I was stunned. I said, "I could start tomorrow. I am unemployed"!'

He then went on to attend the final round of interviews at Philips, and they told him they'd get back to him in two months' time. This helped make Suresh's decision to start with HCL a complete no-brainer. 'I think they hired me was because I'd been to an IIT and also held a Masters' degree from the United States—this was way back in 1987, and HCL was considering going into the body-shopping business. While they were trying to do something in the hardware space in the US, it was going nowhere. I think I had the right sort of background that they could sell to potential clients in the US.'

It was at HCL that he was first exposed to software. 'It wasn't easy, but I found it interesting. In six months, I did a massive amount of reading in order to catch up with the guys who had done their Masters' in Computer Science. I must have read half the books in the HCL library during that period, going through a book a day. It was then that I realised I liked software.'

By the end of 1987, he was sent to the US to work for HCL software. 'It was easier for me to go to the US this time around, as there were other Indian guys out there with me. That said, I was just the fourth or the fifth guy from the firm to go over.'

After having spent three and a half years in the US, he chose to come back to India. 'At that time, body-shopping had not quite kicked off just yet. Infosys was nowhere to be seen, and TCS were doing a little work out there. US immigration officials were not ready for the coming onslaught of Indian IT engineers. When in the US, I was on a B1 (business) visa. And then, in 1989, the government decided that those who worked in the US would have to have an H1B visa. I decided it would be a semi-permanent move for me, and made my mind up to return to India.'

After he came back to India, he found that database did not exist at all in India. 'I used to be paid $60 an hour in the US for the onsite work I did there. In contrast, the average monthly salary for a software engineer in India was a mere Rs 9,000 ($1 was Rs17 then). This was a huge cost differential; with my experience of working in the US, I knew how things worked and that one required only three months of hard work to pick up what the market there required.'

Becoming an entrepreneur

Looking at this made Suresh realise that there was pent-up demand in the west for highly trained IT professionals; a demand India was very well equipped to fill. He looked around the IT training market and realised that the established institutions—the NIITs and Aptechs—offered only beginners courses in subjects that were not in demand outside of India.

'When at HCL, I'd seen the sheer scale of the demands in the market due to my work pitching to potential customers. So I knew what they wanted. When I moved Stateside, there were just four or five of us. When I left three-and-a-half years on, there were eighty of us over there. TCS and Wipro were beginning to build volumes, as there was a huge demand for engineers in the US—but I knew there was a big gap in supply and demand. But I knew we could train people to do the work required in a matter of three or four months. I also knew that there were no courses available in India to train guys in high-end IT work catering to the US market. That's when I decided to set up a small place to train guys for the US market.'

On the 1st of January 1990, with a small initial investment of Rs 1.5 lakh, he started SSI.

'We used the ground floor of the house I lived in as our centre, so we didn't have to hunt for a space first. With the money I'd saved up, I bought the necessary equipment, computers, books and furniture. When we had to get around to painting the house, we ran out of money and could not afford to hire professional painters. The members of my joint family then pitched in and helped me paint the place up, ready for the first students.'

He still remembers the shock on the faces of his father and uncle when they came back from a summer holiday in Shimla at the time Suresh was preparing the ground floor of the house to become an IT training centre.

Once the house/office was ready, they put an ad in *The Hindu* newspaper; something that cost them quite a bit of money. They also distributed flyers at local engineering colleges. With all of this effort, they managed to attract enough students to join the first batch of SSI students.

The course material was designed by Suresh as he was well aware of the market requirements in the US. He was their teacher too. He also chose to target Engineering graduates to start with. 'We had fifteen students in the first batch, who paid Rs 3,500 each for the course. Our first graduates went on to become our biggest marketers. They went around and spread the word that the course was excellent.'

This word-of-mouth publicity began to attract a whole new demography to SSI—IT professionals who were considering moving to the US.

The demand for SSI's services then began to come from outsourcers that wanted to send their engineers abroad. As the demand grew and he could no longer teach all of the students himself, he recruited a couple of engineers and trained them himself to run the course.

The demand for his course from the Indian IT industry was so high that SSI broke even in the very first year. His brother, who was then working in the Finance department of Best and Crompton and helping him out with the accounts after office hours, quit his job and began to work full-time for SSI. Another brother who was working with Sterling Computers also quit and joined him soon after.

The word-of-mouth publicity then brought in a second demography: SSI graduates began to tell their juniors in college about the value to be gained going to SSI courses, thereby resulting in huge demand from final year Engineering students who were about to graduate.

In no time at all, SSI—now with seven instructors in addition to Suresh himself—found itself teaching students in four batches a day; two in the morning and another two in the evening.

By the end of the second year of SSI's existence, he grew ever more confident. 'It was only then we realised that we were on to something really big and significant. We'd had an auditor come in. The auditor then called me and asked me if I could get him a seat on one of our courses. Apparently, our office had told him there were no vacancies. He asked me whether we had a 'management quota' to accommodate this one person! We were amused to find that demand was high enough that people were willing to try and use recommendations to gain a seat in a private coaching institute! This was how high the demand was! We had no place to accommodate all the students that wished to study with us.'

That was what prompted the move out of Suresh's house to the first floor of a rented place that they converted to classrooms. Subsequently, they went on to convert the terrace too. The facility was open 24 hours, 7 days a week so that students could come in and use the library and machines at any time to practise their skills. 'We had a thousand kids studying at any given time in that building. It was choc-o-bloc full of people. That was when I knew for sure that we were heading in the right direction. We realised that the demand for our courses was far, far higher than what we had expected.' This prompted SSI to switch to expansion mode.

Expansion

Suresh decided to approach banks for loans to expand his business. But the problem he faced was that the banks didn't understand his business model. For instance, he needed to purchase licenses for the

Sybase software and went to many banks for a loan of a mere Rs 2.5 lakh, even offering his house as collateral. The banks he approached first wanted to know the rate of depreciation of the software and asked the resale value of the product. When they wanted to see the product, he showed them the cartridge and the horrified bank people asked, 'you mean to say this costs 2.5 lakh?' He had to explain to them that the cartridge cost only Rs 750, and that it was the software contained therein that cost lakhs. In the end, in spite of his efforts, the banks refused to lend him any money—except for a ridiculously low Rs 400 loan to purchase hardware; money that would only cover 60% of the cost of the hardware itself!

'The banks just didn't understand software in those days!'

But by the end of second year of operations, the banks began to see the cash flows into the business, and grew gradually convinced of the solidity of SSI's business model. So, when the time came for SSI to expand again, a bank lent him two-thirds of his monetary requirements, labelling it as a project. 'It is not that they understood software any better than they did before, but because our cash flow was robust, they were okay to support us.'

The IPO

Into the third year of its existence, SSI was making a huge amount of money. Sales had rocketed from Rs 12 lakh in the first year to almost a crore.

'We could not manage the growth. From 7 in the morning till 9 at night, we were running classes.' In 1994, when there was a lot of movement in the stock market, someone asked Suresh, 'Why don't you go for an IPO?'

Suresh remembers, 'They said listing on the stock market would help us raise funds. We understood nothing about the stock market. We didn't know how we were going to raise money when banks were not ready to fund us! A merchant bank came in and asked me what our future plans were. I said, after five years, my plan is to start sending people to the US directly and not through other companies. My plan was to set up an office in the US and place people there directly.'

Then they went on roadshows and met outside investors for the first time. After the meetings, though he realised that he could sell the public issue at a premium, Suresh decided to list it at the par price of Rs 10 per share. And they raised Rs 2.5 crore by selling 60% of the company.

'Many people asked me, "What? Did you sell 60% of your company for just 2.5 crores? In reply I told them that if I had not done that, the remaining 40% would have been worth nothing!'

After the money came in, they opened a second facility of SSI in Chennai itself, much bigger, with 2-3 floors and 16 classrooms, more than 100 employees, a library, and a dedicated team to develop content for the course. In three months' time, this new facility was also full with 6 batches and over 400 students.

In 1995, they expanded to Hyderabad. 'Hyderabad was a turning point for us. Within just 48 hours of our launch, we were full. Students just came and joined without asking us anything about the course. It was really heart warming; it was recognition of the fact that what we were doing worked for them.'

After Hyderabad, it was Bangalore, and then they opened another eight centres in Chennai.

One thing they noticed was as credit cards were not in vogue, the majority of the students were paying cash. 'My brother was managing the finance. On the day the batches started, mainly on the 1st and the 15th, especially during summer months, we were overflowing with cash. All of our branch managers would deposit the cash at our house and go away in the evening and all of my family members would sit around a table and count the money till 1:30 in the morning. There were days when we had Rs 60-70 lakh of cash in the house! It was a messy affair. We didn't have any safe deposit boxes at home or in any of our branches.'

With their rate of expansion, the question many people asked Suresh was how he would fight the behemoths that were NIIT and Aptech? Suresh told all of them that while they taught students the basics, SSI was more like a finishing school.

'We were miles ahead of what they were doing. We understood software. It was not that I just taught Sybase, I understood the database inside out as I used to build Sybase. So our content was that good. We used to get a royalty of Rs 25 lakh on the sales of books alone! Developing content was a very important component for us and we had a team of 75 people focused solely on developing content.'

In 1997, when they became the number one in South India, Suresh thought it was time to move northwards to Mumbai. In six months time, their centres in Mumbai were fully subscribed, and within a year, they opened five more centres there.

Next came Ahmedabad and then by the end of 1999, they were in Calcutta and Delhi. Soon, they had over fifty centres all across the country. Then they decided to expand through the franchise route.

As it came towards marking its first decade of existence, SSI had become a Rs 150 cr company.

Operations in the US in 1997

In 1997, they entered the US market through a 100% subsidiary under the name Client Soft that focused on placing people in American companies. 'I took the person who was to run our US subsidiary with me to the US, and I sat with him for three months in the US, training him and making him understand what was required. Three months later, he placed our first person at Intel. I stayed on until he placed our fifth engineer. At the end of the first year, we moved some of the most trusted people in our company to the US to help out.'

In the first year, they had placed about 25 people onsite, and three years hence, they had 75 people working through them in the US.

Developing software solutions for the stock market

This was when Suresh, with an eye on the future, decided to diversify into developing bespoke software solutions. He knew that teaching youngsters to work in the US market was not a business model that would last very long. After acquiring a company that did software work for various stock exchanges including the Dhaka Stock Exchange, they went for a joint venture with NASDAQ in 2000 as Indigo Markets to develop software solutions for stock exchanges.

'NASDAQ wanted to set up stock exchanges in Japan and Europe and we were to build the solutions worldwide. We set up an office at the NASDAQ stock market office itself for this purpose. We listed ourselves on the London Stock Exchange in early 2000 to raise money to hire the 5,000 people that NASDAQ was expecting us to grow to. We were the first software company from India to list on the London Stock Exchange. The markets were roaring then and we raised US$100 million, the most any Indian company at the time had raised in the UK. The software company we listed became a separate entity called SSI Technology with a different CEO.'

By this time SSI Education had 500 centres with over 1,000 people working for it.

Accolades began to flow his way. In 2000, Suresh received the Best Entrepreneur of the Year award from Ernst and Young, and in the same year SSI were named the biggest wealth creators in India. Everything was going as per Suresh's plans, and in a big way.

The burst of the bubble

In April 2000, the bubble burst.

'For most funds in India, SSI was either number 1 or number 2 in their investment list. But, when the bubble burst, valuations came crashing down. I used to sit in our office at NASDAQ and watch the index drop by 10% everyday. By 2001, the markets had crashed to the tune of 90% below their peak. A lot of wealth was destroyed during this time, and those who thought they were wealthy were left with a bunch of worthless paper. The volumes traded on NASDAQ shrank and they—our biggest customer—rolled back on their expansion plans. That meant our biggest customer had rolled back. From expecting us to provide them with 5,000 engineers, it now looked like they may not even need 500! At the same time, we had built an office ready to accommodate 5,000 people. Suddenly, everything fell apart.'

As they tried to recover from the bursting of the bubble, a second disaster struck: the 9/11 attacks. '9/11 had a massive effect on our US acquisition plans. Companies that had come and seen our facilities in India and promised to offshore their projects were suddenly fighting for their survival. One of our customers was Marriot and in December 2001, they said, "Forget about offshoring, we are not even sure whether we could pay for your onshore work!" Another taxi company that was supposed to offshore their work to us wound up after 9/11. A third customer, Sun Country Airlines, shut down too. We somehow managed to make it through the dotcom bust, only for 9/11 to be another major setback.'

At the end of 2002, while SSI had revenues of Rs 400 crores, it was not growing as originally planned, especially given the investments Suresh had ploughed into hiring people.

The big turning point

2003-04 turned out to be a big turning point for Suresh personally.

His mother was diagnosed with cancer and Suresh and his brothers had taken her to the US for treatment. 'There was an emergency in the hospital one morning and my brother, who was at the hospital asked us to get there as soon as possible if we wished to see her one last time. As we were speeding towards the hospital, I got a call from Merrill Lynch in Hong Kong and was forced to join a 45-minute conference call.

'My mother had played a great role in my life. She was the driving force all my life. When we needed extra money to keep us going in that first year, she pledged her jewels and raised Rs 2 lakh for me. I was rushing to see my mother alive for one last time, and there I was, forced to take a business call. That was when I decided enough was enough, and that I would sell everything. The business was intruding into my personal space. I knew I had to restructure my life. Though I had structured the business well, on a personal front, it was not structured as well.'

But he planned his exit in a structured manner. When he returned from the US, he purchased Aptech.

'We bought Aptech because we knew that there was no space for three companies in India, especially in the current climate. We merged our education business SSI Education with Aptech and subsequently sold it to Rakesh Jhunjhunwala. I just wanted to make sure that the business was in safe hands.'

When the news of Kalpathi Suresh selling his business appeared in the papers the next morning, his son was truly shocked and said, 'Appa, how could you sell your baby?'

'It was only then that I looked at the sale from that perspective. I was never attached to anything in my business. I'd decided I wanted a break and when I got a good offer, I sold it; it was as simple as that. I wanted to sell everything.'

By early 2006, he had indeed done so and invested the proceeds into his real estate company, SSI Real Estate. Finally, in 2007, he sold SSI Real Estate too for around Rs 1,000 crore. At this point, there were 4,000 people working for all the different SSI companies. 'After that, I felt completely relaxed', Suresh reminisces.

Becoming an Angel Investor

After making sure that he would not be a slave to business and would work only at his pace and on what he wanted to work on, without outside forces taking control of his life, he decided to become an angel investor.

'Everything I got into, I achieved a reasonable amount of success before I exited from them. I had identified the right opportunities and the right time to enter and exit.

'After having gone through the journey that I had, I know that it took so little to build something meaningful. I didn't see myself as an extraordinary person and I saw lot of people like myself looking for help. I felt if they had a spark and if it's lit, it could become huge. It doesn't take a lot of money to build something interesting. I feel that if someone has a meaningful idea, they could build something big out of it, even with a small injection of capital. For me, investing in an idea as an angel investor is in a way an opportunity for me to share my experiences with youngsters starting out down the path I set out on all these years ago. I know that when you invest in companies, some may fail and others succeed. Whatever the outcome is, we have to move on. I tell young entrepreneurs, "if you strongly believe in an idea, go for it; you will get recognised and will be amazed at the kind of success you can achieve".'

Pat's Prawn Pickles, Beach Kiosk & Food Courts

There is only one way to describe the story of Patricia Thomas, and that is 'simply amazing'.

She started her entrepreneurial career thirty four years ago by selling tea, coffee and snacks out of a kiosk on the Marina beach in Chennai. She did this at a time when she was faced with a multitude of challenges: a failed marriage, coping with a husband addicted to multiple substances and bringing up two small children.

One thing Patricia remembers today is how she never accepted defeat when faced with challenges. She didn't rest until she achieved success. Today, she owns a restaurant, a food court and also corporate catering, having overcome all of the hurdles life threw her way.

Patricia Thomas, a pioneer in corporate catering, runs a restaurant and food court in Chennai

Hotel Prasan Sandeepha

PATRICIA GREW up in a middle class Christian family with two working parents. Growing up, she was the apple of everyone's eye as she was the first grandchild in the family.

'I was pampered by everybody in my extended family as all of us lived together in a joint household, and ours was a joint family with my father's brother and family also staying with us. There was nothing lacking in my life. Till I got married, I had only experienced happiness in my life,' she remembered wistfully.

Evcn as a child, what interested her was cooking. She derived immense pleasure from trying out new dishes, often without the knowledge of the adults in the family.

The first time she experimented with cooking was when she was just eight.

'My uncle loved rearing hens at home, as a result of which we had fresh eggs everyday. The routine was that in the evening when my aunt would come back from work, she would collect the eggs from the chicken coop and use them to cook dinner. One day, before my aunt had come home, my siblings and cousins heard the hens squawk after laying eggs. We ran out and picked the eggs. But we didn't know what to do with them. I then remembered that ice cream was made of egg, milk and sugar. So, I mixed all of those ingredients together and put the mixture in the freezer. Once frozen, everybody in the family tried it and attested to it tasting very good!'

Having tasted success with her first experiment, she made caramel custard next, and after that, the other kids in the house were perpetually after her to make something new.

But she never ever imagined that what started off as a fun afternoon game would one day become her profession. However, even at that early age, the appreciation from the rest of her family—both the children and the adults—gave her the confidence that what she cooked was edible and also tasty!

'My father was never the most vocal person, but I could see from his facial expressions when eating my cooking that he loved what I made. But my grandfather used to be very vocal about his appreciation.'

At that time, she had no idea that cooking could be anybody's livelihood. 'I thought women cooked only for the family. The thought of becoming a businesswoman never came to my mind at all, as I do not come from a business family and both my parents were government servants. In fact, my mother wanted me to become an IAS officer.'

But falling in love with a person from a different religion and eventually getting married to him in 1977 changed her life dramatically. Both the families opposed the marriage vehemently because they belonged to different religions. Unfortunately, the marriage ended in disaster after he became addicted to alcohol and drugs. She didn't know how to cope with an abusive alcoholic husband who physically abused her everyday. However hard she tried, she could not get him out of the spiral of addiction.

Two years into the marriage and with two small children in tow, she had no option but walk out of her home and the only shelter she could think of was of her own parents. 'Though my father, who was a very conservative Christian, never forgave me, he gave me refuge when I had nowhere else to go. I was literally out on the road with two very small children. It was a question of survival for me. I knew I should either succumb to the burden or fight; I decided to fight my lonely battle.'

From day one, she decided that she would not become a burden on her parents. For that, she had to be economically independent, and she could only think of doing what she knew, and what she was passionate about.

'The first thought that came to my mind was, people use pickles and jams everyday. At the time, the market was not flooded with pickles, squashes and jams as it is today. Moreover, people always preferred homemade stuff and most people liked my cooking, so I knew there would be a demand for whatever I made. Thus began my first venture: making pickles, squashes and jams at home.'

She borrowed Rs 200 from her mother and bought the essential ingredients. It was not small quantities she had in mind; she chose to plunge into it on a commercial scale, making 50-60 bottles at a time. That she sold out her entire stock in just one day was a real confidence boost.

If experimenting with ice cream as an eight-year-old was the first turning point in her life, this—way back in 1979—was the second.

The income from pickles and jams was good and she used whatever she earned to make more pickles, squashes and jams. 'It was quite lucrative in the sense, even an income of ten rupees was a blessing for me. I had no ambition at that time except that the needs of my children should be taken care of. I just wanted each day to pass. I was not even thinking of the next day.'

But her days were extremely tiresome as she had to do everything from shopping and washing the ingredients to drying them and grinding the spices. She was very particular that she cleaned, dried and sterilised each bottle herself before packing it.

'It was 24x7 work. I had to do everything manually and all alone. That said, my brother used to help me a lot by chopping vegetables and grinding spices after he came back home from college.'

Prawn pickles, her signature dish

She considers the prawn pickles she made as her signature dish. 'I used to buy all of my ingredients from a Muslim man who ran a grocery store nearby. He also bought my pickles and displayed them in his store. He used to tell me that my prawn pickles sold like hot cakes! He often travelled to Singapore. Before one of these trips, he asked me to give him a few bottles of my prawn pickles so that he could give them to some of his friends there. It was such a huge hit there, that he ordered as many as 150 bottles to take with him to Singapore the next time! But I could only give him fifty bottles and just making those fifty bottles drained me out.'

After some time, Patricia ended up having to stop making her extremely popular prawn pickles, in spite of the demand. She felt the money she made was not adequate recompense for the time and energy she put into the process. The underlying problem, however, was that she did not have anybody to help her come up with a plan to scale up and commercialise her process. 'Those were the '70s. As I was not from a business family, there was nobody in the family who could guide me. I am happy that today's entrepreneurs have mentors from whom they get proper guidance. Imagine, there I was trying to make 50 bottles of prawn pickles on a small kerosene stove!' The complete lack of guidance to first time entrepreneurs is what she feels is the biggest difference between India in the '70s and '80s and India today. She thinks if she had proper guidance in those early days, she could have been running a successful prawn pickle factory today!

Though she started off her venture purely in order to be independent, her ambitions began to grow with her business. That is when she began to consider moving into the catering business.

Starting catering service

Along with supplying pickles, jams and squashes, she also started catering to small birthday parties. 'The number of people who used my catering services began to grow rapidly, purely through the power of word-of-mouth publicity. But I would not have been able to cope with the demand if it weren't for how my brother and sister helped me and how my parents took care of my children.' In those difficult early days, she began work at five in the morning and continued to work until thirty minutes past midnight the next day. One some days, she'd bemoan her situation as she lay back in bed—those were the days that sleep eluded her.

But normally, though, she fell asleep the moment her head touched the pillow. 'The only thought in my mind on most nights was trying to mentally keep track of all of the orders I'd received.'

The first step as a proper entrepreneur

While she was fully immersed in making jams, squashes and pickles, her father's friend, who ran a school for handicapped children, told her that he was handing out kiosks to people who would employ at least two handicapped people. He needed somebody who could run the kiosk, and asked her whether she could run one such kiosk. On seeing her enthusiasm, he gave her one such cart for free. What she had to do was to train handicapped children to make coffee and tea and serve them to customers.

When the question of where to locate the kiosk arose, she decided on Anna Square on Marina beach, close to where she lived. 'I had seen people thronging the beach in the evenings and thought that it was the best place to have a kiosk. But I had to make umpteen trips to the Public Works Department and wait a whole year before I received permission to park my cart there.'

Finally, on 21 June 1982, she was all ready to start working—this was a day she would never forget. 'The previous night itself, with the help of the local rickshaw drivers, I rolled the cart to the beach. My entire family was with me as it was moved to its place. It was a thrilling experience as the kiosk was my own, and it was an overwhelming thought that I was going to be a business woman the next day. I felt like I was the owner of a 5-star hotel.'

Initially she had the permission to open only in the evenings. While most such kiosks sold only tea and cigarettes, she decided to sell cutlets, samosas, bhajis, and fresh juice in addition to coffee and tea.

First day as the kiosk owner

To her disappointment, on the first day, she could sell only one cup of coffee for a mere fifty paise! 'All through the evening, nobody came to buy anything until at 7:30, a man came along and asked me whether we had coffee. I told him that we had both tea and coffee. He bought a cup of coffee for fifty paisa. While he was having coffee, he said he was a railway employee from Kerala, and was on his way to the railway station. My very first customer.'

Patricia came back home crying and told her mother that she did not want to continue the business. But her mother consoled her saying that at least she could sell one cup of coffee, 'Is that not a good sign? You will do better tomorrow.'

Her mother was adamant that she went the next day too. 'If not for my mother, I would have given up on being a businesswoman on the very first day.'

And her mother was right—the next day was very different indeed. She sold snacks worth Rs 600-700—big money for her in those days! There was no looking back after that.

'As my sales grew and the money began to roll in, I added ice creams, sandwiches, french fries and fruit juices to the menu. I was always thinking of new dishes I could add to the menu!'

At no point did she feel awkward or embarrassed standing on the beach selling coffee, tea and snacks. 'It was my workplace and my work was my God. I used to wash glasses and plates in front of my customers and I never felt embarrassed. I never asked myself, "What are you doing?" I was thankful to God that He gave me a chance to work and be independent. Today, everybody talks about open kitchens in restaurants. Well, thirty years ago, I had an open kitchen and I cut onion and tomatoes right in front of my clients. I always kept my kitchen very clean and my workers and I always wore gloves. Nobody taught me how to run an open kitchen; I learnt all of that on my own.'

Even at night, when she'd close the kitchen, Patricia continued to stand at the beach and sell all the stuff she personally made. 'I never felt scared to stand there alone late at night. My only thought was to prove myself and move ahead. There was a fire in my belly that made me believe that I could be successful without anyone's help. I did not want to be a failure. I feel if you have that fire, nothing in the world can stop you from succeeding.'

Though she never felt embarrassed or awkward, many of her customers were initially shocked to see a middle class, well-dressed, English-speaking woman managing a kiosk at the beach. 'Today, you see women everywhere, but thirty years ago, the scene was different. It was unusual to see an educated woman selling tea and snacks on the beach! I was way ahead of times! But I would say, nobody ridiculed me; I only received respect and appreciation for my efforts.'

In the beginning, her kiosk was open from 3 pm to 11 pm for the evening crowds at the beach but later she found that many people came to the beach to walk in the morning. Sensing a good business opportunity, she got permission to stay open from 5 am to 9 am also.

The days she sold the most was when there was a general strike (bandh). On those days, when nobody could commute to work, she raked in as much as Rs 25,000! She ran the kiosk from 1982 to 2003.

Running a canteen at the Slum Clearance Board

On seeing her work at the beach, the chairman of the Slum Clearance Board gave her an offer to run the canteen at their office: a canteen with a proper kitchen. He used to meet her on his morning walk everyday, and impressed by her professionalism, he put forward the offer to her.

This was the third turning point. For the first time, she was running something on a big scale. The canteen also grew to become a huge success.

'Wednesdays were public grievance days when people came in to file complaints with the Slum Clearance Board. On those days, at least 3,000 people used to come to the office. Those were the best days for business; I used to sell as many as 1,000 idlis through the course of the day.'

Having to run both the kiosk and the canteen, she had to start her day as early as 4 in the morning. She made idlis and went to the beach by 5 am. From 9 am she would be at the canteen. From 3.30 pm she would again be at the kiosk and would be there till 11 pm.

By then, she had people to cook and clean, and even the cooking for the kiosk was done in the canteen kitchen. Her monthly income in those days was around Rs 20,000! She was happy though she did not have a single moment to herself.

Running a canteen for a bank

As she was running the canteen at the Slum Clearance Board, she got an offer to run the Bank of Madurai canteen, and she chose it over the Slum Clearance Board canteen. At the Bank canteen, she had to serve food to around 300 people daily.

'Running the bank canteen was a big step forward in my career as an entrepreneur. Every step I took was a step forward. But I couldn't manage two places at the same time, and I preferred running a canteen at the bank than at the Slum Clearance Board. As the news of my food spread, bankers from other offices nearby began to come along to my canteen!'

But she never discontinued running her kiosk at the beach in the evenings.

Another turning point

Looking back, Patricia believes every turning point in her career as an entrepreneur was linked to her personal life. When she was faced with huge challenges in her personal life, those challenges helped her indirectly move forward in her career too.

'When my husband fell seriously ill and there was no one to take care of him, I took the responsibility of taking care of him though we were separated. This additional responsibility—and the daily fights that ensued—put a lot of pressure on me in those days.'

One day, after an argument with her husband, a distraught Patricia came out of the house and stood at the bus stop crying. She boarded the first bus that came along and travelled on it till the last stop. It took her more than one and a half hours to reach the last stop. When she got down, she saw signs for the National Port Management Training School run by the Central government.

'On the spur of the moment, I told the security guard that I wanted to meet the administrative officer. I had heard from my uncle that they were looking for someone to run their canteen, but my trip was unplanned. I met the officer and told him that I was a caterer and that I'd heard they were looking for one.

'I still believe it was God who took me there. I got the offer and I was to serve three meals a day to about 700 students.'

The training school gave her accommodation as they wanted someone within the premises. It was a new life for her and she got into the groove very quickly.

'It was successful from day one, and I took care of the canteen from 1991 till 1996. I used to be paid every week and not monthly, and my first weekly payment was Rs 80,000. I felt so elated to receive so much money, having never seen nearly as much before then. Soon I was earning almost a lakh a week.'

From catering to restaurants

Her connection with restaurants started in 1998 when she met the people who ran the Sangeetha group of restaurants at a fair in Singapore. They offered her a partnership whereby she got to run one of their restaurants. She took it up as an opportunity. It was her first step into the restaurant industry.

From then on, along with her catering business, she began running the restaurant also. 'I enjoy both, as they are both basically about serving food to people.'

But yet again, fate played a cruel trick on her. In 2004, her daughter Pradheepha Sandra and her husband died in a car crash a mere month after their marriage. Her entire world crumbled around her. 'It shattered me, and I withdrew from all that I was doing. I just couldn't accept my loss. I lived for my children. Even today, I think of her every single moment of my life. This isn't something time will heal; nothing will heal this wound.'

What shocked her was the way the accident victims were treated by the ambulance operators. When the ambulance operators found that all the four in the car were dead, they said they could not carry four dead bodies. Finally, somebody carried all the four dead bodies in the boot of a car.

'When I saw the body of my daughter in the boot of a car, I just broke down. No mother can bear to see such a scene. That is when I decided to buy and keep an ambulance on that very spot in order to help people in accidents, whether the victims are alive or dead. It is in memory of my daughter.'

Back to business

While she retreated from her business, her son Praveen quit his job as a marine engineer and took over her business. It was he who made the decision to start a restaurant of their own, and name it 'Sandeepha', a business in his sister's memory.

It took some time for Patricia to come out of her shell and start helping her son out. She decided to take up offers for corporate catering, and in no time at all, she was managing four food courts in four places, serving 8,000 people and turning over about Rs 2 lakh a day.

Slowly, life started limping back to normalcy.

She started her business with just her slaving over a kerosene stove in the kitchen and now, she has 200 people working for her. Her lifestyle also has changed in the last three decades. 'From travelling in a cycle rickshaw, I moved to auto rickshaws and now I have my own car. From 50 paise a day, my revenue went up to Rs 2 lakh. But I have not changed, I am still an ambitious businesswoman.

'When I became successful, many people tried to pull me down; that was because I was a woman in an industry that was very male dominated. If I had the backing of a huge family business house, nobody would have done this to me.'

Words of wisdom indeed!

The Next Wave

The new century came with new challenges and with it new opportunities. By the time the entrepreneurs included in this section came on to the scene, the startup scene in India had changed immensely. Some of the entrepreneurs in this section who came from underprivileged backgrounds—Mustafa and Sarathbabu spring to mind—had to overcome several social, financial and professional hurdles to establish themselves. Each story epitomises the power and potential of the human spirit and the impact their efforts had on society.

When Teaching is a Passionate Teacher's Business

Though the son of teachers, teaching never fascinated Byju Raveendran when he was young; his passion was sports.

After working for a couple of years as a globetrotting service engineer for a shipping firm, Byju became a teacher by accident. When on holiday from his job, he helped some of his friends pass the Common Aptitude Test (CAT) entrance examination into the Indian Institute of Management. From then on, requests started pouring in from friends of friends, and their friends. In no time, 'Byju's classes' became so popular that he quit his job and began flying from one city to another to take classes. His classrooms grew from a single room, to a hall, and then an auditorium and at one point even a stadium! When 'Byju's classes' became a popular brand, he launched Byju's Learning App for school students in 2015.

The learning app also coaches for CAT, Civil Service examination, the Joint Entrance Examination (JEE) into an Indian Institutes of Technology, the National Eligibility and Entrance Test (NEET) for entry into medical colleges and the Graduate Record Examination (GRE) and Graduate Management Admission Test (GMAT) for admission into US universities.

The latest investment into Byju's firm (September 2016), that has been written about extensively, is the $50 million from the Chan Zuckerberg Initiative (CZI), the philanthropic organisation created by Facebook founder Mark Zuckerberg and his wife Priscilla Chan in 2015.

This is the story of how Byju's became a successful brand, in Byju Raveendran's own words.

Teaching never fascinated Byju Raveendran. When on holiday, he helped some of his friends pass the Common Aptitude Test (CAT). In no time, 'Byju's classes' became popular

BYJU'S
THE LEARNING APP

I GREW UP in Azhikode, a small village in Kannur, Kerala, the bastion of communism. I do not know whether it was the influence of communism or the face of any typical village, the social fabric was very closely knit and people were politically and socially active.

I grew up in a joint family where my father's brother and sister and their children also lived. In fact, there were sixteen of us in the house and we used to joke that us children could have our own football team. I feel children growing up in a joint family are generally not self-centric as they learn to share everything.

Both my parents were teachers at the school I studied. My father Raveendran was a Physics teacher and my mother, Shobhanavalli, taught Maths. Normally, children of teachers are pressured to concentrate on academics but my parents were so open minded that they let me participate and excel in sports which was my major passion as a student.

Other than life skills, they never gave me any coaching in any subject. Though some of my teachers used to complain to my parents that I was missing a lot of classes due to my sports activities, they supported me to pursue what I liked. If given a chance, I would have lived my entire childhood life outside the home playing games! In Kannur, football is a passion for everyone, but I played almost every sport available when in school, and football, cricket and table tennis at the university level.

I had my education in a Malayalam medium school and I learnt English on my own, mainly by listening to cricket commentary. It was quite common that many students who studied in Malayalam medium schools felt inferior in front of those who studied in English medium schools while in college.

My father's influence was tremendous in my life as he let me be free of the confinement of classrooms and I feel you learn a lot more outside the classrooms than inside.

The biggest lessons I learnt from my sporting days were how to lead a team, teamwork, and how to perform under pressure. All these helped me immensely when I became an entrepreneur. In addition, I learnt the value of controlled aggression, how to be extremely positive, and that losing and winning are both part of the game.

We played games for fun and not in the structured way most kids play these days. Unlike children who play video games inside their homes, those who run around and play outdoor games learn a lot more life skills. There is no substitute for playing outdoor games with other children.

Though I played sports well, I did not have any ambition to be a cricketer or a football player. I played games because I enjoyed playing them. In fact, I enjoy every moment of my life; I do not do anything expecting anything in return. Maybe I inherited this attitude from my father who is super cool about everything in life.

The choices in front of all the students at that time were, either be an engineer or a doctor, and I chose to study engineering. One reason why I chose engineering was, I knew I would get more time to play as students of Medicine hardly got time for sports.

From a village in Kerala to travelling all around the world

After studying Mechanical Engineering, I got a job in a multinational shipping firm and started travelling all around the world as a service engineer. It was a very challenging and exciting job, and as I travelled to new places, I became more and more aspirational.

If anyone had asked me at that time whether I would be an entrepreneur in future, I would have said, no. The desire to be an entrepreneur never even crossed my mind.

After two years of working, I was on holiday in Bangalore, where many of my friends worked. It so happened that they were preparing for the CAT exam then and as I was good at Maths, they asked for my help. While I helped them prepare, I also wrote the exam just for fun to see how I fared. To my surprise, I scored in the 100 percentile but I had no plans to do an MBA in an IIM. My friends also did well and some of them even got admission at the IIMs.

I was back in India again in 2005 on holiday. This time, more friends of my friends came to me for help to prepare for the CAT exams. I was in Bangalore for six weeks and I might have trained more than a 1000 students during the period.

As the numbers grew, the venue moved from the terrace of a friend's house to a classroom, and then to an auditorium. The initial workshops were free but students paid for advanced workshops once they liked it. Because of the enormous response to my teaching, I didn't go back to my job after that. Once I started teaching, I realised that I enjoyed teaching tremendously which I was not aware of till then.

Becoming a full time teacher

When I decided to resign from my highly paid job and start teaching, my parents supported me. Never did they question me once. They supported all the decisions I took, like not joining an IIM, quitting my job to start teaching while there were many people who questioned my parents' indulgence of me.

In those days, I taught CAT aspirants on weekends while I prepared myself on weekdays by trying to come up with innovative ways to solve problems. I travelled to Pune, Delhi, Chennai and Mumbai during the weekends and in no time, I had to add five more cities on weekdays due to constant demand. Wherever I went, I addressed a packed audience in auditoriums; a few times, I ran classes in a stadium. As time passed by, I even took maths workshops for 20,000 students at one time.

I became a popular teacher and I was doing this all by myself. It was an overwhelming experience when thousands of students wait eagerly in various cities for your classes. Sometimes I wondered whether I deserved the kind of respect and importance they bestowed upon me.

Funnily, a person who had never addressed any group of even ten during my school or college days, was taking classes for thousands of students in auditoriums. When you take classes in stadiums, teaching gets elevated to become almost like a performance art.

Soon I started making lots of money, much more than I ever thought I would make as a teacher. As I was a one-man army then, I didn't have to spend any money on anything except my own efforts.

In 2009, I made videos of my lectures and used V-SAT to beam them to students in 45 cities where I could not travel to.

Byju's classes becomes a brand

My classes were referred to as Byju's Classes from the time the classes became popular. In 2007 itself, without me knowing, the brand name Byju's Classes was created by my students and I decided to capitalise on the brand name later. I didn't want to lose the popularity and the good name the brand had achieved.

In 2011, the idea to form a team came from some of my students who contacted me after finishing their courses at various IIMs. We started the company Think and Learn with 25-30 people but the team grew in numbers every month to more than a 1,000 today.

The product our company planned to create was content for school students and the decision to move from CAT to creating content for school students came from my observation of the students I taught. I had felt that most of the students lacked conceptual clarity and a proper foundation. I found that there was a huge gap in how the subjects could be learnt and how they were taught. That is why I wanted to create something that could fill the gap.

Looking back, I feel I excelled in exams because I wrote exams for fun, the same way I played games. Exams never intimidated me. There was no stress or pressure to perform well in the exams. I looked at exams as a part of the learning process.

Instead of memorising stuff, I used to learn the concepts well, something I found was lacking in many of my students. So, I decided to target the crucial years in a student's life from the 8th to the 12th standard.

Today, my classes are for children from the 4th standard itself. They are in Maths, Physics, Chemistry and Biology. Maths and Science are two subjects for which I had special aptitude and I enjoyed both, especially solving Maths problems. I never learnt Maths and Science to write exams; I loved learning on my own and understanding the concepts.

I noticed then and even now that majority of the students learn a subject to score good marks. You lose the pleasure you derive from solving, say a Maths problem, by studying for the exam. These students don't realise the fun they are losing out on by studying only to score high marks. I was a Maths Olympiad winner in school only because I enjoyed solving Maths problems.

The problem with our education system is that it gives more importance to breadth than depth. We tend to create many generalists and very few specialists. They tell you to work hard on your weaknesses. On the contrary, I would argue that you should also build on your strengths!

Asking questions is the key to a student's success. You see 2-3 year olds learning things by asking questions all the time but as they grow, adults discourage them from asking questions. I feel all schools should encourage students to ask questions. Your thought process is alive only when you ask the right questions.

I love Maths and sports equally and it's tough for me to choose one. My love for Maths has helped me a lot in life; for example, I used my strength in solving Maths problems to start my own company, attract investors and on a lighter note, even impress the girl I loved to become my wife.

From 2011 to 2015, we immersed ourselves in creating content mainly for school students from classes 6-12.

Our content is very contextual and visual. Instead of focusing on the whats of learning, we pay attention to the whys and hows as well. We created each chapter in a subject like a movie. And its not just me, a lot more teachers take such classes these days. We have a 150-strong Content team to develop the content, a 200-member media team to make it into interesting videos and a technology team of 150 to personalise it. In all, we are a 500-member Product Development team now.

By August 2015, Byju's Learning App was ready to be launched, and in one year, we have had 5.5 million downloads with 250,000 plus students using it on an annual subscription basis. We have also found that students spend an average of 40 minutes per session and more than ninety per cent of the students who came on board last year renewed their subscription, acknowledging the fact that they benefited from the learning programme.

Investment over the years

We didn't invest much initially; the Rs 2 lakh I invested first came from what I made from my classes. The first investment came in 2013 when surprisingly, Mohandas and Ranjan Pai decided to invest Rs 50 crore in Byju's Classes. It was after Ranjan Pai saw how students at the Manipal Institute of Technology attended our video classes in large numbers. We used the money to scale up the team and accelerate product development.

The latest and the most publicised investment was the $50 million invested by the Chan Zuckerberg Initiative (CZI). I do not know how we came on to their radar; I assume it must be through some reference. Two things got them excited in our company: the first was how we use technology to personalise learning and the second was the impact our App has had on students not just in cities, but also in small towns. Naturally, I was very excited to be noticed by one of the world's most dynamic young entrepreneurs.

Mark Zuckerberg wrote on his Facebook post, 'As part of the Chan Zuckerberg Initiative, Priscilla and I are investing in an Indian education technology company we're excited about called BYJU's.

BYJU's was started by a teacher and entrepreneur named Byju Raveendran as a way to help students from different backgrounds across India learn in a way that works best for them. The mobile app uses a mix of video lessons and interactive tools to help teach subjects like math and science for a fraction of what other services cost. So far, BYJU's has 250,000 subscribers who use the app for an average of 40 minutes a day—and it's working. A survey found that almost 80% of parents said it improved their children's learning dramatically.

I'm optimistic about personalised learning and the difference it can make for students everywhere. That's why it's a major focus of our education efforts, and why we're looking forward to working with companies like Byju's to get these tools into the hands of more students and teachers around the world.'

Social impact

With a father who is a communist, and having grown up in a village in Kannur, money is not really important to me; I am more concerned and interested in seeing our App make a strong social impact.

I didn't have any drive or passion to start a business but when I started teaching, I realised that it was my passion and it gave me a lot of satisfaction and enjoyment. When my classes started creating an impact, it became a business proposition.

In the sector that we are in, the real fun is not in creating a billion dollar company but changing the way millions of students learn. The most satisfying aspect for me is that we are able to reach out to tens of thousands of students. I always say, I am a teacher by choice and an entrepreneur by chance.

Making money has never been a priority for me but giving something back to society is. That's why I take care of the education and healthcare of the underprivileged in my village. I grew up there and I feel it is my duty to help others come up in life.

I am of the opinion that a business cannot be driven by the passion to make money; the passion to change society is far more important. After a certain point, what value does money have for a person?

He Gave Voice to Autistic Children

Even when Ajit Narayanan packed his bags for the United States in 2003 after graduating from the Indian Institute of Technology-Madras, his plan was to come back after a few years and become an entrepreneur.

His inspiration was his professor, Ashok Jhunjhunwala, and the numerous conversations he had with him.

In 2007, he along with his friends, founded Invention Labs Labs. Today, they have two companies, Invention Labs and Avaz Inc.

Many accolades have come Ajit Narayanan's way after Invention Labs came out with the device Avaz that gave voice to the children affected with autism, cerebral palsy, and mental retardation. Today, 30,000 Avaz apps help many children suffering from autism all over the world. In 2010, he won the President's Medal for inventing Avaz for people with disabilities. MIT's *Technology Review* gave him the Innovator of the Year award for empowering those with speech disabilities in 2011, and in 2013 he was nominated globally as one of the top innovators. He was also invited to give a TED Talk in California in 2013.

The latest interesting and revolutionary app from the Invention Labs is Free Speech, an app that can be used to learn and communicate in many languages. Ever since it was launched in February 2016, it has been the number one app on Apple Store.

Ajit Narayanan, the founder of Invention Labs, is the creator of Avaz, an app that gives voice to autistic children all around the world, and also Free Speech

avaz

I WAS part of the group under Prof Ashok Jhunjhunwala and it was natural for a student who worked with him to dream of starting a company. When I told him about my dream, he said it was a good decision.

In 2003, after I passed out, I had four months to go to the United States to work. He got me in touch with one Mr Kannan, who was trying to make low-cost ATMs for rural India. I helped him make the electronic prototype while he worked on the mechanical prototype. The four months' experience I had with Kannan also solidified my thinking about what I wanted to do later on in life.

I went to the US to see the world, get a professional perspective on engineering, make some money to start a venture and then come back to India.

Impressed with use of technology in daily life in US

While in the US, I was in touch with some of my old friends from IIT-M—Ashwin Chandrasekharan and Adib Ibrahim—who also had similar ambitions of starting a venture in India. I was also in regular touch with Prof Jhunjhunwala.

I was very impressed with the way America had adopted technology in day-to-day life. I once saw a man sweeping the road using a sophisticated machine. I admired how technology had provided solutions to their problems and made their lives easier.

It is not so in India even today. I wanted to invent things that would improve the lives of Indians. So it was my dream that I should start a company that would create products which are useful to the people of India.

Back in India

After four years of working in the US, it was not a difficult decision to come back to India, as I had decided earlier itself that I would come back.

I didn't ask the advice of many people before taking the decision. Perhaps, it was impulsive. One day I just packed my bags and came back. Looking back, I feel I was a bit naive about coming back to be an entrepreneur without any idea about what I wanted to do.

Starting a company

In June 2007, I along with Ashwin and Pritam Shivanna, who was our junior, started a company. Adib joined us later. We wanted to call our startup 'Inventors' Inc'. The idea was that a lot of inventors from all over India should join hands under one umbrella so that we could all contribute to the country.

But we were not allowed to have the name by the Registrar. He said Inc. meant something else in America and we could not have the same name. When we named it Invention Labs also, we were asked why there was no equipment in the lab!

We started in a disorganised way on the first floor of my parent's house with an initial investment of Rs 5 lakh, the money we had saved up for this. When we invaded the garage, my mother felt we would soon take over the entire house! We didn't. Very soon, we rented a place at the SIDCO Electronics Complex and moved there.

We had this dream of making a product for India but we didn't have any particular product in mind. So, we spoke to Prof Jhunjhunwala, and he in turn spoke to Kannan. By now, the ATM had progressed a lot but he needed some help.

By helping him, we started making money. So, we didn't have to touch the corpus. In a sense, we started making profit from day one. We did some other work also to sustain ourselves till we knew what we wanted to actually do.

Milk packet vending machine for MILMA

It was by the end of 2007 that we got a proposition from the Milk Marketing co-operative, MILMA, from Kerala. They wanted to have milk packet vending machines in apartment complexes which worked like ATM machines. They called it Any Time Milk (ATM). So from Kannan's money vending ATM, we moved to milk packet vending ATM! Prof Jhunjhunwala also encouraged us to take up the offer.

It went on for more time than we had expected but it was not a good product from a business point of view for us. It was not a product we could sell in large numbers. More than that, customers were satisfied with the ecosystem of milkmen delivering packets at home.

We didn't get paid by the government also, which we didn't anticipate when we got into it.

Avaz, for those who do not have avaaz

In the middle of 2008, a golden opportunity came to us.

One day, Anil Prabhakar, a professor at IIT-M, asked us to visit Vidyasagar (formerly called the Spastic Society of India). He did a lot of voluntary work for the disabled at Vidyasagar, with his wife Namita Jacob and Prof Hema Murthy.

Rajul Padmanabhan, the director of Vidyasagar, gave us a detailed view of what affects the children with cerebral palsy and autism. It was an eye-opening experience for us: all those children were with normal intelligence but they could not express themselves in words.

He said if only the children were able to communicate, they could achieve so many things in life. We knew this was not a problem confined to India but children all over the world.

Rajul told us to design a communication device similar to what is used in the US but was affordable to people here.

Designing Avaz for the CP children

Children with cerebral palsy cannot communicate or move their hands in a coordinated way; they cannot even hold a pen and write. But they can make gross muscle movements. We decided to convert the muscle movements of the head, hands or legs into speech.

We made a prototype and spent hours with the children of Vidyasagar to find out where they were frustrated, what they were happy about, where they were comfortable etc.

We went back to them with a better prototype after each session. The teachers there were very helpful with the feedback. It was tough because we were working for those whose feelings we don't experience and who do not communicate to us effectively. We cannot even imagine what the world is for a person with cerebral palsy or autism.

Interaction with the children was absolutely essential; it was not like sitting in a lab and coming out with a product.

We started work on the device by the middle of 2008. By the beginning of 2009, we had the first prototype ready. It took us two years to develop the product.

We called it Avaz as in many Indian languages, it means 'speech'. Our product gives speech to a child, and that is how we decided on the name. It was a boy called Rohit who used the device first and gave us the feedback. He was the boy who demonstrated to us that such a device could have an impact on someone's life.

From a hardware device to a software app

Avaz was a hardware device aimed at children afflicted with cerebral palsy but in no time, we faced difficulties running a hardware business and selling them in low volumes.

Luckily for us, the tablet revolution happened.

Immediately we decided to move from hardware to software, and converted the hardware into an ipad app. It took us six months to do so but it turned out to be quite an effective app not only from the user's perspective but from our business perspective too. The effectiveness was mainly because when we put it on the App Store, people from anywhere in the world could download it and use it.

Within a month of us launching the product on the App Store by the end of 2012, we sold more than what we had done in an entire year. We had sold only around 200 hardware devices in India at that time but we sold the same number of apps within a month.

Avaz app creates a sensation in the US

As ipad itself was a revolution, ours was one of the first such apps available in the market.

In India, we had to create a demand for our app while there was already a demand in the US. It was the US government that purchased all the Avaz apps because if a child is born with autism, the government has an obligation to purchase whatever is good for the child so that he can have normal education. Because of this, they are all the time looking for products that will help an autistic child.

Though there were some competitors when we entered the market, we were able to do quite well there. Our product was priced at $200 which was Rs10,000 then and was quite low compared to the devices that were available for Rs 5 lakh there.

Though we initially spoke of Avaz as a device that would help children with Cerebral Palsy, we found that it worked for children with autism too.

We chose to concentrate on autism when our app became much sought after in the US, as the number of children with autism is large in the US. One in every 66 children in America is autistic. So, autism is a high priority area in America.

Getting the award from MIT

The response was phenomenal from the people of the US, once they started using it. We got some excellent press and also awards there. Every year the Massachusetts Institute of Technology (MIT) releases a list of 35 innovators under the age of 35 who will change the world, called MIT TR 35. In 2012, I was named by the MIT *Technology Review* as the Innovator of the Year from India, and in 2013, I was globally nominated as one of the top innovators.

In 2013, I was also invited to give a TED Talk on the Avaz app in the main TED conference in California.

How Avaz helps children with autism

Pictures are the universal way to communicate whether you are disabled or not. If you look back, we have seen the images painted and carved on caves and stones by the ancient man.

Most children with autism have difficulty in understanding the abstraction in language and also in communication. We use pictures which are not abstract, and children are able to use pictures as reference and communicate. When they pick the picture of say, a dog, Avaz says, Dog. They can also sequence more pictures to construct sentences and thus say what they want to.

After doing exhaustive research on the words frequently used by us, especially children, we have created around 14,000 pictures in the app. The beauty of the app is that users can add their own symbols too like the names of people.

Avaz is like real voice for an autistic child.

Avaz App not accepted well in India due to various reasons

Though we worked hard to see that the app worked in multiple languages like English, Hindi, Tamil etc. for the Indian market, the app was not accepted well in India. One reason could be that while the government purchases it in the US, it is the individuals who have to buy it for his/her child in our country.

Another reason is, in India, the concept itself was totally new while you see thousands and thousands of children using apps like this in the US. People know the way their lives have changed dramatically because of that. But in India, inclusion is still a distant reality.

India is today where the US was 30-40 years ago but I am sure it will not take that long for us to reach where they are now. Even parents do not know the potential their children can have with a technology like Avaz. They do not understand what a child can do if you give Avaz to a child.

Many Indian parents are sceptical, thinking communication is not that important for their child. On the other hand, in the US, they have seen people using such devices for 30-40 years and they have become role models for society. Stephen Hawking is one example.

Another problem India faces is, we do not have qualified speech therapists to help even if a parent buys the app. There are only 2,000 speech therapists in the whole of India, while a city in America has more than 2,000 speech therapists. These speech therapists patiently train the children to use it. That is the kind of support system they have.

When one has the ecosystem, we could see the full potential of the technology being exploited there. We saw children reaching several milestones with the help of Avaz. They even went to regular class rooms and competed with other children.

Training module for children

Seeing the situation in India, in 2014, we came up with an entire training module for parents to use the app so that they themselves can be the speech therapist for their children. We are also conducting training programmes for parents and teachers in India. With great effort, finally we have been able to convince the Tamil Nadu government to buy the app for the government schools aimed at special children.

From US to Europe

Now, we have 30,000 children all over the world getting a voice using Avaz app out of which 25,000 are in the US.

The research we had done to add Indian languages to the app came in useful for the European market. The first European language we added was Danish for Denmark. I was in Denmark for a conference and met with a person who headed the Autism Society there. On listening to Avaz, she said, 'I can't believe that children in India have better technology than the children of Denmark'. She wanted me to make it available in Denmark. With her help, we translated everything to Danish. Today, we have the app available in French, Spanish, Italian and Swedish.

Early intervention is essential

By the time a child is two, we can find out whether the child suffers from autism or not. Avaz targets young children because it is essential to help them develop speech at two if you want better results. Unless they get quality intervention at a very young age, it is difficult for them to get these skills at a later stage. By two, children start talking and that is the ideal age to start with the app.

Free Speech is the new app from Invention Labs

We realised that we cannot use pictures to communicate a complicated message or sentence. When you want to communicate an entire thought in a sentence, using pictures, it can be very challenging.

That led me to inventing a new technology called Free Speech. By using Free Speech, anyone can communicate using pictures, not just single words but entire sentences. In this app, you arrange pictures in the way you want so that it can give meaning to what you want to express. Then I came up with an algorithm that converts the meaning to the language that people want to communicate in.

This is a powerful tool which anybody can use to communicate in any language they want. It took a lot of effort and time, and my TED Talk in 2013 was about this.

We launched Free Speech priced at $10 in February 2016 on Apple app store and in no time, it became the number one app in the App store across all categories and all countries.

Who can benefit from Free Speech

People with dyslexia, and also people who are deaf can use this app. This also can be used by anyone to learn languages, and we already have the Chinese version of Free Speech ready. You can talk and learn Chinese with the help of English and vice versa. Soon, we plan to have many other languages also. The idea is to show the number of languages a computer can speak. Though we started Free Speech with the aim of giving autistic children grammatical capabilities, we soon found that the frontiers are quite big. It was at my TED Talk that I realised the real potential of the app.

Now that we have both Avaz and Free Speech as our products, we have two different markets to cater to. Other than targeting autistic children, we are also targeting people who want to learn languages.

Growth of Free Speech has been faster than that of Avaz. In the first month itself, there were thousands of downloads, and we have made lakhs of rupees!

With Avaz and Free Speech, Invention Labs is doing quite well with 15 people working for us, and offices in the US and Chennai.

Being a socially impactful company, we like to measure our success more in terms of the number of people impacted than the revenue earned.

Job Seekers Become Job Creators

The year was 2008. The entire world was suffering from an economic meltdown that started in the United States of America. India also did not escape from the effect albeit a bit more mildly. Indian companies that were recruiting in thousands every year from college campuses, suddenly found themselves with more employees on the bench with no work. Naturally, recruitment was temporarily shelved.

Among thousands of engineering graduates who passed out that year with a placement order in hand but no joining date were Aniket Jain and Ashish Agarwal in Bangalore, majoring in Computer Science.

After waiting for six months, they decided to join hands and become job creators and not job seekers. Today, their enterprise Solutions Infini has more than a hundred employees working for them.

These two youngsters converted an adversity to their advantage and made a success of it.

Their story in Aniket's words:

Aniket Jain and Ashish Agarwal of Solutions Infini

SOLUTIONS INFINI

COMING FROM a family of entrepreneurs, entrepreneurship was in our blood. We come from a typical Marwari business family and business is in our DNA. But both of us had no inclination to be part of our family businesses. I felt if you had your own family business, you had to be working 365 days a year. That was why we decided to do Engineering in Computer Science and our plan was to work for some big company.

Ashish was a techie who used to make software products, and create and host websites even as a student, and I was always the marketing person. I used to sell his products and also get clients who wanted websites to be created. We also did poster designs for companies. We must have made around Rs 20,000 this way as students, yet we had no plan to become entrepreneurs.

Our final year project was a product that sent sms or text messages to parents from schools and colleges if their children bunked class, and it was well appreciated.

Placed but there was a long wait to join the company

Like the previous years, both of us got placed from campus interviews in very good companies, and we were quite happy. Then started the long wait for the joining date. It just went on getting postponed. That was when we decided to do something on our own and not waste time till they called us to join.

Why not become entrepreneurs?

As we had the previous experience of creating websites, in December 2008, we got an order worth Rs 50,000 to design a website from a company that sold flowers online. We knew we would not be able to do this work all alone, and needed people to help Ashish. We took the decision to hire a few hands. That meant we had to start a company and have an office.

We collected Rs 4 lakh from family and friends, and decided to float a company of our own. We named it Solutions Infini and registered it.

Ashish's family offered us a small space in their office building free till we established ourselves, and we bought some office furniture and computers to start our work.

The first employee of the company

The first person who came to the interview was an MCA graduate, and he asked for a salary of Rs 6000. We thought the salary he was asking was high and let him go. After a month, when we didn't get a good hand to help Ashish, we called him and found that he was still searching for a job. We offered him Rs 6000 and asked him to join us. He became our first employee but he is not with us now.

An interesting employee we hired was after two-three months; he was the fourth person we hired. When he came for the interview, he didn't know the technology we were working on. So we couldn't take him but he came back after a month mastering the technology, and we hired him. We are proud that he is still with us.

Designing websites did not excite them

We got many orders to create websites, and there was a steady flow. After 18 months of designing websites, we knew what we were doing was not right. It was not economically viable to continue and also satisfy clients.

After 18 months, a mentor comes and helps them dream big

In the first eighteen months, we didn't have any vision for the company. We were rather clueless. That was when we decided to take the help of a mentor. We had seen our people only do traditional business and what we were doing was so different.

Our mentor helped us realise that we could take Solutions Infini to higher levels. He showed us the potential of the market, where we were and how far we could go. That was when we started dreaming of building a Rs 100 crore company.

The first thing he asked us to do was to concentrate on what we wanted to do and only after that, we should start expanding.

Infi-Buzz: Technology to send bulk sms to customers

In the meanwhile, Ashish was working on the sms project we did as students and fine-tuning it. We felt that was where the future lay.

Today, when you book a bus ticket or a train ticket, you get the details on your phone. When you draw money from the ATM, you get and sms from the bank.

Similarly, our product Infi-Buzz helps companies to send bulk sms's to their customers. They integrate our technology into the system so that the moment their customer does a transaction—say draw money from a bank, or buy something or book a ticket—he gets an sms.

Advice to expand to conquer the market

Even today, there are only four-five players in the Indian market who create this technology. In India with 1.5 billion people, sms is the most used mode of information transmission. Only urban India is in the sms loop and we are yet to tap the huge rural market. For example, the Grameen banks are still not active on sms.

So, in our second year, we started our first operations outside Bangalore, in Mumbai. In no time, we had branches in Delhi and Hyderabad too; all sales and service offices. First, we had only one person in each city working from home. With them bringing more customers, we opened our own offices in those cities too. Now, all our centres are contributing handsomely to our revenue.

One more product

With Infi Buzz a huge success, we decided to include one more add-on product to it. It is the welcome audio message you hear when you call most of the companies. We named it Dial Street first and later changed the name to Voice as a part of the cloud business solutions. Our aim is to simplify communication for businesses as we work with B2B customers.

6100 customers in eight years

The first customer of Infi Buzz was a lights and bulbs manufacturer in 2009 and our charge was Rs 2,300. I still remember going and collecting a cheque for Rs 2,300 from them, depositing in the bank and feeling so proud of it.

One of our earliest and biggest customers was Tata Communications. Then, we got United Colours of Bennetton and many banks like the Vijaya Bank, Syndicate Bank, Bank of Baroda, Dhanalakshmi Bank etc. as customers.

2015 had been quite good for us as we added 2,000 customers in that one year, and today we have 6,100 customers.

The Indian market is so huge that 80-85% of our revenue comes from the domestic market. Though we had a plan to focus on public sector banks initially, we found that it was very hard and painstakingly slow for them to take decisions. Instead, we decided to focus on new age companies in e-commerce, logistics, retail, and SaaS based companies where decision-making is faster. Some of our big customers include Ola, Flipkart etc.

Becoming a global player

We started dreaming of becoming a global player in the beginning itself as we knew our product could be used anywhere in the world. But we understood that if we wanted to be a global player, we had to have a strong base somewhere outside India.

In our third year, we became a truly global player after we bagged a few customers, and our global footprint expanded in June 2015 when we set up an office in Dubai. We picked Dubai as our first global office because Dubai is very supportive of entrepreneurs in terms of taxation, and it is quite easy to set up a business there while in the US the taxation is high. Dubai, in a way, was our stepping stone to the global market. Another advantage we had was, even before we set up our office in Dubai we already had our customers there.

Today, Dubai gives us 15% of our revenue through five customers, and ever since we set up our office in Dubai, we have 50 customers from the Middle East, European countries, Malaysia and Singapore. Having an office in Dubai helps us get customers in other markets of the Middle East and also Europe.

In the next two years, we plan to have offices in Singapore, the US and also in UK.

Becoming a 100 crore company

We made a revenue of Rs 50,000 in the first month and that was mainly because we didn't have to pay for our office space and both of us were not drawing any salary.

In the next 6 months, our revenue increased to Rs 2 lakh a month, and in 2014, we made Rs 58 crore which jumped to Rs100 crore in 2015. So our dream to be a 100 crore company happened in 2015!

Giving employment to 120 people

In the first year, we had eight people working for us and in the second year, it became twelve. By the end of the third year, we had twenty five people. It was then that we decided to move out of the old premises and have a spacious office space. Today, we have as many as 120 employees.

The biggest challenge we faced was to function without any support, and lots of interference from the various departments in the government in the initial days. Doing business in India is not easy. We have to deal with multiple departments and we waste so much time and money on this though we are 100% compliant.

The next big challenge is the highly competitive market, with new players entering the field at regular intervals. This can be overcome only by innovation and that means you have to be innovating all the time, which we are doing.

For more startups to come, there should be ease in doing business. We should be able to start a business in 24 hours but there are rules and regulations that stop you from moving ahead fast. Many startups shut down because of government regulations and interference. They should understand how startups function; we need only a little space and a couple of people and a great idea to start with. India's ecosystem has to change urgently if we need more entrepreneurs to come up.

We also need a better education system. Imagine, we still teach age-old technology in schools and colleges. It is high time to update the syllabus. So, it is a challenge to get good quality talent as we cannot offer huge salaries like the MNCs.

Despite all the shortcomings, we feel this is the right time to be an entrepreneur in India.

Sometimes, we look back at the days when we looked forward to joining the company that recruited us and the call didn't come, and the frustration felt. Today, we give employment to 120 people and run a Rs100 crore company because we decided not to wait for that call. The journey so far has been very interesting and it will be even more interesting in the next couple of years!

An Entrepreneur who Runs Marathons

Karthikeyan Vijayakumar, an alumnus of BITS, Pilani, had only one dream; to be an entrepreneur. In fact, as a school boy, he felt if he did not become an entrepreneur, he would be a failure in life.

Though he became an entrepreneur in 2007, his most successful venture twenty19 was born in 2009.

twenty19 is a start up in the educational space helping students get internship in companies; in a way connecting job seekers and job providers.

Karthikeyan is not just an entrepreneur—community service and running marathons also run parallel in his life.

Karthikeyan Vijayakumar is the Founder of twenty19 that connects job seekers and job providers

twenty19

MY FATHER, an agriculturist, is a first generation entrepreneur. As a child, I have seen him build his dream project of electrical contracting from scratch.

At that age itself, I felt that he had made a positive difference in the lives of those who worked for him. This was a big inspiration for me. I also wanted to do something that would have an impact on the lives of people when I grew up.

My father also made sure that I was groomed to be an entrepreneur. I still remember how he talked to us about transforming an idea into reality and the benefits of entrepreneurship, when we went for long drives during our school vacations.

It would be a surprise if you grew up in Coimbatore, a city full of entrepreneurs and not become one. So, somehow even at that young age, I believed that if I did not become an entrepreneur, I would be a failure in life.

How BITS Pilani helped him become an entrepreneur

On hearing some of my seniors talk very highly of BITS, Pilani in the school assembly one day, I decided that I would study technology and it would only be at BITS . It became my dream.

Like I had dreamed, studying at BITS Pilani was a great experience. It helped me get to know a wide variety of people and they turned out to be a big support to me later on in life. When I started my career as an entrepreneur, it was my seniors there who mentored me and they have always been there for me.

In 2004, I graduated and worked in a business consulting firm for a short period to experience the business world before I started something of my own.

First step as an entrepreneur

In 2007, I started Exedos, a business consulting firm along with a friend of mine with a capital of Rs 60,000 and two laptops. We didn't have an office; we worked from our one room apartment. That was the time many international companies were starting their operations in India.

We got our first client two months after we launched, by sheer luck. A semiconductor firm from the US had contacted a friend of ours and he referred us for a job in the company.

We told the company officials about our venture and they were ready to have us as their consultants. We evaluated the market for them and they were quite impressed with our work. With their reference, we got the opportunity to work with many Fortune 500 companies and that included Google, in the next five-six months. We helped many big companies launch in India by evaluating the market for them.

In the first month itself, we started making profits. Within a year, there were 100 people working on various projects for us, across India. We worked with multiple partners and were generating revenues to the tune of $150,000 within a year.

Idea to start another venture

Though our company was making profits, I felt that it was not making any significant difference to the lives of people or any impact on society. We wanted to make an impact on society with our for-profit company. And to make such a difference, we had to be a product company and not a service company.

It so happened that I got a chance to talk to a few college students on entrepreneurship and after that, some of them started working as interns for us. We found that being a small company, they made a lot of difference to our work.

Many of the small and medium companies we were working with also needed interns but didn't have access to them. On the other side, there were students who were looking for internship. Though initially, we connected the students to the companies known to us, soon we found that there was a huge potential in the space.

First, we went and talked to many students about the idea of internship, and found that they were extremely interested but had no idea how to contact companies.

Starting twenty19

By the end of 2009, my friend Rahul and I decided to launch an online portal connecting students in need of internship with companies that needed interns.

We chose to name the portal twenty19 because the students in search of internship are those in their late teens and early twenties. We also thought students would identify with such a name.

With around Rs 4 lakh, the money we saved from the previous venture, we started twenty19.

The beginning was from my rented one bedroom apartment, the living room as the office space. I slept in the bedroom, and the hall became the office room during the day where both of us sat down and discussed our strategies. I had to get ready and come to the living room before my partner turned up for business discussions!

Within three months, we recruited three more people, but our office still continued to be my living room. Once we launched the website in March 2010, we frequented colleges, hung around in the college canteens and talked to students to understand their problems so that we could incorporate all that in our website.

The exciting part of the new entrepreneurial journey was that we were working closely with those who used our website, and it was beneficial to the users. Even the smallest words of appreciation were big motivation for us because it was just an idea before, and the thought that the idea really worked when it was executed, was a big thing for us. When we got the first mail from one of the students thanking us for helping him find an internship, we were as excited as winning an award! It gave us the confidence that we were moving in the right direction.

Searching for a good revenue model

The idea might have been good but our revenue model was not exemplary, as we were not making big money. In the first six-eight months, we had very little money coming in. We were only surviving on what we had saved. I was not taking any salary so that we could pay the team. In fact, the team also agreed for a pay cut in the initial days. That was the biggest blessing we had; a great committed team. In the first couple of years, our revenue was around Rs 20 lakh only.

Other than the five-member team, we also had a few interns working for us. After the first six-eight months, we were charging the corporates who had tied up with us but it was not enough to survive. Charging companies also was difficult, as they were not used to paying to get interns—they had only seen students reaching out to them. They didn't see much value in the service we offered.

We were driven mainly by the adrenaline.

We worked exclusively with college students and they registered on our website with a list of their interests, preferences and the industry they wanted to work in.

We had a tool— a Quiz Challenge tool which the students filled in and it was from this that companies identified the suitable students and it helped them save eighty per cent of their time.

Companies also posted their requirement for interns on our site. Once the students register, they get timely alerts on the availability in the industry.

Though it was free registration for students, the companies paid us for the Quiz Challenge tool they used.

In the first six months, we had 300 companies registering on our portal and more than 5,000 students using the platform.

Around seventy per cent of the interns got their internship converted as job offers. Many of the companies looked at internship to gauge whether the student fitted into their requirements.

When we started in 2010, only ten per cent of the companies paid a stipend. But, noticing the quality of students and work done by them, ninety per cent of the companies started paying them a stipend, albeit slowly.

Our plan was to reach out to venture capitalists after attaining a sustainable model. Till 2013, we didn't contact any of them as we were struggling. The advice we got was, instead of going for seed funding, we should wait for late stage funding when we were more clear about how we wanted to go about it. Till then, we were advised to go lean and mean.

By 2012, I moved out of the one-bedroom apartment and converted it into our office. In 2013, we moved to a smaller corporate office.

Two changes

By 2012-13, a startup boom had taken off in India and all the startups were facing a huge shortage of talented interns. Earlier companies were not ready to pay for recruiting interns, but after the startup boom, we found that they were willing to pay for good people. Without us asking, they moved to our pay-plan.

We also observed then that only less than ten per cent of the students who applied for internship were shortlisted. We started thinking of how we could equip the rest of the ninety per cent who applied for internships, but did not have the skills to get internship.

It was then that we decided to start online courses for students to equip them better. We first thought of involving experts to create the course, but finally we ourselves designed the course. After all, we knew what the companies required and what the students lacked. This knowledge helped us design a course that could bridge the gap. It took us about eight-nine months to design the first course material, which was aimed mainly at engineering, arts and science students.

In 2014, we launched the study material and today we have 200,000 students taking up the course. Though we have 80 courses live, ten courses are free and the rest are priced between Rs 1,400-2,800.

Small and medium companies need talented people

From our experience, we found that it is the small and medium companies that suffer from a massive shortage of talented people.

Out of the 18,000 companies who are registered with us, five to ten per cent are large companies, twenty per cent are small and medium companies and the rest are small companies.

When we started, less than five per cent of the companies offered stipend but today, as many as ninety eight per cent of the companies offer a minimum stipend of Rs 5000. When the companies realised that these students could add value to the company, they started paying them well. Today, students have the option to choose companies that pay good stipend. Naturally, if companies need good interns, they have to shell out money. Out of the 500,000 students who have used our website, we noticed that nearly forty to sixty per cent of these students converted their internship to jobs.

Finally, a good revenue model

Today, our revenue model comes from students as well as companies; students using the course material and companies using the data to get interns.

In 2014-15, after we launched the course materials, we grew by 300% and 85% of the revenue was coming from the course material.

Another interesting statistic we have found is, out of all the students who use our website, around forty per cent are from the north of India, thirty six per cent from the south, fifteen per cent from the western region and only five from the eastern region while the companies are mainly located in the metros.

Most of the opportunities are in the technology sector, but we also have media houses, NGOs, content writing companies, ad companies, services, and even some in the core sector use our portal.

The startup scene in India 2016

Because we deal with the small and medium companies and students, we have noticed that there is a massive growth in startups in India. By looking at the number of startups that have registered on twenty19, I can say that from 2013-15, there is a 190% increase in the number of startups using our website. They are the ones who first offer internships and stipend to students.

Ups and downs

We did go through a lot of ups and downs, especially in 2013-14. Though we were growing, we wanted to grow more and impact more people and more students but that did not happen for a long time.

Our experiences taught us that if you wanted to be in the education sector, you could only have a long-term model unlike consumer startups. Also, funding is very difficult to come by in education. We realised that education startups have lots of limitations because here, spending is only for learning and not for buying something.

The temptation is to spend money on a phone than on educating oneself. But we are confident of our startup impacting students for years to come as there are 1.5 crore students doing higher studies in India, and only less than five per cent get to do internship. So, there is a huge market out there. I expect this market to grow several times in the next two years.

Starting Deepam, an NGO

One day in 2008, I was running with a mentor friend of mine, and when we ran past a government school, our discussion turned to the children of the school. We felt if the kids of those schools also got similar opportunities like we had, they could also achieve many things.

We felt that children from the underprivileged background are lacking in the two key skills that are required—in the field of IT-knowledge of computers and English. We also felt that if these children had these two skills, they could go anywhere in the world.

We then decided to volunteer our time during the weekends to help these children equip themselves with these two skills.

That was how we started Deepam. It is a voluntary community effort. Many of our friends also joined the effort. Within a year, we taught over a hundred students. It was an enriching experience for us to see the kids coming back week after week to learn from us.

We are into our eighth year now and around 550 people from all walks of life—retired persons to students—are part of Deepam. We teach in six schools and we have taught 1500-2000 students so far. We are also supporting some of our students financially when they go to college.

Running marathons

Right from my school days, I have been a sports person. But when in school, I had an accident and after that, I had to start my life from scratch. That made me focus on running.

In 2006, I ran my first marathon. The first marathon gave me the confidence that I could do anything. I have completed three full marathons of 42 km and over forty half marathons.

In addition to running, I also do yoga, swimming and cycling. This has helped me remain calm, focused on the tasks I do and remain fit physically and mentally.

There is a lot of correlation between running a marathon and running a business. Both are about picking the right path, persevering through and staying focussed for a longer period till the finish.

She Helps Women Find a Career After a Break

A few startling statistics.

India is ranked 123rd in the female-male ratio at work place.

India has 48% of its women aborting their careers mid-way, which is twenty per cent more than the global average.

The Indian woman's contribution to the national GDP is at 17%, which is much lower than the global average of 37%. This is the lowest among all the ten regions in the world.

If India's women's workforce participation rate can be increased to 41% by 2025, it can add an estimated Rs 46 lakh crore ($700 billion) to India's GDP. It is in this background that the efforts of Saundarya Rajesh to help women find a career after a break, becomes significant. She was chosen as one of the hundred woman for the #100Women Initiative started by the Union Ministry of Women and Child Development in collaboration with Facebook to recognise and acknowledge women who are making a difference in their communities, across the country.

Saundarya's journey as an entrepreneur started in 2000 when she co-founded AVTAR with K Umasankar and five employees.

In 2005, she started the initiative AVTAR I-Win to help women find a second career after a break. Ten years later, it has about 40,000 women professionals in the network and more than 8,000 women have re-entered the workforce because of Saundarya and her team. In the meantime, she also did her PhD on women's work force participation. Here is the story of how Saundarya Rajesh decided to help women find a career after a break.

Saundarya Rajesh is the Founder President of Avtar that helps women find a career after a break

AVTAR

The Power of Change

I NEVER wanted to be an entrepreneur as a student though my father, who was a successful entrepreneur in pharmaceuticals, was my inspiration. Even when I studied English literature, my father saw an entrepreneur in me and asked me to do an MBA.

I met my husband there and both of us joined Citi Bank later. When I had my first baby, I had to take a break from my career from 1993-96.

Becoming an entrepreneur after taking a break in career

After the break, while I was working as a guest faculty in the Management department of a city college, I started doing projects for corporates like planning training, creating business plans etc.

I would say, I had no other option but to become an entrepreneur! I felt entrepreneurship was the only answer to all the problems I faced at the work place. So it was necessity that made me an entrepreneur.

Founding AVTAR

After doing projects for various recruiting agencies, I decided to start an enterprise in the human resource area with my friend Umasankar in 2000 December. He became the co-founder of AVTAR.

We decided to name it AVTAR as it meant incarnation or metamorphosis. It is to say we take different AVTARs all the time, personally, professionally and spiritually. That is why our byline is, the power of change. AVTAR has many meanings for the corporates and also for a woman. We have the butterfly in our logo as it depicts nature's yearning to constantly reinvent and improve, and become a different version of itself. My mother-in-law became my first investor when she gave me a cheque for Rs 60,000, and with that we took a flat on rent for our office. Till today, we are not funded by any external agency.

We grew into three units in the course of time. In 2008, we started AVTAR Human Capital Trust, and in 2011 we started AVTAR Flexi Career India.

How corporates help their employees in the US and the UK

In 2005, I got the Chevning Scholarship in the UK and also the International Visitor Leadership Program (IVLP Program) in the US, sponsored by the American Consulate. Visits to these two countries were eye openers for me. I saw how these developed economies leveraged the power of women to give advantage to the country.

From my interactions with successful women there, I found that the problems women face were the same all over the world. The woman who has a baby in the US also goes through the same problems as a woman in India. But I found that corporates were actively engaged with these women to find solutions to their problems in their private lives by giving them flexi time, part time and many such support systems. This kind of involvement of the corporates in the lives of their employees was laudable, and it was gender agnostic and not concerning women alone. This made me think, why can't Indian corporates also do the same thing?

Women who were looking for a second career after a break

I came back and did a study on employment of women after they take a break by talking to as many as twenty five corporate houses. I asked them, why didn't they leverage the huge group of talented women workforce to their advantage?

Even today, a break in your resume is a cardinal, unpardonable sin. I tried to make the corporates realise that women returning to work are more energetic, reliable and hard working. Moreover, they are familiar with the corporate world too.

First time, a second career programme in the country

In December 2005, we decided to conduct a second career programme for women, and it was the first of its kind in India. We started our initiative by launching the portal www.AVTARiwin.com and within days, 4,000 women registered. Today, we have 42,000 women on the network. Our focus was women who had taken a break and wanted a second career but we didn't want this to be another job site. So we decided to profile the women who had registered, and set up a small team to speak to them. What started off as profiling became counselling for women who wanted to have a new second career. Most of them, we found, were confused and suffered from depression. So, all of us got trained in counselling.

8,000 women find a second career through AVTAR I-Win

Today, we are the largest providers of second career for women. As many as 8,000 women found jobs for a second time through us.

I would say the corporate sector is still very apprehensive about women taking a break. They think that women should not get pregnant, take a break and then come back even though we are so advanced technologically. The mind-set is still the same. It is very tough, making them think differently. We have to ask questions like, what if your daughter has to take a break...?

I tell the corporate sector that it makes phenomenal business sense to engage women after a break. I also point out how corporates stand to benefit more than the talented woman, as she has more opportunities and she will flourish wherever she goes.

Winning the #100Women Initiative contest

I am happy about the #100Women Initiative started by the Union Ministry of Women and Child Development in collaboration with Facebook to recognise and acknowledge women who are making a difference in their communities, across the country. It was a contest to select 100 women achievers in India through public nominations via social media. I was selected for my initiative to help women find a second career. I am sure this contest and my selection will make the industry and the country aware of this issue and our initiative.

With the President at the Rashtrapati Bhavan

I have received several awards in my career; some of them were for my academic achievements and some for my work but receiving the Scroll saying 100 Women Achievers from the President of India at the Rashtrapati Bhavan was a big moment for me.

I still recall the Gold Medal received from the hands of the then Governor of Tamil Nadu, Dr PC Alexander when I came out First in Madras University in English Literature in 1990.

In 2011, I received the Business Wizards of Tamil Nadu award from the then Governor, Dr Rosiah. In 2014, I received my Doctorate in women's workforce participation from Narendra Modi, a couple of months before he became the Prime Minister. I was also in the UN's list of 25 Women Transforming India in 2016. But what I still cherish was a card I received in 2008, after we finished conducting an assessment centre for women to re-enter the career. This card was made by an 11-year old boy thanking me for finding his mom a job, after an eight year break! That was the best award I would ever get!

'Best Companies for Women' project in India

Increasing women's workforce participation in India is a personal mission of mine. In 1985, the Working Mother Group of US created the world's first tool to collate information about companies that were the best employers for women. Today, 30 years later, I take great pride in bringing the Best Companies for Women project to India.

'Best Companies for Women in India' project is India's very first assessment and benchmarking exercise that helps companies check how welcoming their workplaces are for women. It is a completely self-rating and self-evaluating mechanism as there are no external auditors or employee surveys or any ranking of companies. All companies that participate in the Best Companies project get an individual, private scorecard informing them of their relative position.

I have been a researcher in the field of women's careers for over fifteen years. My own PhD dissertation was about how companies could increase gender diversity in their workplaces. It was always a point of deep anguish for me that there was zero information on companies in gender diversity.

Vision to achieve 50-50 gender balance at work place

We are driven by the vision to achieve 50-50 gender balance in all workplaces. A United Nations report says how a country's GDP can increase significantly through the presence of women in work place. This can be early career women, mid-career women or women coming after a break. Brazil has shown that it has gone up several notches in human development index, GDP index and gender balance index by including women.

Message to the government

The government should give incentives to the Small and Medium Enterprises (SME) to employ women. The large enterprises generally look for talent and by default, they employ women but not the SMEs. While twenty five per cent of the employees in the large enterprises are women, it is less than ten per cent in SMEs.

I feel the six-month maternity leave further alienates the SMEs from employing women and I don't blame them also. So, what the government should do is to give incentives like tax rebate or exemption under some category to the SME sector for employing women.

Advice to women who want a second career break

Let me be quite frank. It is not easy to get a second break in your career. If possible, try not to take a break; instead negotiate for flexibility or part time work with your employer, so that you have the job even when you are away on a break.

If you have taken a break, keep yourselves skilled and update your knowledge and skills even when you are on a break. Women tend to stop skilling themselves, once they become a wife and a mother.

You should not to be obstinate about the kind of job you want to do after the break. There are so many women who have become professionals and entrepreneurs and chosen unconventional areas after the break. You should have an open mind and be flexible in your choice.

A Serial Entrepreneur

Kalyan Manyam is a true serial entrepreneur, having created four startups so far. His tryst with entrepreneurship began as a college student when he started designing websites along with a friend of his.

His next venture was after his graduation when he co-founded a telemedicine company with his brother way back in 2001. Perhaps they were well ahead with the product. This venture failed.

Nothing deters Kalyan from experimenting with new ideas, without bothering much about its destiny. One thing stands out: he is always well ahead of times whether it is the telemedicine venture or indyarocks or Mojostreet.

Today, he is more involved in his new venture, TrueSemantic Labs but he admits that he will never get tired of new ideas and creating new ventures.

The journey as an entrepreneur which started in 2001 still continues…

Kalyan Manyan, a serial entrepreneur has founded Indyarocks and Mojostreet before TrueSemantic Labs, his present venture

TrueSemantic

THOUGH MY father was working with the State Bank of India, he was always interested in doing something on his own. He used to help other family members start businesses. In fact, he himself started a business, but unfortunately that did not succeed.

At the dining table, the discussion always revolved around business. I think I inherited the entrepreneurial streak from him. He was my inspiration and the consequence of my father's failed business venture taught me how essential family support is to tide over difficult times. My first step as an entrepreneur was when I was doing my graduation in International Business in Hyderabad. Along with a friend of mine, I started my first business, that of creating websites. Making money was not my intention at that time; it was more to get a first hand experience of being an entrepreneur.

But we got cheated by the person who took care of the business side of the enterprise as we were ignorant that we needed to have a proper business agreement. That was a first-hand learning experience.

The telemedicine venture also failed

After my graduation, I wanted to go to the United States to pursue my Master's but could not do so because of lack of funds. Then, somebody who knew us very well came forward to funded us with Rs 200,000 and that was how we started Innova Health Systems, a company on telemedicine in 2001

The second lesson I learnt was, it is not a good idea to start an enterprise with money from friends and relatives. If the business fails, it will result in strained relationships, which is dangerous. The pressure to succeed and give the money back to people close to you will not allow you to focus well on the company. The idea to start a telemedicine company came from my brother, Vishnu, who is a doctor. We decided to work together as he had exposure in the field of medicine, and I knew the technology space.

The product was excellent, but the problem was, we were way ahead of time in 2001. Even today, there is no mass market unless you are working with the WHO (World Health Organization) or the UN (United Nations). In India, more than anything, there is a strong need for telemedicine, but not many people are working in that area.

When we started to sell the product, many people felt we were too young to manage such a huge project. Unable to run the business the way we wanted, we decided to sell the company. We could do that easily as we had a good product. Fortunately, we recovered the investor's money, which gave us the confidence that our idea was good. The lesson we learnt this time was, there was lot more to business than building a product. Although many people say entrepreneurs should not get attached to the product, you do get attached as you work on it day in and day out. Even now, my family complains that I am always with my work but the fact is an entrepreneur gets obsessed with his creation. I know it is dangerous.

Back to studies

After selling our company, my brother and I sat back and thought, what should we do now? One thing we realised was, we needed more experience to be successful entrepreneurs.

My brother went to the US to study and then chose to practise there. I sat for GMAT and fortunately, I got funding from the university to do my Master's in Information Systems.

Soon after my Master's, I got a job with a big company with a pay packet of $70,000. At the same time, I got a call from a startup in Silicon Valley for an internship but the pay was much less. What attracted me to the Valley job was that it was a startup. I wanted to gain all-round experience and then start my own venture, and this can happen only in a startup.

When we first started our enterprise, we found that we didn't have experience in anything, except designing products. That was why I was keen on getting experience in all the areas. I told my boss in the beginning itself that I would start something of my own soon; I didn't want him to invest too much in me. I went to the Valley, deep into the world of entrepreneurs. As expected, the company gave me the opportunity to work in multiple areas.

I came back to Hyderabad as part of the company, but was travelling all over the world.

Active member of TiE (The Indus Entrepreneurs)

Even when I was in the US, I was an active member of TiE as my aim in life was to be an entrepreneur. In India also, I am an active member of TiE, Hyderabad chapter and that was how I met the Dean of ISB (Indian School of Business). ISB had started just then in Hyderabad. I told him that I had two options—either I would do an MBA there, or start something of my own. I was not sure whether I was ready to plunge into entrepreneurship. When he came to know about my previous attempts, he told me that I didn't need to study MBA to start something on my own. He felt I was ready for my third innings.

His words gave me a lot of confidence and my brother, who was practising in the US, and I started to ideate once again.

Idea to start indyarocks

The year was 2006; that was the time Orkut was growing rapidly. A lot of people were unhappy about lack of privacy on Orkut; only scrapping was available. Still, they were the only big one in that space, and there was no one to challenge them. We felt there was a huge opportunity out there. That was when we decided to get into that space and started indyarocks.com. We borrowed Rs 500,000 from someone we knew in the US, and registered the company as PhoneLinx Communications Ltd with four employees.

First, we thought we would connect those in the special networking via mobile. We then realised we were repeating the mistakes we had made with our telemedicine venture. At that time, it was dangerous to be only on the mobile platform as mobiles had not become all pervasive. Once again, we were a little ahead of times! So we decided to start an online machine first and then slowly move to mobile capabilities.

We also decided to change the name to indyarocks as we wanted to build a site for the Indian audience. We heard many people say, 'India rocks' and we decided to name our venture indyarocks. People loved the name.

Within three and a half months, we built a social networking platform with privacy capabilities, and I think we were the first to do so. The other thing we did was to integrate user-generated content like videos, photos, audio, blogs and classified all on a single platform.

The initial marketing became very easy as everybody wanted their blogs to be read and photos to be seen by their friends. We looked at the portals in the US and China and found that they never advertised. We also decided not to advertise but we kept tools that would help those who use the platform to spread the word.

Launching 'indyarocks' in 2007

We had a private launch of indyarocks in April 2007 and we first introduced it to bloggers. It was very well reviewed by international bloggers. Then, Indian bloggers also wrote about us. After that, there were many requests for accounts in indyarocks. We created 18,000 accounts and they helped us a lot in finetuning the product. We decided to bring in the Indian flavour by introducing entertainment on to the platform in the form of '360 degrees Bollywood'. It had trailers, profiles of the stars, reviews; everything about every movie that got released. For this, we partnered with various channels for content.

Attending TiE-ISB Connect

The turning point was at TiE-ISB Connect in 2007 where we raised Rs10 lakh from JA Chowdhary of TiE, an angel investor. He also introduced us to other people and we went on networking with as many people as possible.

Despite the media coverage we got, we got only 50,000 members in six months which was not enough. From the feedback, we understood that we were lacking in usability. International bloggers called indyarocks an advanced site. Yes, it was not simple; users had to learn to use it. Nobody likes to learn and use; it has to be intuitive. We made the necessary changes.

From December 2007 onwards, the number of members just jumped. We started adding 200 members everyday and it went up to 13,000 new accounts everyday. In three months, we added 1 million users from all across India, from the smallest town in Jammu & Kashmir to the north-east to the south. We started getting ads and earned good revenues. In 2008 alone, we added 2.6 million members. Then JA Chowdhary brought two more investors whom we met at the TiE-ISB Connect and the investment went up to Rs 1 crore and we broke even.

By 2010, we had more than 8 million members. One of the investors in indyarocks wanted to get into the digital consumer space then and expressed a desire to acquire our company. At that time, we were a profitable company with a turnover of half a million dollars. Most of the companies in the space had closed down or were in the process of closing down while we were making profits. Eventually, Value First, a Delhi based company acquired indyarocks in 2011 end. It was a profitable acquisition. In 2010-11, in India mergers and acquisitions were not happening much but we felt it was the right time to exit and if we remained a boot strap company, we would not have survived. Indyarocks which we started in 2007, got sold in 2011 and we made good money.

Mojostreet

In fact, in January 2011, even before we sold indyarocks, my brother Vishu and I got interested in the mobile consumer space and started Mojostreet. Srini Koppuu, former director of Microsoft India and JA Chowdhary joined us as investors. We raised $350,000 and started building the product.

It was mainly to help people discover movie theatres, restaurants etc. and also to provide more information on all of them. As we were only on the mobile consumer space, this information was available only on mobile phones.

This idea came when we found that if we wanted to go out somewhere to a new place, there was very little information available online about the place. There was Just Dial that gave only the phone numbers. As we hadn't sold indyarocks then, we thought we could make use of the user base and ask them to write restaurant and theatre reviews. We didn't want to rely on what a restaurant says on its website.

Mojostreet was designed to give you suggestions like the place to go for breakfast, the tourist locations etc. For example, if a person was looking for a hair cutting saloon, it would give that information too. In fact, it helps you locate anything in a place. We had information on 2,500 cities across the world and the product became quite popular and was featured in many international media and also in the Google app store. Looking back, I feel we were a bit too early to enter the mobile space. We could not commercialise the product by making the Indian local shop owners pay to be visible on the mobile platform.

We still have a small team that manages Mojostreet but we are not actively pursuing the product. It is still not a profitable venture, though it has a goldmine of information with so many people feeding information on so many places continuously.

TrueSemantic Labs

When we were working with small companies while working on Mojostreet and also seeing reactions of many customers on Facebook, twitter etc. we found that one of the difficulties these companies face is in engaging with their customers.

That made us develop a software product with the help of which companies could find out what exactly their customers want. We sell the software mainly to large chain of companies who have a problem understanding what their customers feel about them, and also what they really want from the companies.

In January 2015, we spoke to many companies and all of them were positive about having such a product at their disposal. In fact many companies had tried making such a product themselves and failed.

In April 2015, we started TrueSemantic Labs as a bootstrap company by investing just Rs 25 lakh with the six people who have been working with me from 2006! In June, we launched the product, Truesemantic at the Uncut Convention in Bangalore. Though we were aiming at large chains, many smaller companies showed interest in buying the product and they were from different areas like education, health, retail etc.

With constant feedback from these companies, we are adding more and more features to the product. More than 250 companies have applied to use the product on trial. The idea is to get at least 50 well paying customers before we go for fund raising.

Four startups and the journey so far

From 2001 when we became entrepreneurs first, the ecosystem in India for startups has evolved a lot. At that time, the word startup was not even heard; we were building a company then. The word entrepreneur was also not popular then. In 2001, we wished there was someone with whom we could talk and get some guidance as we were just out of college. We had this idea to start a company but we didn't know how to execute the idea, scale it up and go to the global market. To get funding was also tough then; the only way anyone could start a company was by borrowing money from friends and relatives. We had a real tough time building our first company.

In 2005, when we came back from the US, the situation had changed a lot. TiE, Hyderabad was quite active and had created a platform to bring all the entrepreneurs in Hyderabad under one umbrella. Through TiE, entrepreneurs could get investments and mentors too. At that time, we were building an online consumer platform, which was again one of the first in India.

From 2008, I started helping budding entrepreneurs by sharing my experiences and guiding them as often as possible. Some youngsters want to be entrepreneurs because they want to become rich fast; that's the worst outlook an entrepreneur can have. He should be passionate about the idea and aware of the challenges ahead.

The startup ecosystem changed so much that by 2014, a lot of people have come forward as angel investors. Outside the ecosystem, a bigger change has taken place; society has become ready to accept startups as a career option, not only as an entrepreneur but also as a place to work.

Parents also have started accepting their son working in a startup. That change has helped many startups to hire good talented people. When my brother and I started our companies soon after college, my father was fine with it but my mother could not accept it. She used to ask us, "Why do you want to take challenges like this when you can work in a big company and earn good money?"

Another important change I see is, many youngsters are ready to accept stock options and grow along with the company.

Challenges over the years

Lack of funds was the biggest challenge I faced all the time. During our first startup days, there was a time when my brother and I used to share the breakfast of one plate of idli in the morning as we didn't have enough money to order two breakfasts. We used to skip lunch, and share dinner again. That was how we saved money as we had three employees and were responsible for giving them salary. We didn't want to take any money from our family. Then there was no source other than a bank loan for technology companies in those days. For a software company, there was no machine or factory to show as collateral to get a bank loan.

Another big challenge in the initial days was getting good talent. In those days, everybody wanted to join big companies like Wipro, TCS or Infosys; nobody wanted to work in a startup. In the last 15 years, the atmosphere has changed tremendously in India and the willingness to join a startup is growing among youngsters now.

Why I am an entrepreneur

If you ask me why I am an entrepreneur, I would say because I love creating new things. The biggest drive for me is the impact my product has on people. The moment I get the feeling that I am not adding anything new to the company, I sell it and start another one, and I will never get tired of starting companies.

Build-to-last Entrepreneur

The journey of Suresh Sambandam, the founder and CEO of OrangeScape as an entrepreneur, started at the age of 19 in Cuddalore, a small town in Tamil Nadu. Today, he is not only a successful entrepreneur but a man with a few patents to his credit and an angel investor to startups in Chennai.

He started OrangeScape in 2004 with Rs 2.4 crore which he got as fees for an assignment and this has been growing at more than 300% every year.

As the CEO of OrangeScape, he shuttles between India, the United States and London.

Suresh Sambandam is the Founder of OrangeScape, builder of Application platform for cloud computing

OrangeScape

I GREW up in Cuddalore, a small town in Tamil Nadu and became an entrepreneur at 19 when I was not even aware what entrepreneurship was. I would say I was an amateur entrepreneur then. It is not that I had this urge to be an entrepreneur; I only wanted to be independent and free even when I was a student, and starting something of my own was the answer to my goal.

When I finished my 12th standard in 1990, my father's real estate business was in trouble. So, I had to opt for distant education in Commerce from the University of Madras. That gave me a lot of free time in the evenings, so I and my friend decided to learn typewriting as that was in vogue then, and that was the turning point in my life.

Other than typewriters, the institute also had one computer. Computers had just entered our lives then and not many knew what it was and where it would take us, especially in a small town like Cuddalore. When the institute manager offered to teach me computers for Rs 50 a month, I joined the course immediately, though I had no idea what I was going to learn about computers. Once I started learning, I knew it was opening a new world for me.

From Basic, I soon moved to dBase and sitting in a remote corner of India, I created a programme for the airline reservation system. Imagine, I had never travelled in an aircraft or seen it at close quarters.

I was so fascinated by computers that I went in the afternoons also to the institute when it was deserted, so that I got more time to learn.

Starting a computer centre

The idea to start a computer centre came to my mind when I felt that was the only way I would get to work on computers all the time. Five of us friends decided to pool in Rs 25,000 each and start a centre.

When I asked my father for Rs 25,000, he refused at first, but my persistence worked and I borrowed the amount from him with the promise that I would give it back soon.

I was so happy when we opened the centre in 1993. The other four guys were only financial partners as they had other work. The advantage was, I got the centre all to myself.

Our plan was to teach students in the mornings and evenings, and also create some software products. We had already gone to some industries at the SIPCOT in Cuddalore with proposals, and we got offers to do automation process in many companies.

The centre used to make Rs 30-35,000 every month which was just break-even for all of us. The only one who had fun was me.

I went to Pondicherry and bought computer books as there were no such books available in Cuddalore. I was like Ekalavya, I learnt Basic, dBase, Cobol, C, C++, and Unix by reading books.

In 1996, when we decided to close it down, all of us got back what we had invested. It was in addition to what we made every month.

Had Internet arrived in Cuddalore at that time, we would have been able to continue the centre for some more time. Anyway, after we closed the centre, I gave the money back to my father!

From Cuddalore to Bangalore

After finishing my graduation, I decided to work in a company so that I would get an idea of how the corporate sector worked.

At that time, only Bangalore and Mumbai were the places to be if you wanted a career in computers. Chennai was not in the picture at all. So, off I went to Bangalore.

Going from a small town to a place like Bangalore was very intimidating then. Even the way I dressed was so different from what others did. Luckily, I had a good command over English as I studied in a convent school.

I literally roamed the streets looking for a job. I must say it was by sheer luck that I got one. Java was just becoming popular and I had learnt it. I saw an ad in the paper that Hewlett-Packard was looking for people who knew Java, and I applied immediately.

I did well in the test and interview, and was offered the job. It so happened that I was the only one among the applicants who knew Java!

I came to know later that HP selected me because in one portion of a project, they needed someone who knew Java. Later, they and I found out that they needed only 10 lines of Java code! Anyway, as I was proficient in C and C++, I also did the rest of the 10 million lines.

I started off as a Software Engineer and got three promotions and in three years I became a Software Analyst.

Applying for a patent

When I left the job in 2000, I had already applied for a patent. It was about a compression technique and not in the area I was working on. When we were running a huge programme, I found that the data communication between the server and the client was very slow as a large amount of text data was being transmitted. I felt there had to be an automatic way to compress the data without actually writing any programme. The client and server could automatically negotiate between themselves and determine a compression algorithm and then compress and decompress the data automatically.

I wrote a paper on this and gave it to the HP patent office, and they felt it was a patentable idea and applied for one. Much later, I realised that the patent would go only to HP and not me! But it is in my name as the inventor but assigned to HP.

Leaving Hewlett-Packard

At that time my boss Ayee Goundan, who was known as the father of R&D labs, and was with HP for 16-17 years, left to start Selectica, a company of his own in Silicon Valley with an office in Chennai. The company was in rule-engine space where I wanted to be. I joined as Software Analyst at Selectica in Chennai and became the Director of Product Engineering in three years.

Starting OrangeScape

The trigger to start my own company was, Accenture taking over our division. That made me think it was high time I started something of my own. I never wanted to work for any large consulting company.

Accenture did many blunders while acquiring the business. They did not add a clause that employees also should go with the acquisition. They actually thought it being such a big company, everybody would flock to them. After the acquisition, I along with a group of people who were working in my team told them that we were leaving. They were shocked to hear the news.

Vision behind OrangeScape

When I was trying to name my company, I asked my boss at Selectica what it should be. He said, find a name that is international but with a Tamil or Indian root. That is when I thought of Orange and named it OrangeScape. In Selectica, we used rule-based engines. Though rule-engines were used by high-end programmers, they were invented so that people who are not programmers also can use the engine.

So, we thought, why not create a product which would help ordinary people use business rules? That continues to be the vision behind OrangeScape. We call this democratisation of computing.

Funding for OrangeScape

I asked my boss whether he would fund OrangeScape and he readily agreed to be the first angel investor and gave us a couple of crores over a period of time. With five people, and Mani Doraisamy as the co-founder, OrangeScape was launched in December 2004. After we started our company, Accenture came to us for consulting and we charged them Rs 2.5 crore for nine months. That became our capital.

First product

It took us a couple of years to develop our first product, Dimension, a pre-cloud version product. We first signed up Numeric UPS in Chennai as our first customer followed by the Rane group of companies, Unilever and Citibank.

In fact, we sold it to a large number of top IT companies. It was a high end product that companies with more than a revenue of Rs 500 crore (Rs 5 billion) could only buy. Business was good, we made a revenue of Rs 1 crore in the first year.

Cloud computing and cloud-based products

Cloud computing came around that time and became very popular with companies. We had encountered a few problems earlier which needed a solution like the cloud, and when it came, we felt this was what we were looking for.

Then, we decided to write a complete new platform. This time, we decided to launch the product as 'OrangScape' itself instead of 'Dimension'. We also made it browser based; Dimension had to be installed from a CD. We were one of the pioneers who created a browser-based development environment which could run on the cloud and deploy on the cloud.

Platform as a Service (PaaS)

The cloud has three layers; one is hardware, which is at the bottom. The software application is at the top. In the middle is the platform and OrangeScape is at the platform level.

At that time, we also made some big decisions like betting on the Google App engine when it was just a beta version. It paid off well and we ended up closer to Google.

We used the Google App engine as the cloud platform technology. Our strategy was to partner with software application developers to create Software as a Service (SaaS) and work on the Google cloud engine. The application belongs to Platform as a Service (PaaS).

Our customers grew, and one of the largest deals OrangeScape got then was with ESIC from Wipro for Rs 5 crore. At one point, we had 100 developers working on a single project which is ESIC, accessed by 20,000 employees all over India.

Google's technology partner

In 2008, we had bet on the Google App engine and in 2012, we were listed as the first and only technology partner on Google

App Engine. In the Google announcement, OrangeScape got a prominent mention, and it showed the kind of confidence Google has in OrangeScape.

Though we are a technology partner to Amazon too, ninety per cent of our work has been done with Google as our partner. In fact, we are in the premier partner category of Google.

Kissflow, the product

We developed Kissflow just for Google App users but in due course, we added Microsoft users also and eventually it became a product for anyone who signs up. Within a year of its launching, we became the number one in Google work store marketplace for B2B products of about Rs 3,000-4,000.

Kissflow has around 10,000 customers from around 121 countries. Because it was the number one product on Google store, people from far away places buy the product and use it.

One of our pastimes was to search for the country on the globe when a new customer from a country we haven't even heard of buys our product! For example, I didn't even know that there was a tiny island country called Aruba in the Caribbean Sea.

We continued to add language support to Kissflow, based on the customer base. After English, we added Portuguese and Spanish when there was a huge demand from customers. Then we added French, German and Arabic, and today we are in ten languages.

As we grew, we opened offices in India, US and London though most of the product development happened in Chennai.

Journey so far

It has been a roller coaster ride. I saw both highs and lows in my journey as an entrepreneur and in 2008 during the recession, I would say, we hit rock bottom. Then in 2012 before the launch of Kissflow also, we were in a very bad shape. I have faced a lot of challenges as an entrepreneur but when I look back, I thank the team for standing behind me. None of them left us when we faced rough weather; in fact some of the senior people even took a salary cut. We kept going through all the difficult times, believing they would pass and they did pass.

Investing in startups

I became an Investor in startups as a social cause; I don't call myself a mentor or an Angel Investor. I am more like a hands-on coach to the young entrepreneurs and I get fully involved in them and their product.

I want to help young entrepreneurs so that they don't make the same mistakes I made or somebody else made. If somebody is there to guide them, they will not lose any time to move ahead as time is very precious for a startup.

I have noticed that many of the young entrepreneurs who come from the tech background spend a lot of time coding the product rather than trying to understand what the customer really wants. They believe what they think is what the customer or the market wants, which is not true. The most important thing is to understand the customer. This is what I tell all young entrepreneurs.

I also tell them to draw a mission chart before they start looking for funding. If they feel that there is a good market for their product, they should go to Venture Capitalists for funding.

The startup scene in India

The startup scene in India is very bullish now. There was a time when we lost even bright youngsters to the big service companies, not anymore. Today's youngsters do realise that product development is what they should be doing. I am seeing this change from 2013 onwards.

That is why I decided to be a part of the I-Spread team that popularised the idea of a Product Nation.

I feel the startup India initiative will create more visibility for startups. Because more startups are succeeding, youngsters are also ready to take the risk and become entrepreneurs.

When I became an entrepreneur, I had not heard of the word entrepreneur; even terms like mentor, VC, pitching and angel investor were alien to me. I only knew if I needed money, I had to borrow from the bank or friends and family.

I think I am one of the few who belong to the build-to-last kind of an entrepreneur.

The Ticketing Genius

Phanindra Sama is only 36, but he says he has 'purified' himself as an entrepreneur after having come to the end of a very successful eight-year entrepreneurial journey.

After having sold his highly successful venture, redBus—India's largest online bus ticketing system—to a multinational company based in South Africa for an undisclosed amount, he says, 'An entrepreneurial journey is worth taking just for the experience. Entrepreneurship has completely changed my perspective on society.'

For him, being an entrepreneur is tantamount to self-purification. 'As I finish this journey, I find that I am a completely different person to the one that embarked upon it. I have become more patient and tolerant; I understand people better and can inspire them. Without understanding people and inspiring them to give their best, you can't run a company.

'In an entrepreneur's life, tough times come suddenly and leave you with the feeling that your business is going to vanish into the ether. But you come back through sheer resilience. With experiences like that, you become stronger and more stable. It is a high-pressure job. You have to visualise what is going to be happening to the industry in five years.

'If I was just an engineer, I would never have got an opportunity to take these tough decisions and stretch myself.'

Phanindra Sama founded redBus, the most successful online bus ticket booking company in India

THE BEGINNING of the journey was in the village of Tadpakal in the Nizamabad district of Andhra Pradesh (now in Telengana).

Interestingly, if we were to look at Phanindra's life, we will see that it changed dramatically several times. But each change was for the better, as he came out of it with new experiences and learning.

If his parents had decided to educate him in the village when he was small, his life would have been different.

But his father, a farmer, was very particular that his son received an English education. The problem was that there were no English-medium schools in the village. So, he was packed off to Nizamabad at the tender age of three. He stayed in a boarding school all the way through to his first year of primary school.

Because of the health problems he encountered in the boarding school, he was sent to live with his uncle working for an insurance company in Adilabad. When he was 11 and in the 7th standard, his uncle was transferred to Hyderabad. From then on, he got to study in the capital city of the then-undivided state of Andhra Pradesh.

The next big change in his life was going back to the boarding school at the age of 15 for his 11th and 12th standards. He now says that if he had not gone to the boarding school then, he would not have got into the renowned Birla Institute of Technology and Science (BITS) in Pilani, Rajasthan, to pursue a degree in Engineering.

'It was in boarding school that I heard the other students say great things about BITS Pilani. So, when they applied, I decided to as well. Nobody in my family had ever heard of BITS Pilani. There was nobody to guide me through my academic decisions. So, I would have to thank my friends in boarding school for my having secured entry into BITS Pilani. In fact, I came to know of the IITs only after I had joined BITS,' says Phanindra.

Life changed dramatically yet again after he joined BITS Pilani. 'This was a time of many firsts. I was travelling outside Andhra Pradesh for the first time. It was the first time I was meeting students from all over the country. It was so enriching to meet toppers from every state.'

His first steps as an entrepreneur were also taken there. Phanindra recalls, 'Every decision was taken by the students there, from the kitchen menu to the cook's salary. Students had a major role in managing the departments and the institution. There is not much else in Pilani other than BITS; it is a small village. The nearest town is some 200 km away. So we spent a lot of time amongst ourselves. Naturally, the student community was quite close-knit, and I made some very good friendships with people from different parts of the country. That gave me the greatest exposure in my life, both as an entrepreneur and as an Indian.'

But when he was in BITS Pilani, Phanindra never thought of becoming an entrepreneur; not even in his wildest dreams. 'In 2002, when I passed out, not many youngsters chose the path of becoming entrepreneurs. It was only after 2007 or 2008, that the National Entrepreneurship Network, that played a significant role encouraging young entrepreneurs in colleges and universities, became active by setting up E-cells at all of India's major educational institutions.'

His ambition was to become an electronics engineer and he was happy working for Texas Instruments in Bangalore. But the story couldn't end there. Phanindra was destined to be an entrepreneur.

It was a long Diwali weekend in 2005. All his friends had gone home for the holidays, except for Phanindra who had decided to stay on in Bangalore. Bored, he suddenly decided to go to Hyderabad to see his family, except there were no bus tickets available. He had a gut feeling that there had to have been a vacant seat on some bus or the other going to Hyderabad, but there was no way he could find out.

'As I had nothing else to do, I went to a bus ticket agent and asked how the whole process of bus ticketing worked. When he explained the working of the system to me, I could immediately see that there were many inefficiencies in the system. Just suppose there were hundreds of buses from 30 operators running from Bangalore to Hyderabad, the agents did not have access to all the operators. When an agent received a customer, he called a bus operator to find out whether there were tickets available. The operator would then look at the chart and tell him the number of vacant seats he had on the bus he was plying. The number of agents a bus operator could have on book was limited as he needed to communicate with each of them on the phone. The customers could not always choose the seats they wanted as there was no transparency. Another problem was that the fares were not published in one central location, which meant that there was no fixed fare a customer could expect to pay. But the major problem was booking return tickets. Every time you went somewhere, you had to call someone at your destination and ask them to book the tickets for the return leg. Travelling from Bangalore to Hyderabad was harder than travelling between two countries!'

As an engineer, he started thinking of various solutions that could fix the problems he saw. He felt that computers could solve these problems easily. Still, starting a company was not on his mind. 'It was like, there is a problem and as an engineer, I felt it could—and should—be solved.'

Later that weekend, he wrote an e-mail to his roommates telling them about the problems he'd faced at the booking office, and why he'd had to stay back in Bangalore. He also wrote, 'I see a solution to this problem. Could we work on this?'

His friends were also game for some extra work for fun.

His original plan was to write a piece of software, sell it to the bus operators and give the money he received to some NGO. It excited the entire group of friends to find a solution to a problem that concerned thousands of people.

In January, 2006, seven of them divided the work amongst themselves and started working weekends on the project. When the prototype was ready, they went to the bus operators and tried selling it to them, but they were not even willing to take it for free. 'We were trying to upset the status quo, and they didn't like it. We didn't know what to do then.'

With a solution that they felt was pathbreaking but one that had no takers, the friends felt a bit disappointed. But this was around the time The Indus Entrepreneurs (TiE) Bangalore was established. So, they decided to go to TiE with the idea. TiE gave the young men three mentors to advise them on what to do. 'The mentors changed our mindset completely; especially Sanjay Ananthram. Soon, the idea became a business plan. They encouraged us to start a business of our own.'

To start with, the mentors gave them assignments every week, starting with a market survey. 'We were very prompt in doing all the assignments because we felt that we had to be meticulous, given that such big businessmen were taking time out to help us. We collected data such as the number of buses, the number of routes, the average price of a ticket, how people buy tickets, the profile of customers, how much commission a bus operator pays to an agent etc. It might not have been comprehensive, but it gave us a general idea of the industry', Phanindra said.

It was tough for them to work in the office on weekdays and then do the assignments over weekends. Naturally, only the tough ones survived. In August 2006, Phanindra Sama, Charan Padmaraju and Sudhakar Pasupunuri decided to quit their well-paid jobs and take an entrepreneurial plunge deep into the world of business. With Rs 500,000 (the savings the three of them had in hand), they started redBus.

Why redBus? At the time, Phanindra was reading the autobiography of Richard Branson, the British entrepreneur who built the Virgin conglomerate from scratch. 'The way he rose from the depths of poverty fascinated me. His Virgin brand is red. Marketing becomes easier if you have a colour. Another reason was, as we are an Internet-based company, people would have to type our name in. So, it was a good idea to have an easy-to-remember name. That was another reason we zeroed in on red. The third reason was that as students in BITS Pilani, we used to go home via Delhi, where you have the red line and white line buses. Though we first thought of redline, the name was already booked. So we finally decided on redBus. I am glad we chose such a striking name.'

A room in the house they stayed in was turned into their first office. In the morning, they closed the rest of the house down so that the room looked like an office. The first thing they did was design a logo for the company, which was done by Angeline, a friend of a classmate. They then registered redbus.in and created a web site.

Soon, three young relatives of theirs who were on the lookout for jobs joined them.

The friends never anticipated the difficulties they were going to face as entrepreneurs. 'Life after we started redBus was very tough; from a pampered corporate life, we were thrown into a life of uncertainties where we had to go to people begging for things. To the bus operators, we were like the hundreds of sales people who made a beeline to their offices every day. The world of business is totally different from the world you see as an employee. We faced huge challenges.'

They went to the IT companies, stood outside when the employees came out for lunch and then gave them their redBus cards. 'For the first time, we were on the other side of the fence. Just a few weeks ago, we were inside a campus and we used to ignore such salespeople or brush them aside. Now, we had to kill our egos. It was a moment of truth for us. In entrepreneurial life, you have many such humbling experiences.' After several visits and many requests, one operator agreed to give them five seats to book online using their website. The operator told them, if you sell five seats in one week, its fine. If you don't, don't bother me again. Thus, the young entrepreneurs got one week to prove themselves.

August 18 dawned, the day they opened their website for ticket booking. 'We put the seats up! We told all our friends and colleagues and asked them to buy from us. We also requested one of our friends to write about us on the Infosys discussion board.' But no one bought a seat.

The five seats remained unbooked till the 22nd of August. On that day, they would sell their first seat. A woman working at Infosys booked a ticket to go to Tirupati. All three of them were so stressed that they went to the bus station and waited till she boarded the bus. 'We saw to it that she sat inside the bus. But we didn't tell her that we were from redBus!'

It took them another five days to sell the rest of the seats and then they went back to the operator confidently. Naturally, the operator was happy. Slowly, they added more operators to their inventory.

In early 2007, TiE picked redBus as one of the three bright ideas (out of 300) that deserved further mentoring. This caused redBus to become news among the Venture Capitalist (VC) community who found the idea interesting. Soon, they started contacting redBus to invest in the idea.

'Till then, we knew nothing of venture capitalists! That was a time when there were many VCs and very few ideas. So, people were willing to put up money for our idea.'

But they were unsure about VCs investing in redBus. So they took the advice of their mentors who told them to take the money and begin developing the idea. The mentors also asked them to diversify and change from an online bus ticketing company to just being a bus ticketing company.

When the VCs asked them how much money they needed, they said Rs 30 lakh (Rs 3 million) which they thought was big money. 'Then one of the VCs spent several hours with us and we revised the plan seven times. At last, we found that we needed Rs 3 crore (Rs 30 milion) to scale up the business.'

The agreement was that money would be invested in three years and it was supposed to last till February 2010. But they spent all of the Rs 3 crore in just a year and a half.

In the meanwhile, Phanindra also understood one thing; that 'when you take money from someone, it becomes a business and you have to return profits on that money.'

Phanindra remembers with gratitude the role that Sanjay Ananthram, one of the mentors, played in their becoming entrepreneurs. 'When we went to him with the idea, he said it could be a good business idea and connected us to the VCs. He brought in the credibility factor that got the VCs to invest in our idea. Once we got the money, he taught us how to recruit people, and helped us formulate what the company should stand for, its strategy, and its culture.'

When they were trying to sell the software to bus operators, he advised them to change gear and start selling tickets online. That was the best idea he could give them. 'For me, turning into an entrepreneur from being an engineer was like sculpting. I had to change a lot. He insisted on us being transparent and valuing only talent.' As an entrepreneur, was he able to remain fair and transparent all the time?

'Absolutely', says Phanindra. 'I am thankful to Sanjay for that too. I was under the impression that a businessman had to be shrewd. I had heard people say that it was a war between competitors, that one had to win, and that everything was fair in war. If Sanjay wasn't around, I would have believed all that. If he was not there, I also would have used words like, "I have to win the war, and to win the war, I have to kill them". I had also heard stories of how bribes have to be paid to government officials to build a company. But Sanjay told me many stories on how Premji built Wipro while staying honest. As a former Wipro employee, he knew Wipro very well.'

RedBus later on also collaborated with many government transport organisations. In the beginning, people at the lower end asked for bribes to move their requests along, but they refused to pay up. Yes, it took them longer to get contracts, but he stayed firm in his belief that redBus wouldn't pay bribes. Once, when they were negotiating with a state government, the government of the state of Goa contacted them and asked for a demo of their software. They were so happy with their work that they spoke about redBus at some meeting. That was the spark they needed. After that, many State Road Transport Corporations contacted them to establish partnerships.

'We never paid a single paisa as a bribe to get any of those government contracts. Now, the entire company has a different view of the world. But that was only because we followed what Sanjay said and remained patient.' Phanindra also confessed that before he started redBus, he never cared to stop at a red signal if there was no one at a junction. He was only scared of the policeman. But today, he says his ethics do not permit him to break rules. 'I also found that even at midnight, when I stop at traffic lights, the vehicles behind me also stop.'

Phanindra advises all those young ambitious entrepreneurs out there to find a good mentor, 'that wise man, that teacher, then your journey becomes much easier. Like Einstein said, he saw further than most only by standing on the shoulders of giants. So, find those shoulders to stand on. We need those giants and their shoulders.'

In addition to having an innovative idea, redBus leveraged open source software as far as possible, including for their call centres. When they were setting up their call centres, many people told them to buy software. But as it would have cost them a lot of money, they decided to use open source software instead. 'We looked around and came across this software called Asterisk, which is an open source software for telephony. Because it was freely available, we could evaluate it quickly and find that it worked! Like any startup, we faced criticism, and many condemned us for "our ignorance". Even then, we pursued it. In fact, many industry players started saying, "if redBus uses it, that probably means it works!"'

Another interesting thing they did was keep all their IT infrastructure and servers on a cloud platform. They chose to move to the cloud when hardly anyone in India was doing that. Compared to those who moved bit by bit, redBus moved their entire IT infrastructure to the public cloud in one go. By doing so, they were able to cut costs by forty per cent.

And when Endeavor, a non-profit organisation started by Harvard alumni, identified redBus as a high-impact venture and provided them help in scaling their business, it was yet another feather in their cap.

'We were selected because of the revolution we wrought in the bus transportation industry in India. They helped us connect to potential joint venture opportunities in Uruguay, Argentina and Europe. They also provided us the opportunity to take Harvard MBA students in for internships, something that would have otherwise been impossible for a company such as ours. Besides, they also connected us to some very famous people in India who helped us with scaling our business.'

When they made the first business plan, their ambition was to have a turnover of Rs 1 crore (Rs 10 million). 'The inspiration was the reality show Kaun Banega Crorepati. The prize money that was offered on the show was Rs 1 crore. We thought it was a magical figure, and we felt that if ever our company made Rs 1 crore turnover, we would have achieved something.' And they hit that magic figure in just the second year of their operation!

Though their first financial year was shorter than 12 months, they did Rs 50 lakh (Rs 5 million) worth of business in the first financial year without turning a profit. Their second, ending March 2008, was a huge success—turnover hit Rs 5 crore (Rs 50 million). In 2009, they grew six-fold, turning a profit and increasing turnover to Rs 30 crore (Rs 300 million). In 2010 March, redBus turnover was up to Rs 60 crore (Rs 600 million)!

In 2012, Business magazine Fast Company listed redBus as one of the World's 50 most innovative companies. That came as a big surprise and boost to Phanindra and Co. 'Not even in our wildest dreams did we ever imagine that we would be chosen as one of the world's 50 most innovative companies. This recognition gave the team a whole new fount of inspiration to work harder.'

FY 2013 ended with redBus employing 600 people and turning over Rs 600 crore (Rs 6 billion). Thousands of bus operators worked with them and more than a crore (10 million) tickets were sold on their websites every year. RedBus had a presence in 24 Indian states with 64% of the market share in online bus tickets (6-7% of bus tickets overall).

That was when Phanindra decided to sell redBus. After working so hard on an idea and making it a roaring success in eight years, why did they want to sell it? 'When you have VCs investing in your company, you give them the permission to sell it if they deem it appropriate. It has to either be sold or go for IPO to make money. When we raised the first round of money, we knew we would have to sell the company one day. We were prepared for the eventuality.'

After redBus became successful, Phanindra says they used to receive buy-out offers every six-seven months. But finally in June 2013, they agreed to sell for an undisclosed amount to the Naspers Ibibo Group's holding company MIH Ltd, owned by South Africa's media house Naspers, which has operations in hundred countries.

In June 2014, Phanindra and the other cofounders exited completely from redBus. 'With the new management wanting to take redBus international, it is a proud moment for us Indians. It is not often that a company that started in India has gone global, unlike many successful companies who came to India from elsewhere. Now, when someone in Brazil buys a ticket using redBus, the profit comes back to India unlike the MNCs like McDonalds or Pizza Hut or Dominos, who take profit from India. When you export ideas, technology and companies, it will help our economy.'

Phanindra and his friends decided to come out of redBus though they had the option to stay on. 'As entrepreneurs, we want to create something new and innovative. We enjoyed creating redBus and taking it to this level. But we felt, if it had to be taken to a very higher level globally, it would have to become more managerial than entrepreneurial, something we would not be able to do quite as well. We want to do something new.'

As is the case for every entrepreneur, the last eight years saw ups and downs in Phanindra's life. 'In 2008, when the global economy collapsed, we were not able to raise money. Those were the most difficult of times for redBus. Many of our staff wanted to quit as we were all so demotivated. It was one of the most stressful periods of my life. What helped me was meditation. I went to Vipasana meditation camp for ten days. If not for it, I would have fallen into depression. After ten days, I came back a different person.'

The highest point was, 'Personally, the most heartening thing for me was when my parents read an article about me in the Telugu newspaper *Eenadu*. That was the first time they read about us and understood what we were doing. They were so happy.'

Now that redBus was behind him, Phanidra began feeling a kind of emptiness in life. 'For 8 years, every moment of my life was about redBus. But it feels so empty now! I am okay with selling it as I am a little practical. We sold redBus and we knew we had to exit. I am fine with it emotionally.'

The advice his entrepreneurial friends gave him was to relax and not think about anything till serendipity hits. 'They don't want me to plan or look for any new ideas. The money will take care of the family, so I am relaxed. Now whatever I do next, I don't have to look at the financial angle. But I am waiting for an epiphany...'

Cloud Computing as Service

It was in 2010 that 35-year-old Girish Mathrubootham founded freshdesk Inc. with his friend Shan Krishnasamy as co-founder. In no time, the venture attracted major venture capitalists in India, quite rare in those days. The reason was the quality of the product, freshdesk, a cloud-based help desk software that allows organisations to support their customers through email, phone, website, Facebook and Twitter. Started in just a 1000 sq ft space at home, freshdesk has moved to a 1,20,000 sq ft space today.

It is also the fastest growing SaaS based (Software as a Service) company in the world.

Girish Mathrubootham is the Founder and CEO of freshdesk, the fastest growing SaaS based company in the world

freshdesk

I BECAME an entrepreneur soon after I finished my MBA in 1999. Though I had done my Engineering in Electronics, I felt then itself that the future was in Information Technology. By the time I finished my engineering in Electronics, I had learnt all the software tools and languages on my own. In a way, I became an entrepreneur because my friends wanted me to teach them Java. Fully funded by my students who were my friends, I started my first venture, Xpert Labs, a training institute. In fact, the institute 'walked' into my house. It all started initially when five of my friends paid me Rs 3,000 each and with that Rs 15,000, we rented out tables, computers etc.

As the number of students grew, I resigned from my job and started teaching multiple batches. After sometime, I got bored with teaching and decided to go to the US to get some exposure. I parted with my venture (gave it to a friend) and went to the US. I worked in the US for a year and when I came back, Xpert Labs was about to be closed as it was not doing well. That was after the dotcom bust, and my efforts to revive it did not work.

Working for Zoho

I decided to move from training students to product development, and got a job as a Presales Engineer with Zoho and that was where I met Shan Krishnasamy, who joined a year after me as the Technical Lead.

Though I was only an employee, I looked at my job as running a company, in the sense that the product was my company and I was responsible for it. It was like being an entrepreneur except that I was being paid a salary.

I worked with Zoho with that mindset for 10 years only because the company gave its employees that kind of freedom.

But by 2010, I started feeling restless and bored.

Entrepreneurial life starts again

I read an article about Zendesk raising their prices, and how their users were unhappy about it. The news woke up the entrepreneur in me as I saw a huge opportunity in that space. Zendesk at that time was earning a few million dollars in revenue.

I knew that the massive transition to cloud was happening. In my team, we were developing similar products but we were building on-premise products, not SaaS (Software as a Service on cloud). With the domain knowledge and the talent available in India, I knew we could develop a good product here. It was exciting to think about the idea itself and I started researching on all the companies in the space.

Customer support market is like restaurant business

When we started our first help desk for Zoho, there were 600 help desks in the market. Yet we created a multi-million dollar product!

I would say that Software business is more like a restaurant business. What differentiates a dosa made in one restaurant from another? It is only a dosa, still people may like one over the other. Good product is like good food. Just as any restaurant serving good food will never go out of business, a great product will always do well in the market.

Customer support traditionally is customers talking over phone and email, and companies responding to it. But what we thought was about those people who talk about the company on social media. Social support was a new phenomenon then, and customer support was the new marketing tool. Engaging the customer community is also important today. So, we decided to go beyond traditional customer support and build a 360-degree customer service platform.

Software as a Service (SaaS)

We chose to develop a cloud based SaaS as customer support system. Software as a Service (SaaS) is a software distribution model in which applications hosted by a vendor or service provider are made available to customers on the cloud.

We saw many Small and Medium companies moving to cloud computing, and we chose to target them. They do not have the money to invest in huge infrastructure so, our cloud based system could be of great support to them.

Starting freshdesk

I needed a co-founder to start a venture, and asked Shan Krishnasamy whether he was interested in joining me. He didn't think twice before saying yes. We complement each other very well; while I take care of product management, he takes care of the technical aspects. In hindsight, I feel if he had said no, would freshdesk have happened? I don't know.

I zeroed in on some potential domain names and found that freshdesk.com was actually expiring in a couple of weeks. So I back-ordered it, and waited. It was almost a month before the domain was officially transferred to me.

It was October 2010. We were just the two of us and started freshdesk with Rs 30 lakh. By February 2011, we hired four employees and moved to a rented place.

From day one, our dreams were big; we wanted to sell our product to the world.

First customer

Though the product was not fully ready, we posted a blog on the Freshdesk page. The blog was picked up by Hacker News, a community of geeks, and that made many people get attracted to the story. In two days, close to 30,000 people visited our site and 175 people signed up for the product.

On March 24, we released the beta version to all those who had signed in. We were happy with the response and by May, we were ready with the public beta.

We got our first customer two days after our launch. He was from Australia. In no time, we started getting enquiries from all over the world.

We had three plans - sprout, blossom and garden. The price was based on the customer supporting agents; like $9, $19 and $29 per agent per month. For example, if you choose the $9 plan, and you have 5 agents, you pay $45.

Interest among venture capitalists

Hacker News writing about us made us visible to venture capitalists all over the world. Angel List also brought us some interest among the VCs. By May, we were talking to some investors.

In June 2011, we won the Microsoft BizSpark India Startup challenge in the Cloud category and the prize money we got was US$ 40,000. There were VCs among the judges which also helped us later. We were the finalists at another event called Unpluggd in Bangalore. All these events brought significant interest among investors in freshdesk.

Funding from Accel and Tiger Global

After Accel Partners invested $1 million (Series A) in freshdesk in December 2011, Tiger Global Management joined in the next investment round along with Accel Partners, and they invested $5 million (Series B) five months later. We then expanded our team and also moved to a good office.

Apart from them, Google Capital also has invested in our company. Today, Accel, Tiger and Google have collectively invested up to $94 million in our company.

Most of the money we raise, we just keep in the bank saving it for the rainy day. Because we are generating revenue, we have not burnt a lot of cash we raised from investors.

Of course, we have invested in people, product development and global marketing. When I say rainy day, I mean the day when funding goes dry. For example, suppose a company needs money now, funding is not easily available. It is a tough situation for any startup that doesn't have any money in the bank.

In 2014-15, there was a big frenzy to invest in Indian startups, and we also made use of the environment and accepted the investment.

Funding always goes through cycles. In 1999-2000, there was a lull after the dotcom bust. In 2008, again there was a crash in the market after the Lehman Brothers went bust. When such things happen, funds become hard to come by for startups. Once the economy recovers, funding becomes active. In 2014-15, it was very bullish. According to me, it is always better to ride such cycles with a cash reserve.

Stupendous growth

In 2012, we were not even a one million dollar company. We started with Rs 30 lakh with just the two of us in a small space at a friend's office. Today, we have more than 800 employees and have an office space of 1,20,000 sq ft.

Nobody expected us to grow like this. Truth be told, we also did not expect this kind of a growth.

When you are catering to the global market, huge opportunities await you. We had a great product for the global market, and we could sell it globally and that was the reason for our amazing growth.

When we started, our plan was to target small and medium companies. Even today, after six years, our target customers are small and medium companies only but some big companies are also coming to us and buying our product.

We knew that when we were a small company, it was better to target small and medium companies. In the global market, we didn't face any prejudice, luckily. When customers come online and buy a product, they don't look at whether it is created in India or somewhere else. From the customer's perspective, we are a global company.

Then and now

In 2010, there was no ecosystem in Chennai. Today, it is much more mature. In 2010, VCs never came to Chennai. Even if they set up appointments, they used to cancel at the last minute saying there was not many startups in Chennai. Today, they are looking for interesting companies in Chennai too. We have been fortunate as we were at the right place at the right time.

Investing in office space

From day one, our office space looked different from the usual offices. At that time, we didn't have the finances to design it so well except colour the walls with bright colours like green, yellow and blue. Throughout, we were trying to creatively design our office within the constraints of our budget. Because we can afford to spend a little bit more, we do that.

I would say we are a little more creative in designing to make our office look different and not just plain cubicles. That is why the way we have designed our office space is written about a lot; it is unique, creative and unconventional. One thing is, we want freshdesk to be a happy work environment. Yes, first the work people do should make them happy but when they walk in, the fresh, vibrant colours they see, should make them feel happy.

Just like all the family members are involved in the design of the interiors of your home, many of our employees are also involved in the design of our office space.

Acquiring companies

We are only six years old but we have acquired five startups in quick succession, in a span of 12 months. We acquired the live video chat provider 1CLICK.io in August 2015, social recommendation app Frilp in October 2015, the messaging app Konotor in December 2015, online collaboration platform, Framebench in February, 2016 and the fifth acquisition Airwoot, a startup that helps deliver customer service on social media, in April 2016.

These are opportunities that come to us when good companies and teams with good ideas are unable to grow by themselves when they run out of money. When we acquire a company, we look at whether we are acquiring the product or technology or people or the business.

If you take 1CLICK or Konotor we acquired, they were for both the product and people that attracted us. Sometimes, it may take some time for us to build a product like that, which will add value to us. In the case of 1CLICK, we wanted to acquire it for customer support because of the video streaming facility they had, which we felt would add a lot of value to our product.

So it was a good opportunity for us to get good products with value and people through these acquisitions. When so many teams come to our fold, we have to make sure that they integrate.

Fastest growing company in the world

We didn't expect to grow like this, at this breath-taking speed. We have 80,000 customers and four products now—freshdesk, freshservice, hotline and freshsales. We have been growing 5X, 3X and 2X over the last three years. I don't think anybody can say it is easy to tackle this kind of growth.

It's like playing cricket, and we are like the batsman who goes out to face new deliveries bowled at him everyday, from yorkers to bouncers to googlies. Like a good batsman, we tackle growth and the challenges that come with it.

The challenges are in the form of good problems and bad problems. Luckily, almost all the problems we face are good problems which only helped us grow. When you are growing fast, the wheel is also spinning fast, and customers ask for a lot more new features, which is a good problem.

We have been running so fast, rather driving so fast that sometimes we gasp for breath. I feel maybe it's a good idea to pause for say, six weeks and celebrate what we have done so far and then resume the run again.

But it has been a phenomenal journey so far. To me, a company is like a living organism which shows different characteristics with each passing month, and it is amazing to observe Freshdesk from that perspective.

Freshdesk is like a 6-year-old child who grew so fast to be an active, beautiful, smart and strong child—a global child.

The Idli Dosa Man

This is the story of a boy who hailed from a remote village in Wayanad whose father was a coolie and mother hardly went to school.
This is the story of a boy who failed in 6th standard but went on to join the REC and IIM-B.
This is the story of a man who decided to be an entrepreneur along with his cousins and employ people from rural India.
Today, fresh idli and dosa batter made from their company ID Fresh reaches the homes of Bangalore, Chennai, Pune, Mumbai, Mysore, Hyderabad, Mangalore and Dubai.
He is PC Musthafa and this is his incredibly inspiring story.

PC Mustafa is the Founder of ID Fresh, one of the most popular fresh food producers in India

I GREW up in a remote village called Chennalode near Kalpatta in Wayanad. The village was so remote that we had only a primary school there, and we had to walk at least three kilometers to the nearby high school. So, most of the kids dropped out after primary school. In those days, there was no electricity or roads in our village.

My father, Ahmed, also stopped studying after 4th standard, and worked as a coolie in the coffee plantation and my mother, Fathima hardly went to school. I was the eldest and I had three younger sisters.

Failing in 6th standard

I was not very interested in studies and after school, I liked helping my father in his work rather than doing homework or studying. And there was no question of opening the books at night as there was no electricity at home; only kerosene lamps. The weekends were also spent working with my father as a daily-wage worker. Though I was below average in all the subjects, one subject I was good at was Mathematics. When I failed in the 6th standard, I lost interest in going to school.

A school master motivates to go back to school

When I failed, I decided to join my father as a daily-wage worker. When my Maths teacher, Mathew Sir saw me roaming around, he didn't like it a bit and tried to motivate me to go back to school. Sir also spoke to my father and he was okay with giving me one more chance.

Mathew Sir asked me a question; 'do you want to be a coolie or a teacher?' I looked at him, and I could see the difference between my father and my teacher. So my answer to his question was, 'Sir, I want to be a teacher like you'. My father was a great inspiration in the sense that he persuaded me to go back to school, citing his own example.

When I went back to school, I found that I had to sit with my juniors and all my classmates were in a class higher than me. I felt humiliated to be with my juniors, and the humiliation was so much that I became attentive in class. My language skills were very poor and I was very weak in both English and Hindi, and seeing my discomfiture, Mathew Sir helped me after school.

From a failure to a topper

Sir's help worked, and in the 7th standard, I was the class topper, surprising all the teachers. From that day, they saw a different me; a boy who was willing to work hard and there was no looking back after that. I was the school topper in 10th standard.

In those days, I had only one ambition; I wanted to be a Maths teacher like Mathew Sir. He was my role model.

Stepping out of the village to a city for the first time

Till I completed my 10th standard, I had not stepped out of Wayanad. But if I wanted to go to college (it was Pre-Degree in those days), I had to go to Kozhikode. When my father's friend suggested I go to Kozhikode to study in college, my father said he had no problem with me studying but he didn't have any money to fund my education. My parents were committed to educating me, even skipping a meal to educate me.

Staying in the charity hostel and getting free meals

I got admission in Farooq College in Kozhikode where my father's friend arranged for a free meal scheme in the college charity hostel. I was one of the 15 students who were offered free stay and free food, as we could not afford to pay.

There were four hostels in the college, and we were to go to different hostels for breakfast, lunch and dinner as we were on charity. Naturally, other students looked at us in disdain, and it upset me a lot. It was like we were eating somebody else's food. Some students made fun of us and it was not a pleasant experience at all but then I had to swallow all the humiliation for the sake of my education. Looking back, I feel the college management did a great job by taking care of poor students like us.

Though my father had no means to support my daily meal in the hostel, he used to bring me home-grown bananas and jackfruits. He was very worried about my situation in the hostel.

Coming from a village, I was very weak in English and it was a big handicap in college where all the lectures were in English. A good friend of mine used to translate everything for my benefit. I also worked extremely hard, and scoring good marks energised me.

Studying Engineering at REC, Calicut

I wrote the engineering entrance exam after my college and scored 63rd rank in the state and got admission at REC, Calicut (now called NIT). When I look back, I feel three factors helped me get admission at the REC. Yes, I had the potential in me as I was good in Maths. I also worked hard. Third and the most important reason was, God was with me.

I was very lucky to have secured such a good rank and got to study what I really liked; Computer Science. There was no one to guide me in those days except the God Almighty. Life was not that bad at REC; I got a scholarship and also took a student's loan. I didn't have to pay any tuition fees, and had to take care of only the hostel fees. That was a big burden off me. Only thing was, unlike many other students, I had to be very careful about spending money but then that was okay with me.

I had no dreams to be an entrepreneur then but I wanted to be a well-known engineer. I worked hard and did well in studies. When I passed out in 1995, I got placed at Manhattan Associates, an Indian startup in the US.

Starting to work at Motorola in Ireland

After a few days of working at the startup in Bangalore, I got an offer from Motorola, which was a dream offer for a person from a remote village in Wayanad. After working for a short period in Bangalore for Motorola, I was sent to Ireland.

First flight

As a young boy, I stepped out of Wayanad for the first time to study in a college. Now, for the first time in my life, I boarded a flight and went out of the country. It was 6.30 in the evening and when the flight took off, I looked down and saw Bangalore from atop. I will never be able to forget the image; the aerial view of Bangalore.

Missing India when in Ireland and Dubai

Though I loved Ireland and the Irish people, I missed my people and country a lot. I also missed Indian food, as there were no Indian restaurants there. I was used to praying five times a day, which I found difficult to do there. After three months, I got a very good offer from Citi Bank, and I jumped at it and moved to Dubai. In 1996, a salary in lakhs was quite alluring.

The first thing I did after I paid off my loan was sending one lakh rupees in cash in a bag to my father through a friend of mine! I was told he cried seeing so much cash sent by his son.

He paid off his debts and started planning the wedding of my sister. One of my sisters had dropped out after school but the others went to college. In 2000, I also got married.

Building a house for his parents

Soon, I built a house for my parents in the village. People in my village, who had seen me as a small child, could not believe the change that had taken place in my life. The positive effect of that change was, many kids in the village look up to me, and they also dream of achieving something big in life.

Coming back to India for three reasons

In 2003, after having lived in Dubai for so long, I decided to come back to India. There were three reasons to take such a decision.

I wanted to come back and spend time with my parents.

I also wanted to study further. Though I had a very good GATE score, I couldn't study after my Engineering due to the financial condition I was in. After working for a few years, I decided to study Business Administration.

The third reason was, I wanted to give something back to society. I got this feeling after seeing so many smart youngsters in many villages not getting a good break in life. I wanted to give them that opportunity, the break so that they also could come up in life. Initially, I didn't know how I could help them. Soon, I realised the best way I could help them was by providing them jobs.

To offer jobs to them, I have to be a job provider; an entrepreneur.

Quitting a job to study and be an entrepreneur

To quit my well-paying job was the toughest decision I took in my life. It was not an easy decision for a person coming from a poor background. My father couldn't digest my decision to quit a high paid job. So also my family. But one person who supported me wholeheartedly was my cousin Nazer.

I was very close to my maternal cousins and always shared every single detail about my life with them. We grew up together and they also came from very poor families. Unlike me, they didn't go for any higher studies.

Nazer ran away from home to Bangalore and started a small kirana store in Thippasandra. He had a good network with stores in Bangalore as he was also running a small-scale spices and dry fruits business. He gave me the courage to listen to my heart. He said, 'if it does not work out, you can go back to work anytime. It is not that quitting the job is the end of the world. But you shouldn't feel that you didn't try to do what you wanted to'.

The funny thing was, I knew I wanted to do something but I had no idea what I was going to do. I came to back to India with a savings of Rs 15 lakh.

Studying MBA at IIM-B

I met with my first objective by going to my village every weekend to be with my parents. Instead of studying technology, I decided to do MBA as I found management more interesting than technology and I got admission at IIM-B.

Starting an enterprise to make idli, dosa batter

Even while studying at IIM-B, I was constantly discussing with my cousins what business we should start. Shamsuddin, one of my cousins, suggested that we should make dosa batter and supply it. He had seen dosa batter in plastic bags tied with a rubber band in the nearby stores. We saw a big opportunity in this.

That was an aha moment!

When we found the idea appealing, we decided to invest Rs 25,000 and start a company immediately. Five of us cousins—Nazer, Shamsu, Jaffer and Naushad and me—decided to join hands. We found a small place of around 550sq ft and started with 1 grinder, 1 mixer and 1 sealing machine.

ID is identity and not Idli Dosa

We discussed so many names and suddenly one cousin suggested the name ID. We preferred to call it our enterprise, our ID, our identity. We named the venture ID Fresh as we planned to supply fresh dosa and idli batter.

First business plan

Our first target was 20 stores in the neighbouring area and the business plan was, if we were able to sell 100 packets a day in 6 months, we would invest more in our venture and buy more machines.

We didn't employ anyone at the factory. My cousin was in charge of our small factory. We started very small with just 10 packets a day. Initially, the shop keepers were not willing to keep a new brand. So, we gave them a special offer; cash after sales.

When the customers asked for ID repeatedly, the nearby stores also started asking us to supply them. But we stuck to the first twenty stores and waited to touch the number 100. In the 9th month, we were selling an average of 100 packets a day.

Making profit from day one

The best part of our venture was that we were making profit from day one as none of us took any salary initially. Our profit was Rs 400 in the first month. Once we reached the target, we decided to invest Rs 6 lakh and move to a bigger kitchen of 800 sq ft that has 2000kg capacity, that is 2000 packets with 15 wet grinders.

We employed five people, all of them were our relatives. Nazer was the all-round player for the first three years when I studied.

Joining as the CEO

In 2007, I received my MBA from Mukesh Ambani and officially joined as the CEO in charge of marketing and finance. Till then, I was only remotely participating in the operation along with my cousins.

In two years, we increased the capacity to 3,500 kg a day and the number of stores also increased to 300-400. By then, we had 30 employees working for us. We were operating our kitchen in a residential area till then. As the demand increased, we decided to have a proper manufacturing plant in an industrial area. We were making a decent 10-12% profit every month.

Moving to the industrial area

In 2008, we invested another Rs 40 lakh and bought a 2500 sq ft shed in the Hoskote Industrial Area, and instead of small grinders, we imported large wet grinders from America and customised for our requirements.

From dosa, idli to parathas and from Bangalore to other cities

In 2008, we added parathas to our list of products, and we plan to introduce vada batter and rawa idli batter. What is unique about ID fresh is, we deal only with fresh food and we do not add any preservatives in any of our products; we supply only natural fresh food.

In 2012, we expanded our horizon to other cities like Chennai, Mangalore, Mumbai, Pune, and Hyderabad. It was our friends and relatives who joined us to take ID Fresh to the next level. We follow the partnership model in other cities with a local manufacturing plant in each city, and each partner becomes a shareholder in the parent company.

In Dubai also

In 2013, we started our operations in Dubai. We see the maximum demand for iD products in the Dubai market and we are not able to match up to the demand; always in shortage there.

It is our experience in Bangalore that helped us in replicating the model in other places; same raw materials, same manufacturing process and same business model. Once you have a successful working model in one city, it is not difficult to replicate the model in other cities. It is a bit tough when you are not locally present.

We are not looking at any other international market right now, as India is such a huge market to explore.

Rs100 crore company

Today, we produce around 50,000 kg in our plant. The total investment must be around Rs 4 crore and our revenue is Rs 100crore.

When our company became a Rs 100 crore company in October 2015, we celebrated it in grand scale. We have grown from producing 10 packets a day in 2005 with just my cousin managing the kitchen to 50,000 packets a day and 1,100 employees, in ten years.

Employs smart youths from rural areas

What do we look for in an employee when we recruit him is—he has to be smart, honest and committed. Some of them who work in the sales make around Rs 50,000 a month.

Biggest challenge

The biggest challenge any startup faces is getting the right people, the right team. I was lucky to have my cousins with me as business partners. Balancing work and personal life is, by far the toughest challenge.

Future plans

Our aim is to make ID the most popular and trusted brand in the fresh food segment and take it to a Rs 1000 crore company in the next 5-6 years. By then, I am sure we will be able to give employment to at least 5,000 people.

Advice to entrepreneurs

If you have the passion in you to start something, do it immediately and don't wait for tomorrow. I had the passion in me to be an entrepreneur but it took me a few years to take the decision and I still regret that. I feel I should have taken the decision five years earlier.

My words may sound like management jargons but it is very important to maintain the quality of the product to be successful.

The four things that worked for us are, we were a right team in the right city with the right product at the right time.

Book Bindng to BITS, He has Seen it All

The story of Sarathbabu Elumalai is an inspiration to millions of young Indians. A self-made entrepreneur, his mission in life is to help the poor through job creation.

He hit the headlines when he rejected several high-profile job offers from various MNCs after he passed out of IIM, Ahmedabad, to start a catering business of his own.

His inspiration has been his mother who once sold idlis on the pavements of Chennai, to educate him and his siblings. It was a dream come true for him, when Infosys co-founder N R Narayana Murthy lit the traditional lamp and inaugurated Sarathbabu's enterprise way back in 2006.

This is his story, in his own words.

Sarathbabu Elumalai rose from poverty to become the Food King.
He is the founder and CEO of FoodKing

I WAS born and brought up in a slum in Madipakkam in Chennai. One of my first memories of my childhood was our tiny hut and my mother coating cow dung on the floor.

When I was around 5 or 6, my father disappeared to start a new life with another woman. So I do not have any memory of him at all. Our family was the five of us; my two elder sisters, two younger brothers, and my mother.

Mother was the sole breadwinner of the family. It was really tough for her to bring up five kids on her meagre salary. Because hers was a love marriage, nobody from her family came forward to help her when our father left us. My father's family wanted to drive us away because they wanted to grab the small piece of land we stayed on. But my mother was a brave lady; she fought all odds to bring us up.

As she had studied till the tenth standard, she got a job under the mid-day meal scheme of the Tamil Nadu government in a balwadi on a salary of Rs 30 a month. She made just one rupee a day and with that one rupee, she had to feed five children and herself.

She also sold idlis in the mornings and made around Rs 15-20 daily, but the profit was just Rs 5-10. She would then go to the school and prepare the mid-day meal for the children. We children used to eat the free food along with other children in the balwadi as she could not feed all of us. In the evenings, she taught at the adult education programme of the Indian government; again for a meagre salary.

She did three different jobs to bring us up and educate us. Although she didn't say explicitly that we should study well, we knew she was struggling hard to send us to school. I was determined that her hard work should not go in vain. Our lives were also hard. In the mornings, we went out to sell idlis because people in slums did not come out of their homes to buy idlis. For kids living in a slum, idlis for breakfast is something very special. When we came back from school, there would be some leftover idlis for us to eat. We used to then go to the free tuition centre run by Satya Sai Seva Sangh.

As we lived in a hut, till I reached the 10th standard, we didn't have electricity at home. So I used to do my homework and study till 9-9.30 pm at the Seva Sangh. There were many days we went to bed tired and hungry. The food that was there at home was never enough for five hungry children. We had to use one uniform for three years, which was stitched and mended many times by my mother, for she had no money to buy new uniform every year. I used to feel ashamed, angry and irritated because of my uniform. I tried to hide the stitches with my notebooks when I was amongst other students who came from reasonably well-off families. I didn't know against whom I was angry and irritated but I was angry with the situation we were in.

The first time I topped the class, I knew where I could score over the others. I felt happy when my teachers appreciated my efforts and the other classmates applauded me. I got their respect and attention because I was the topper in the class.

My mother was not aware of institutions like the Birla Institute of Technology and Science, Pilani, or the Indian Institutes of Technology. She only wanted to educate us so that we got a good job. I didn't know what I wanted to do at that time because in my friends-circle, nobody talked about higher education or preparing for the IIT-JEE.

When you constantly worry about the next square meal, you do not dream of becoming a doctor or an engineer. The only thing that was on my mind was to get a good job at the earliest and end my mother's struggles.

I remained a topper throughout my school days and my mother used to be very proud of that. She used to tell her relatives with pride that I got first rank in school.

I got very good marks in the 10th standard exam and stood first in school. Yet it was the most critical moment of my life. Till the 10th, there was no special fee but for the 11th and the 12th, the fee was around Rs 2,000-3,000.

I did book-binding work during the summer vacation and accumulated money for my school fees. When I got many orders, I employed 20 other children and all of us did the work together. That was my first real job as an entrepreneur. Once I saw the opportunity, I continued with the work.

Getting admission at BITS, Pilani

A classmate of mine whose father worked at the Secretariat asked me to apply to BITS, Pilani. He was confident about me getting admission at BITS, as I was the school topper. He also told me that on completion of studies, I would definitely get a job and that piece of news was a big incentive. So it was only because of him that I applied to BITS, Pilani.

When I got the admission, I had mixed feelings. Though I was happy that I got admission in one of India's premier institutions, I was worried about the fees I had to pay. On one hand I was excited about going out of Chennai for the first time, but there was also a sense of uncertainty.

The fees alone were around Rs 28,000, and I had to have around Rs 42,000 before I went to Pilani. It was huge, huge money for us. And there was no one to help us; just my mother and sisters. My mother was such a strong lady that she said somehow, we would manage and that I shouldn't worry. One of my sisters who was married by then, pawned her jewellery to one of our relatives and collected money for my fees. It is another matter that this relative charged her a very high interest.

Journey to BITS, Pilani

I joined BITS, Pilani in 1997. I, who had not travelled even 10km from Chennai, was going to a place 2000 km away with my luggage of two sets of dresses and a demand draft of Rs 48,000! My brother in law had accompanied me the first time. I felt the journey was never ending.

When I saw the college for the first time, I stood in awe. I couldn't believe I was going to study there. I had not seen such a huge campus before. To put it mildly, I was absolutely shocked.

Till then, I had moved only with students from poor families. At Pilani, all the students were from upper class or upper middle class families. Their lifestyle was totally different from mine. The topics they discussed were alien to me. When they talked about the good times they had in school, I thought of my school years which were a big struggle. There was this communication problem also, as I was not conversant in English then. I felt totally out of place, isolated and alone in a place where toppers from India's premier institutions came to study. Everybody would try to fit in a gang first and I also tried, but I found that I didn't fit in at all. The English books they read, the English films they saw, the songs they listened to… I didn't understand any of them. I had only seen a few of black and white MGR films.

When they went out and had food outside, the bill would be around Rs 2000 while I got Rs 50 for my monthly expense. When I could not even afford a samosa, how would I go out with them?

I came from a totally different background. They didn't try to find out why I was not in any of the gangs. Nobody thought of giving me a helping hand as it was a highly competitive place. When some students even ridiculed me, I withdrew from all and just observed them.

I concentrated only on my studies because back home, so many people had sacrificed for me. When I went to the mess to have food, I thought of my mother who would be hungry at home and I found it difficult to eat the good food served there.

Finally, acceptance

And it took a really long time—till the end of the first year—for me to make friends.

By then, I became a little more confident and started opening up. We had an engineering exhibition and I worked really hard for it in the first year. I did a lot of labour-intensive work like welding and cutting, though my subject was chemical engineering. My seniors appreciated my efforts.

In my second year also, I worked really hard for the engineering exhibition. This time, my juniors appreciated me, and they became my close friends, so close that they would be at my beck and call!

In the third year, when there was an election for the post of the coordinator for the exhibition, my juniors wanted me to contest. Thanks to their efforts, I was unanimously elected. That was my first experience of being in the limelight. It was also quite an experience to handle around a hundred students. In those days, I used to practice my English speech in front of a mirror before a speech. And today, I address thousands and thousands of students and give motivational speeches, I have gone to the US several times and addressed many students and entrepreneurs. Seeing my work, slowly my batchmates also came to the fold. All of them said I lead the team very well. By then, three years had passed.

Paying the fees

During this time, my mother found out about an Indian government scholarship scheme through somebody. She sent me the application forms, and I applied for the scholarship, and was successful. So, after the first semester, it was the scholarship that helped me through.

It also helped me pay my debt to the sister who had pawned her jewellery. When the next scholarship came, I repaid the money I had borrowed from my other sister. The scholarship, however, covered only the tuition fees. What about the hostel fees and food? Even small things like a washing soap or a toothbrush or a tube of toothpaste was a burden. My mother borrowed money at high rates of interest and sent it for my expenses.

By the time I finished BITS, Pilani, we had a debt of around Rs 100,000-150,000.

Preparing for CAT

My friends and juniors used to tell me that I could be a good manager and asked me to take an MBA. That was the first time I heard about something called MBA. When I asked them which was the best institution in India, they said, the Indian Institutes of Management. I decided then that if I was going to study MBA, it should be at one of the IIMs, and nowhere else. When I was preparing for CAT, I happened to read in the papers that 30% of India's population does not get two meals a day and I thought of my mother then. I know how it felt to be hungry. What should be done to help them, I wondered. That was when I decided to be an entrepreneur and create jobs so that no one goes hungry.

I also read about Infosys and Narayana Murthy, Reliance and Ambani then. Reliance had employed 20,000-25,000 people at that time, and Infosys, around 15,000. When a single entrepreneur like Ambani employed 25,000 people, he was supporting the family of four or five, of each employee. So he was taking care of 100,000 people indirectly. I felt, I too should become an entrepreneur.

When I was dreaming of becoming an entrepreneur, back at home, my mother was waiting for her engineer son to get a job, pay all the debts, build a pucca house and take care of her.

Getting a job

After a lot of thought, I decided to go for the campus interview, and got a job with Polaris. I also sat for CAT but I failed to clear it in my first attempt. I passed out with very good marks and I knew I had to repay all the loans before I became an entrepreneur. So, I joined Polaris Software in 2001.

When I got my first salary, I bought a sari for my mother and gave the rest of the salary to her in a cover. Then we all went out, and I treated my entire family to Pizza. That was the first time all of us had Pizza. It was like our life was changing.

I worked for 30 months at Polaris. By then, I could pay off all the debts but I hadn't built a proper house for my mother. Still, I decided to pursue my dream of becoming an entrepreneur.

When I took CAT for the third time, I cleared it and got calls from all the six IIMs. I chose to study at IIM, Ahmedabad.

Life at IIM, Ahmedabad

My college helped me get a scholarship for the two years I was at IIM. Unlike in BITS, I was more confident and life at IIM was fantastic. I took up a lot of responsibilities at the college. I was in the mess committee in the first year and in the second year I was elected the mess secretary.

Becoming an entrepreneur

By the end of the second year, there were many lucrative job offers coming our way, but I was determined to start something on my own. As I hadn't built a house for my mother, it was a difficult decision to say 'no' to offers that gave you Rs 800,000 a year. But I was clear in my mind even while I knew the hard realities back home.

My mother had been an entrepreneur, and subconsciously, she must have inspired me but my real inspirations were Dhirubhai Ambani and Narayana Murthy. Nobody at my institute discouraged me in my decision. In fact, at least 30-40 students from IIM wanted to be entrepreneurs and we used to discuss various ideas all the time. My last option was to take up a job.

Foodking Catering Services Pvt Ltd

I decided to be in the food business, perhaps my mother is the inspiration but then, I had also started my life selling idlis in my slum. My experience as the mess secretary at IIM-A also gave me confidence as I must have handled at least a thousand complaints and a thousand suggestions at that time. Every time I solved a problem, they thanked me.

I felt there was a good opportunity in the food industry. If you notice, a lot of people who work in the food business come from the weaker sections of society and understand what it means to be hungry and poor.

The best compliments I received were from Narayana Murthy and my director at IIM, Ahmedabad. When I told him (IIM-A director) about my decision to start a company, he hugged me and wished me luck. They have seen life, they have seen thousands and thousands of students and if they said it was a good decision, I was sure it was a good decision. My friends helped me with registering the company with a capital of Rs 100,000. Because of the IIM brand and also because of the media attention, I could get a loan from the bank without any problem.

I set up an office in Ahmedabad and employed three persons. The first order was from a software company in Ahmedabad; they wanted us to supply tea, coffee and snacks. We transported the items in an auto. When I got the order from IIM, Ahmedabad, I took an additional loan of Rs 11 lakh and started a kitchen. So, my initial capital was Rs 11.75 lakh.

Tough beginning as an entrepreneur

As I am a first-generation entrepreneur, the first year in business was very challenging. I had no experience in handling people in business, and it was difficult to identify the right people.

I had a loan of Rs 20 lakh by the end of the first year.

Though I made losses in the first year, not even once did I regret my decision of not accepting the offers from MNCs and starting an enterprise of my own. I looked at my losses as a learning experience. I was confident then that I would be successful one day.

Sleeping on the railway platform

When we started our second unit in October 2006, I thought my bad days were over, and I would start making money. But I made losses of around Rs 2,000 a day. I knew a first generation entrepreneur could not afford such a loss. I worked really hard, working till 3 am in the morning.

I started the third unit, again in Ahmedabad but it also made losses. All my units were cafeteria and I understood then that the small cafeterias would not work; I needed huge volumes of work. My friends were extremely supportive in the first year when things were difficult for me. I had taken loans from my IIM-A friends as they were earning very well. Birthday party offers also helped me tide over my losses.

In December 2006, an IIM Ahmedabad alumni event took place in Mumbai and I decided to go there mainly to get a contract. I was hopeful of getting it. I also knew that if I got the huge contract, I would come out of all the losses I had been incurring.

I had booked my train ticket from Ahmedabad to Mumbai for Rs 300, after that I had just Rs 200 in my hand. As the meet went on till late at night, I could reach the station only at midnight and I missed the train. As I didn't have the money to check into a hotel, I decided to sit on the platform till the morning and travel by the next train. I didn't want to disturb any of my friends so late at night. It was an unforgettable night, quite insulting and embarrassing too. I was even shoved off by policemen from the platform but, after two hours when people went back, I also moved in.

A man who sat next to me on the platform gave me a newspaper so that I could sleep. I spread the newspaper and slept on the platform! And I slept well. I got my ticket refund in the morning and went back to Ahmedabad. But luck did not favour me, and I didn't get the contract. In March 2007, I got an offer to start a unit at BITS, Pilani. That was the first medium break for me. For the first time, I started making profits there though the other units continued to make losses. The reason for our success at BITS, Pilani was the volume as there were more students. If I made Rs 5000 a day at Ahmedabad in two shifts, at Pilani I made Rs 15,000 a day. BITS Pilani, unit gave me the confidence to move on.

Unless you make money, you can't be confident in business.

Fortune changes

Through BITS, Pilani, I got the BITS, Goa contract and that was the biggest break for me. It was not a cafeteria like the earlier ones; we got the dining hall and had to feed 1,300 students. We started our operations in July 2007. At Rs 50, for 1,300 students, our sales were Rs 65,000 per day. We soon started making a profit of Rs 10-15,000 a day. Around 60 to 70 people worked there. I gave the charge of the Ahmedabad operations to one of my managers and moved to Goa.

Within six months of starting our operations in Goa, I repaid all my debts.

Giving inspiring speeches

It was at that time that I was called to give a motivational speech at the SRM Deemed University. After the speech, I asked the Chancellor, 'can you give me an opportunity to serve in your campus?' He said, 'If not you, to whom will I give such an opportunity?'

It was a food court but a big one, and we had to feed around 17,000 students there.

When I got the first opportunity to speak, I thought God had given me an opportunity to encourage or inspire entrepreneurs. When youngsters tell me they are inspired, I feel good. When you just dish out the theory, nobody believes you. But when you do it, they believe you. What I tell them is based on my own experiences.

When I thought of starting a company, I felt India needed at least a 100 people like Narayana Murthy and Ambani. If 100 such people support 200,000 people each, imagine how many Indians get supported?

Entrepreneurship is needed to uplift the poor. It is not easy to be an entrepreneur, especially a first generation entrepreneur. There will be lots of challenges in the beginning but one should learn to look for the light at the end of the tunnel. It's your determination and tough mind that help cross the initial hurdles.

When I hire 200 people, indirectly, we touch the lives of around a thousand people. Only 10% of my workers are educated, the rest are uneducated. I want to make a change in their lives. If they have any problem, I will take care of it. We support the marriages and education of their families. We pay more to the employees when the company does well.

When I became an entrepreneur, I had only two dreams, not for myself but for my mother. I wanted to buy a car and a house for my mother. I bought a car first. Though I have built a house, I still live in the same old house, the same hut where I lived 25 years of my life. I feel good in the hut; that's where I get my energy. I want to remind myself that money and fame should not take me away from what I want to achieve. The only advice my mother gives is, don't waste money.

My journey so far has been very enriching though sometimes I feel I have been in this for many, many years me. I am living every moment of the last few years as an entrepreneur; from sleeping on the Mumbai railway station platform to this level.

I have seen people from all walks of life—from the slums to the elite in the country. That is why luxuries like a car or a bungalow do not matter to me. Even money doesn't matter to me.

My ambition is to create as many jobs as possible and inspire as many youngsters as possible to be entrepreneurs so that they became job creators.

The New Generation

These young entrepreneurs who started on their journeys after 2010 are lucky in a way. By the time they began to hatch their plans, an ecosystem to help and encourage entrepreneurs was in place, society was knowledgeable enough to accept and applaud their entrepreneurial spirit, and venture capitalists, angel investors and mentors abounded to help them. That, however, does not imply that the journey of an entrepreneur is easy by any means, as the stories in this section illustrate.

An Environmentista

Arun Krishnanmurthy is a social entrepreneur who has only one purpose in life: save the environment, animals, wild life and lakes. When young men of his age enjoy life watching films and dancing in pubs, here is a 30 year old who has dedicated his life to saving the environment and wild animals.

The NGO, Environmentalist Foundation of India (EFI), he has built along with hundreds of school children is purely committed to conserving the environment. If he has other ventures that make money, it is only to sustain his sole aim.

This pursuit makes him work at least 18 hours a day to fulfil his roles as an environmental activist and an entrepreneur.

Arun Krishnamurthy, a social entrepreneur and founder of Environmentalist Foundation of India, is into conserving lakes, environment and animals

SEVERAL FACTORS in my childhood contributed to my getting passionately attached to animals and nature. The first was growing up in a village on the outskirts of Chennai. Then, having my school education in the pristine surroundings of Good Earth, a school run by the J Krishnamurthy Foundation, which taught me how to live in harmony with nature.

The many lakes and ponds I grew up seeing as a child slowly started vanishing when the city swallowed the surrounding villages. Huge concrete structures appeared in place of the pristine lakes and ponds. It also saddened me immensely when high-speed buses that raced through my village mercilessly knocked down cows, dogs and cats on the roads. I could never forget the mutilated bodies of cats and dogs on the roads. In my mind, I took a vow then that I would dedicate my life to preserving the environment, and also help animals live a peaceful life. When my father came to know of my decision, he encouraged me by giving me all the opportunities to chase my dreams. He was a huge inspiration.

Studying at Madras Christian College

I was sad and sceptical when I had to move out of my suburban village to Chennai, a big city, a metro. I had only experienced the serene beauty of nature in my school but Madras Christian College was a pleasant surprise to me. Anybody who has seen the campus of MCC knows how inspiring it can be to nature lovers.

In no time, I became a part of many groups of volunteers that worked to preserve the environment, and I will not say I was fully satisfied with what I was doing. Yet, it gave me a lot of pleasure to live amidst trees, and work to save them for posterity.

Working for Google in Hyderabad

After taking a degree in Microbiology from MCC, I moved to Hyderabad when I got an opportunity to work with Google. I was not even 20 then, but fortunately, the move turned out to be a major breakthrough in my life.

I saw that Hyderabad was a beautiful city but it pained me to see the bad condition of the Gurunadham Lake there. I couldn't bear to see dirty, uncared for lakes so I approached the government for permission to clean it. Luckily for me, the authorities gave me all the support I needed.

The next challenge was to find people who would help me clean the lake. I decided to go to some schools and speak to the students about environment and our duty to protect it. I made a plan; I conducted orientation programmes on environment in schools and in the end I asked them to join me as volunteers to work for protecting the environment.

That was when I realised, it was not only me but many other youngsters who were equally interested in taking care of nature. It was just that somebody had to bring out the passion in them. From then on, it has been my mission to motivate school students through speeches, and I have been doing it all over India.

It was not just one or two but a hundred students joined me in cleaning the Gurunadham Lake, and after 6 to 7 hours of hard work, we came out with 12 tonnes of garbage. The success of our very first effort encouraged me to continue with what I believed in. I didn't look at it as an achievement but a combined effort of the youth of India, and we were playing a small part in taking care of our environment.

From then on, cleaning and saving lakes became a part of my life. I don't look at a lake as just another water body; it has various forms of life in it. When we restore a lake, we save not just water but so many other life forms, and that is the main reason why I am obsessed with cleaning lakes. Ultimately, my goal is also to save animals, especially the animals living in these water bodies.

The three and a half years I spent in Hyderabad working for Google turned out to be one of the most satisfying years of my life. I just didn't work as an employee of Google; we had an excellent relationship. Google was very appreciative of what I was doing for the environment, and even after I left Google and Hyderabad, my association with the organisation continued. In fact, Google went on to partner with me in cleaning the lakes.

I wanted to help not just the animals that live in water but the wild animals trapped in zoos too. I started visiting various zoos with my young friends to keep the environment they live in, clean. I believe that if they live in a clean environment, they will be peaceful.

Moving to Delhi from Hyderabad

When it was time for me to move out of Hyderabad, I felt quite sad. It was a very difficult moment for me as the city had given me an identity. I was financially independent for the first time, and it gave me an opportunity to do something for the environment.

But then I had to quit Google to continue my studies at the Jawaharlal Nehru University in Delhi. Even though I was in a new city and a student once again, my passion did not leave me. There are lakes in every city and the truth is, all the lakes needed cleaning. I continued to go to schools and inspire students to join me in cleaning lakes.

The first lake my young team and I cleaned in Delhi was the Trilokpuri Sanjay Jheel.

Initially we were only cleaning the lakes, but soon we found that people in the nearby areas were making it dirty in no time. Many people we spoke to listened to us but there were many more who didn't care about lakes. That was when we started fencing the lakes and also, planting trees around the water body. It served two purposes; we could not only prevent it from getting dirty but birds could come, nest and live on the trees. By doing this, we felt we were creating awareness among the people to keep their own lakes clean.

Becoming an activist and an entrepreneur

After finishing my studies at JNU in 2011, I decided to come back to Chennai. This time, I didn't try to find any job in any company. My idea was to plunge deep into environmental work, and not do any 9-5 job.

I wanted to do my work more professionally, and the first thing I did was to start an organisation, the Environmentalist Foundation of India (EFI) and register it. Though we share the earth with every other life form, we believe that only we have the right to this planet. Just because we can talk louder and can walk erect, we can't call ourselves the supreme species; other living beings also have exactly the same right as us on this universe. We wanted to spread this message to all the citizens of the world.

We believe that the cause is the hero and not those who work. All of us who are associated with EFI genuinely want to give our time, manpower and volunteering efforts to the world we live in which is not ours alone. As I went along, I also found that more than adults, school children were dedicated, and ready to devote their time and labour for a cause. It is only because of their interest and passion that EFI continues to support many causes; we exist only because of the children.

Funds are needed for activism

I started an organisation to preserve the environment, but the question was, how to fund a completely volunteer-driven organisation? I had to somehow generate money.

That was when I decided to start my own enterprise—Krish Info Media—with a capital of Rs 40,000. I bought a laptop and an Internet connection with the idea to do market research and psephology.

Initially, I had no money to pay a regular salary, so I got six freelancers. But in no time, our company had a turnover of Rs 3 to 4 lakh a month. Today, we have a turnover of Rs 1.55 crores and I feel God is giving us money so we can invest in EFI.

In 2015, I started one more company, Yugeine-Danta that handles digital marketing and curriculum development. The name meant 'A peaceful saint'; I had named it after Hanuman, one God I look up to for energy and power.

EFI all over India

Today, we have EFI branches from Thiruvananthapuram to Jammu & Kashmir, and from Vadodara and Ahmedabad in Gujarat to Shillong. We take a lot of time before starting a centre in one place. For example, it took us a planning of three years in understanding the ground realities before we expanded to Kerala. Once we choose a place for action, we employ a person who will run the organisation there. I only go there to motivate them, and help them run important projects.

Rather than we choose the place, the place chooses us in the sense that the school kids who were with us in the beginning have all grown up and moved to other places. It was they who wanted us to start units in those cities. That way, we know the place is in safe and strong hands. They are, in a way, our Ambassadors in those places.

These days, I have to work at least 18 hours a day, and yes, it is hectic but then this is the journey I have chosen for myself. God has been kind to us by giving us so much work and we want to deliver something big for the future generation.

The modus operandi

We have only one agenda, and that is environment conservation at the community level. Unless the local community is involved, you cannot conserve the environment. So we make sure that the local community who is interested in social work does the conservation work.

We connect the corporates who want to do CSR (Corporate Social Responsibility) activities with conservation projects. Most of the corporates do not know what to do as their CSR work. They make T-shirts, caps etc. and waste a lot of money. We now tell the corporates to invest in our projects and we will run the project for them. This model has turned out to be quite successful so far.

They do not pay our salaries; they only help us in the work. For example, if we need a machine to restore a lake, the company will pay for the machine directly.

Over the years, we have become a lot more professional and mature in our approach to the environment. We do not want society to look at us as some college kids doing something for a hobby. We put in a lot of emphasis on science and logic in our work. Looking broadly, we want all the water bodies like ponds, rivers, lakes and temple tanks to be conserved as fresh water habitat so that all life forms can thrive in them.

I manage both my roles as a business entrepreneur running two companies and also as the social entrepreneur running the most ambitious EFI because I am very passionate about EFI. The companies that I run give me the confidence that I can run organisations; I teach, I design, I strategise for advertising, I do market research and I do psephological analysis for our clients.

I am not much bothered about the money that I make. As long as we can sustain and pay our bills, I am happy. We should not be dependant on anyone for our survival.

I am able to chase my passion because my company acts as my backbone.

It is wonderful to be completely occupied, but without volunteers, EFI is nothing. So many volunteers are coming forward everyday to be a part of EFI. There is no hierarchy here; all are volunteers and there is no President, Secretary or Treasurer at EFI.

I have big dreams and I have nobody to guide me. I am just following my dreams with all these schoolboys. We want to establish Environment Foundation of India as an organisation that does real conservation work all over India. I want to die with the satisfaction of having saved animals, and I know I am destined to do this job

As an environmentalist, my dream is, before I am gone, I want 500 freshwater bodies completely and scientifically restored so that many life forms can thrive in them. Nothing is going to stop me from doing so. Till my last breath, I will continue my efforts to conserve the environment all of us live in.

The Film-maker Milkman!

The story of B Udhaya Krishna and his friends is that of today's aspirational India, the India that encourages entrepreneurial spirit. Hurdles like poverty, discouragement and insults are just temporary hindrances that only make them stronger, pushing them to work hard and move towards achieving their dreams.

29-year-old Udhaya Krishna and his schoolmates dreamt of becoming entrepreneurs when they were in school itself. The dream became big when they were in college. It got bigger and bigger as they established their companies, made them successful, diversified and also helped other friends to realise their dreams as entrepreneurs.

Unlike some young men who preferred to agitate for opportunities, Udhaya Krishna and his friends created opportunities to succeed.

Coimbatore based Udhaya Krishna's story is that of a young hardworking dreamer who believes that if you work hard, nothing is impossible to achieve.

Udhaya Krishna is the founder of mypromovideos and paal.co

paal

AS IT SHOULD BE.

I HAD A difficult childhood after having lost my father at the age of eight. My mother stitched clothes to get us, her two boys, educated, with some help from her mother. It was not very easy; we were subjected to a life of humiliation, insult and neglect in the joint family where we lived with no father providing us any financial support. The other family members looked at us as a burden.

Because of the humiliation we were subjected to, both, my younger brother Vishnu and I wanted to do something that would make the relatives respect us and give us recognition. It was a tough life for us as kids. Unlike the other children of our age, we were deprived of many things; we never had any toys or video games to play with, we never had any chocolates to munch. As children, our dream was to have lots of toys and chocolates like other children.

We felt if we had to succeed in life, we had to make money and for that, we had to be businessmen. So when I was in the 4th standard I decided to be an entrepreneur. When teachers asked me what I wanted to be, I always used to say, a businessman!

My initial dream was to have a dairy farm when I grow up as I loved animals, mainly cows. That was because my mother's sister had cows at home. I loved going to her house and whenever I went there, I would spend time in the cowshed milking cows and feeding them. I was never scared of milking the cows though I was subjected to a few kicks from the cows in the beginning but soon, they became my friends. At that time, I thought I would start a business of selling milk.

Gets a cow from his aunt

As my aunt was getting old, and finding it difficult to look after her cows, she gave me Durga, one of her cows. Durga was a blessing to us; we sold her milk and the money was a big help in continuing my education. But the others in the family, somehow, did not like having a cow in the premises. So we were forced to sell Durga. That day, my mother, brother and I cried a lot. The money we got selling Durga was used for the 11th and 12th standard education of my brother.

After school, a diploma course in Computer Science

After my 12th standard, I got admission in a prestigious college in Coimbatore and my grandmother was willing to help me with the fees. But even that joy was short lived, some of my relatives intervened and prevented me from joining the institute. Their argument was that we were unnecessarily wasting money. Finally, I had to study a Diploma course in a government college in Computer Science.

I was in a hurry to get a job but my mother and her sister forced me to join an Engineering college as a lateral entry after the Diploma. My mother wanted to see me as an Engineer. I also had the desire to study engineering as my old school friends, Anil and Santhosh were there.

First initiative as college students

In college, my friends and I got an opportunity to organise events for various schools and colleges under Rotract, the youth division of the Rotary Club. Till then, nobody could make any profit out of these events, and many dissuaded us. But we organised that year's event and even managed to make it profitable. It was well appreciated by the members of Rotary Club. That was how we got our first job. But even before we passed out, it was recession time and jobs were not available for fresh graduates.

We got our degree in 2009 and joined a small company in Coimbatore, which filed IT returns for the employees of various companies. One good thing was, in the three months we were with the company, we were all the time travelling to Chennai, Bangalore and Hyderabad and meeting the employees of many big companies. It was a great learning experience watching how big companies work.

Becoming an entrepreneur in 2009

People say, many big ideas come over a cup of coffee, in our case, it was while we were sitting on a bench near a bakery and ruminating over our future. Santhosh came up with an idea to start an animation company, and after a lot of deliberation, we also found it appealing.

Though another friend, Mahesh Babu, could not join us due to his commitment to his family, the others resigned from their jobs and moved to a room in Santhosh's house with their computers.

That was how we started our journey as entrepreneurs. Santhosh's brother Gopalakrishnan also joined the team soon.

On the 9th of September 2009, with no capital, we started mypromovideos. Anil was good in animation, I loved designing websites and Santhosh was good at marketing. We designed and uploaded a promo video first. And you won't believe, the video was so impressive that from day one, we started getting orders. The first order was for $5. By the end of the first month, we made Rs 16,000. By the end of first year, the company was making $3000 every month.

Moving to Explainer Video and tasting success

By mid-2010, we could move to a proper office and decided to expand into making movies and animation films. Our research found that there is a huge market for Explainer Videos that explain about the products for companies through videos. Our first video for a startup in Chennai is still quite popular and brought us many customers that include Flipkart, HCL, Aditya Birla money, HDFC etc. With the success of Explainer Videos, revenue of mypromovideos started going up. From Rs70 lakh in 2012, it went up to Rs 1.6 crore in 2015. As we are presently working with 18-19 clients, in the next couple of years, we hope to touch Rs 20 crore annually.

Soon, Santhosh and his brother Gopalakrishna started their own firms and left us. Today, mypromovideos is a private limited company with only Anil Kumar and me as partners and 15 people working for us.

When you work for clients, you will not get the freedom to experiment much. That was why we decided to make a series of videos on Know about India. We realised that we have so many misconceptions about India and like us, there may be other young Indians who are not aware of the many unknown facts about our beautiful country. We hope our series will help people know and understand India better.

Starting a dairy farm in 2015

Animals have always been my first love and starting a dairy farm was my childhood dream. It would have remained a dream if my schoolmate Ramnath had not told me about his desire to start something on his own. Ramnath's parents wanted him to go to Dubai and make money but he was of the opinion that there were plenty of opportunities in India.

He spoke to us about his dilemma, and that was when I gave him the idea of starting a dairy farm. After all, I had been carrying this dream from childhood. Anil and I decided to fund the project, and we made him the working partner. That was how paal.co (paal is the Tamil word for milk) came into existence on 26 January 2015.

We pooled in Rs 4 lakh and bought 1.5 acres of land near Coimbatore on lease from my uncle. We bought six cows and four calves to start with, and in one year, we have increased to 60 cows and calves. In just over a year, we also broke even.

Though the cows have sheds now, eventually, our plan is to let the cows graze on the land itself and also use a part of the land for coconut cultivation. I created a website, a Facebook page and a logo for paal.co. We have developed a mobile app for the customers to track and use milk as per their needs.

We were sure about one thing; that we were going to sell milk only online. Till it happened, we sold milk to the cooperative societies. It took us 4-5 months to supply directly to customers. Now, we market and sell the product online. We realise that if customers come to you, there is more value to your product. We also decided to supply milk in bottles and not in plastic covers. That's how we used to get milk in the old days. So, we wanted to give people the same feeling. It's also a non-polluting way. Our vision is to give good milk to people, that's why we want to have desi cows alone. What we give is not pasteurised milk; just pure cow's milk. Again, we are recreating the same experience we have had in our country where we used to get fresh milk from the cows.

We chose the most elite area in Coimbatore to first supply milk and all the enquiries came through our Facebook page. Today, we have 150 customers and sell around 200 litres of milk everyday but we want to sell 1000 litres in the next 1-2 years. We already have a 10-acre land where we are growing greens for the cows. We know this is going to be a life-long business. As long as human beings are there, milk will be in demand!

We do not want to scale up the project without thinking of our animals because I believe that they also have the right to live with dignity. Only if they are happy co-existing with us, will we get what we want. As an animal lover, I hate slaughtering cows so I will keep my cows and calves till they die.

Changes in life

It may sound crazy but to make up for all the things I missed in life as a child, I bought a car and a house first. I wanted my mother to live in our own house. I wanted to have these materialistic things in life so that my relatives respected me. They treated us badly because we were poor. But now, they talk about us proudly, recognise us, and visit us. I am amazed by the change in the attitude of people when you have money.

But my gift to my mother was freedom from drudgery. When we were young, she did all the work from morning till evening for the entire household, for the joint family. She washed clothes, cleaned the house, washed utensils and cooked food. She did not have a single moment of freedom then. I want to give her that freedom, to do whatever she wants. But she is into spirituality now. Nothing materialistic appeals to her. The only thing she wants from us is to be good human beings. As for me, I am indulging in the simple pleasures that were denied to me as a child. I even buy chocolates and eat to my heart's content. It feels really good to be in a position to buy whatever I yearned for as a child.

Reason for the success

If I am successful today, it is only due to hard work and my thirst for knowledge and nothing else. I do not believe in the word luck; I don't think I am a lucky person also. I haven't got anything in life easily. I believe only in hard work. You have to work really hard if you want to be successful in whatever you do.

I work from 9 in the morning till 8 at night. I think only about work all the time. Now I am trying to find some personal time so that I will be more productive during working hours. I also make it a point to learn something new every day. The biggest lesson I learnt is, we have to have a clear idea of what we need to do and only then we should go ahead. Perseverance is what an entrepreneur needs the most. There will be many moments in the life of an entrepreneur when you feel like leaving everything, but giving up is not the answer; we have to stick to the vision we had.

Then, there has to be a good team for an entrepreneur to be successful. The trust Anil and I have for each other is immense, and that is what makes us succeed as a team. I feel this is the right time for an entrepreneur to be in India, especially when the government is giving a lot of support to startups. My advice to all those who want to be entrepreneurs is to start as early as possible—when you are really young and have no commitments in life. You let yourself fail as much as possible in the early stages so that you learn from the mistakes and succeed as you go ahead.

Dreams as an entrepreneur

As a Diploma student, I had attended a seminar in which one of the speakers told the audience that there were no brands from India which were internationally acclaimed. From that day, it is my dream to create a brand that is recognised all over the world.

We want to make a world class animated film from Coimbatore, from our own studio. I would say, I want mypromovideos to be the Pixar of India.

For a Healthy, Tasty Munch!

Startups in the Information Technology domain is quite common these days but there are only a handful of youngsters who venture into the field of food. Two friends, who studied in the Tamil Nadu Agricultural University in Coimbatore and lived in the same hostel room, belong to this minority.

There were only two choices in front of them as students; either join the Civil Service or become entrepreneurs. They chose to be entrepreneurs.

The seed of the idea for a startup was sown in the hostel room when Arul Murugan and Arun Prakash studied Agriculture. As both of them were from middle-class families, they decided to begin their journey as entrepreneurs only after making some money and also some experience in the corporate world.

Arul Murugan, the CEO of Snackexperts talks about their journey.

Arul Murugan is the founder of Snackexperts that sells healthy snacks

I COME from a small place called Oddanchatram in Dindugal district and my father was a farmer. I have seen the difficulties my parents faced as farmers. From a young age itself, I had decided that I would only study agriculture so that I would be able to do something for the farmers and make agriculture a viable profession for farmers.

It was at the Tamil Nadu Agricultural University in Coimbatore that I met Arun Prakash. Both of us used to sit and talk about starting an enterprise in the field of agriculture. We also knew we had to work for sometime, make some money before venturing into entrepreneurship.

So, after graduating in Horticulture, both of us worked for multinational companies that specialised in food processing and exports to know how the industry worked, before we became entrepreneurs.

I spent seven years with the company, learning the industry and making enough money to fulfil my dream. My dream was to provide a complete business solution where I could source products directly from the farmer, process it in a factory and then supply to the consumer.

I had seen how tough it was for my parents as this kind of a link did not exist in India. I was able to look at it from all angles because I am educated. I understand the missing links; the inefficiencies in the system make the product go through many hands before it reached the consumer but the benefit never reached the farmer.

Even when I was working for the company, I had many discussions over phone on various ideas with Arun and his sister Shamla, who was a software engineer. After a lot of brainstorming, we chose the snack space to be in, as we knew the food market was very crowded.

We found that on an average, 25% of our calorie needs come from snacks; 35% of the urban population and 15% of the rural population enjoy snacks. Though many of us know that we have to eat healthy, we do not do so.

We were sure about one thing; that whatever we did, technology would play a major role. After all, we were from technological background and we included Shamla in the group for that reason. Only technology would be able to clean up the system by eliminating middle men so that the benefit reaches the producer, and here it is the farmer. If we eliminate middle men, we will be able to reach the product faster to the consumer and without any middle man in the middle!

Resistance from the families

When we broke the news of resigning our well-paying jobs and becoming entrepreneurs, our families were shocked, there was stiff resistance. My parents were farmers and I was the first-generation graduate from the family, and their dream was to see me earn a monthly salary and not experience uncertainty. My parents were not at all pleased with my decision. I knew, unless I earn what I was earning before I became an entrepreneur, they would be very upset with me. They wanted to know why I wanted to get into trouble when I was earning a good salary.

So I decided to resign from my job only after the startup started getting orders. Arun and his sister also had to face a similar experience at home and they also had to use all their might to convince their 'middle class parents'.

The beginning

We pooled together a capital of Rs 2.5 lakh and started the company, Chloroplast Foods and named the brand Snackexperts.

Major portion of the capital was spent on developing the website as we had decided that it was going to be an online company. The rest of the money was spent on product development, packaging and shipping.

As we had experience in the field, in two months time, everything was in place. We were confident about the space we were getting into; people loved snacking, and we knew if the consumer liked our products, there would be repeated orders.

Why an online store?

From our experience, we found that while those living in the Tier 1 cities do not have the time to buy healthy snacks though they are available, availability is the problem in the Tier 2 cities. So to cater to all, we came to the conclusion that an online store is the best. In December 2014, the website for our online factory supplying snacks without any preservatives, was ready.

We had researched a lot on the healthy ingredients that are missing from today's food habits. For example, oats and honey. Though oats is used for breakfast and dinner, it is not used as snacks. Honey is very healthy but people use only sugar. Similarly, palm sugar that is used in many traditional recipes, is not in our regular recipes today. We dug out traditional recipes from our agricultural university library; our university has a huge wealth of such information.

We sourced 30 recipes initially under different and alluring names like Flapjack Fairies, Sweety Retreats, Fruits and Nuts Extravaganza, Fruits Fosterage, Scintillating Savourites and Sassy Seeds.

Oats form a major ingredient of almost all the snacks. For example, Nosh n Josh is a flapjack of mixed seeds and dry fruits. Sassy Seeds has pumpkin, cucumber and sunflower seeds.

We also knew that all the recipes would undergo changes depending on the response from the consumers.

We want everyone to know what he/she is eating. So we provide Nutrition facts like total calories, carbohydrates, protein, fibre and fat in each snack so that consumers can choose what they want. We also add 'Fantabulous Facts' about each snack. For example 100gm of 3pm Tea made of Roasted Watermelon seeds contain 557K calorie, 15 gm carbohydrates, 28gm proteins, 47gm fats and 0 fiber. And the fanatbulous fact about it is, Watermelon seeds are good source of vitamin B like Thiamin, niacin, folate, and packed with nutrients including fatty acids, essential proteins and lots of minerals.

A customer could choose any of the five items from the recipes provided in the online store and order. The cost was Rs 700 for a box of five different snacks.

Our principal aim was to remove middlemen from the cycle but as we have only started, it was not possible to source from the farmer directly. But as orders increase, we plan to directly deal with the farmers and realise the dream of buying from the farmer and directly giving it to the customer.

Today we buy the ingredients from the market and outsource them to make the snacks.

Within two months of us starting, the unbelievable happened.

Winning 10 Minute Million at IIT Bombay

The turning point for us was the '10 Minute Million', an Entrepreneurship Summit organised by IIT-Bombay, for the first time in the country to encourage pathbreaking ideas.

In February 2015, within 60 days of us starting the business, we decided to participate in the summit, and I was the one who represented our startup when we became one of the ten ideas short-listed by IIT- Bombay from a list of 260 applicants.

The selected startups were supposed to present their idea to the public that included many investors, in 5 minutes and the next 5 minutes was for the investors to ask questions. What they were looking for was not just game changing ideas that could change the way business functions but products too. We were already two months old and had supplied to quite a few consumers by then. We pitched our idea as one that can connect the producer to the consumer. I said, as our greatest strength was the team that had experience in the industry, we could take care of the entire chain starting from sourcing to production to delivery.

At the summit, we were the only one from the food industry, who spoke about farmers, food, production and technology. I couldn't believe it when after the question and answer session, four investors came forward to fund us and thus we raised Rs 14 lakh. But the competition was designed in such a way that we were allowed to take home only Rs10 lakh.

The trust investors had in us gave so much confidence, and made us realise that what we were thinking of was viable and interesting. That was the first time that we had pitched our idea to any investor.

After the win

Life changed dramatically after the win. Till the previous day, only our friends knew about us, and what we were doing. The day after we won the award, we received 40 orders. Even the food companies and leading VCs started enquiring about our products. An Indian in the US ordered snacks for his old parents in Maharashtra as a present. Our promise is to deliver snacks all over India and anybody from anywhere in the world can order for their dear ones in India, and we deliver snacks at their home. We delivered 70 boxes in February.

Crisis

We had so many plans then but things did not go as we had planned. Two-three months after we won the award, we had exhausted almost all the Rs 25 lakh we had raised from the investors. Though we were getting orders, they were not significant enough to match the investment made. We got only 150 orders per month and when we spent Rs 4-5 lakh, we generated only Rs1 lakh! People did not come online and order snacks.

That was when we got the feedback from many customers that they didn't want to order a food item without tasting it. Since we were an online company, we wondered how we could give a sample product for the customers to taste.

We then identified our target group as those from the age group of 25-60 totally excluding kids and teenagers. Only by 25, people become health conscious and start looking for healthy food.

We realised we had to reach the customers directly and find out the response but our prime idea of an online store was not helping us. We were confident about the quality of our product; the only problem was, our target group was not getting a chance to taste it.

That was when we got an offer to deliver 50gm pouches to Ramco Systems for its employees everyday. They didn't want the Rs 700 box but small pouches. The employer wanted his employees to eat healthy food and not junk food which they were used to till then. He wanted to change the food habits of his employees and have healthy snacks.

We were in a dilemma; we came as an online healthy food store and if we supply everyday to an office, were we not moving away from what we had started with? But our model was not working, funding was going down, and the company was sinking. With Ramco, we were getting a chance to reach out to our customers directly.

We also found that a similar trend was happening in companies that had less than 500 employees. When there are more than 500 employees, they have their own kitchen and pantry.

We had two option; remain an e-commerce company and shut shop after two months, or grab the opportunity and keep our venture alive so that our dream came true. We had a very good product and our main objective was to reach it to the customers, and not just follow a business model.

Finally we decided to grab the opportunity and in October 2015, we started delivering 200 pouches worth Rs 7,000 daily. That meant, from this one customer, we had an earning Rs 1.5 lakh a month. At that time, we had a revenue of just Rs 80,000 from online sales. And with just one customer, we doubled our revenue.

An advantage we had with the Ramco model was, we got instant response from the customers. Also, some of the employees who tasted our product started ordering online for their families. It struck us that we could have both the verticals; B2B and B2C.

Impressed with our product, we got similar orders from Ramco Mumbai and Delhi offices. Since our products have a shelf life of 30 days, we decided to ship pouches for every week. By December, we had a revenue of Rs 3 lakh. Diwali was approaching and we spoke to many companies on festival gifts and we got orders worth Rs 3 lakh.

Our investors also felt what we were doing was right to take Snackexperts to profitability. Other than the money we received at IIT, Mumbai, we have not raised any money as we make 15-18% profit every month which we put back into the venture.

The decision to supply small pouches to various companies turned out to be a good business decision we made as we started growing at 20% every month with a customer base that include companies like Freshdesk, Orangescape, L&T, Paypal, etc other than our first customer Ramco Systems.

Today we supply an average of 1000-1200 pouches everyday and 90% of our business is still in Chennai.

By May 2016, we started making Rs 6.5 lakh every month and look forward to making a revenue of Rs 1.5 crore in 2016.

We are glad that we made the right decision at the right time. We want to expand to other cities only gradually and with caution. We hope to have a pan India presence in the next three years.

Ecosystem for a startup

In India, it has never been so good for an entrepreneur. With the support given by the government, even registration has become much easier. If the single window system becomes operational, it will even be easier.

Social media is a big boom for today's entrepreneurs. You can get connected with even the most well-known investor on social media and they are willing to guide you. The good news is, investors with money are looking out for good ideas. Today, they are ready to even invest in the startups of Tier 3 cities. You can be from a village but if your idea is good, it will take off.

From America to Work for Rural India

They were just two very studious young Americans; not friends, not studied in the same university, didn't even know each other, but were connected by a Professor at the MIT who knew they had similar interests.

After a half hour lunch, they spent another three hours brainstorming on how to start a company that would create essential technologies. In fact, they even decided on the logo of the company they were going to start.

Soon, they became the co-founders of Essmart Global, a company that right now, works with and for rural south India.

They are Diana Jue and Jackie Stenson; both 29 years old.

After four years in India, both Diana and Jackie consider India as their home though they missed home in the beginning. In fact, Diana's husband is an Indian, and she considers Bangalore as her home. In Diana's words:

Diana Jue (right) co-founded Essmart Global that provides Essential Technologies to rural India, with Jackie Stenson (left)

ESSMART

THOUGH BOTH Jackie and I were in Boston, we studied in different universities; I was at MIT and Jackie, at Harvard. I had decided to study engineering as a teenager in high school itself when I saw one of my advisors building a solar water filter. That got me interested in easy technology for community development.

I joined MIT to study designing technologies but I was more fascinated by community development than designing technologies. Anybody studying at MIT, and interested in development ended up in D-Lab, and it helped me design technologies for community development and making products that people can use. My interest in essential technologies grew after my extensive travels to Chile, Argentina, south India, China, Singapore and Thailand as an undergraduate student.

Jackie also used to frequent the D-Lab, although she was a Mechanical Engineer but we never met at the lab. Jackie went to Sub Saharan Africa for her project while I went to China and India. I was at IIT-Madras on my research project of testing technologies in Indian villages.

My fieldwork in Tamil Nadu and Karnataka made me understand how communities develop and in what ways we can help communities develop in the right direction.

That was when a professor who knew both Jackie and me, connected us. In our first meeting itself, we decided on what we should do and a rough business plan also was ready over our lunch meeting.

Our business plan won $7000 from MIT to run a pilot. Prashanth, who was Jackie's classmate in the University of Cambridge, joined us and we floated Essmart Global.

Visiting India for the pilot project

I came to India in January 2012 for our pilot study and we chose Pollachi in Tamil Nadu for our project. That was because Prashanth's family hailed from that area. Also, I had the experience of doing my research project in south India.

The pilot was to understand the needs and willingness of the malligai stores (Kirana stores) to buy essential technologies. When I say 'essential technologies', I mean solar lanterns, water filters, cooking stove, agricultural tools etc., anything that will make the life of a person living in a rural area, easy.

Why Tamil Nadu?

We spoke to around 200 such stores as a part of our survey. We believe that these stores have a strong relationship with the villagers and they could be our channel to sell these technologies. We tried to understand from them what the villagers would like to see in our catalogue. We did a similar survey in Ujire, a village near Mangalore also.

Through our products, we want to make a difference in the lives of rural people but to achieve that, they should be in a position to buy our products. If you have any plans to create products for rural areas, it makes more sense to introduce it in the area where people can pay for them.

We also believe that the first-time customers have to be the ones who are aspiring to be the middle class, and not the poorest. That was why we chose the southern part of India as our area of work. The educational levels of Tamil Nadu are relatively higher than say, the northern part of India. Also, slightly more wealthy communities welcome technologies first, and it will be a stamp of approval for the poor communities who aspire to be like the wealthier people. From our research, we have found that technologies move from richer, urban areas to the rural areas and not in the other direction.

No technology should be given free

Technologies we have in the US are not designed for the lower income group in the rural areas. In the US today, technology is used in non-essential purposes. That is why we, engineers, decided to create Essential Technologies; we believed that technologies could play a role in enhancing the quality of people's lives. We wanted to bring in technologies that will help millions and millions of people. The goal is to give access to useful technologies to everyone and everywhere.

While doing our research, we saw many NGOs buying technologies like Solar lantern, cook stoves etc. and distributing it to the villagers for free. The truth is, when people get things free, they don't value it and they don't use it too. We have seen cook stoves dumped in some corner of their house. But when you buy things, you use it. That is why we were sure that we would only sell essential technologies and not give anything free.

Testing the Pollachi market with Solar lamps

The first technology we kept in the malligai stores in Pollachi, were solar lamps imported from an American company. We wanted to see how people accepted them. The 12 solar lamps were sold in a week. Of course, even in January, there were huge power cuts there!

After the pilot scheme, I went back to MIT to finish my research.

Winning competitions at MIT and Dell

At MIT, our business plan won the MIT Idea Global Challenge competition and got $10,000 as reward. Then, at the Dell Socio Innovation challenge, an international competition for student entrepreneurs, we won another $50,000.

With the money, we decided to start Essmart Global officially in August 2012. Five team members from the Boston area also came down with us initially.

I have been here in India ever since and Jackie joined me later.

Local people recruited to market the products

We know how important it is to have local people who know the area, language and residents, to market our products. We have directors from Coimbatore and Coorg who oversee all operations. Chandru, who joined us as our first sales person, is now in charge of Tamil Nadu.

Initially, we started very small; just 10 outlets, 2 sales people, with our presence only in the villages close to Pollachi and 20 products. We were selling just 1 piece at a time. Our products were not big brands but good quality ones, sourced by us in the US but imported by people from India. We bought from the Indian buyers.

When we sold our 100th product after two months or so, it was like crossing a huge benchmark.

We have 43 people working for us with over 1,000 outlets and 6 offices in Tamil Nadu. Now, we are expanding in Karnataka.

When we started, our catalogue had only 4 products but today, we have 65 products. We had two solar lanterns first, one priced Rs 550 and another at Rs 1,600 but today, we have a whole range of products; solar lanterns, solar powered mobile phone chargers, water filters, agricultural products like mobile phone-controlled water pump controllers and many other agricultural tools; all aimed at rural people.

We found that even villagers are willing to pay more if they find they are getting a quality product; and you are willing to give good after-sales service. That is one of the areas we stress a lot. There is no point in selling products without providing any after-sales service, the product just gets dumped in a corner after sometime. That is why we offer proper service for each one of our products.

We must have sold more than 13,000 products so far, selling an average 500 to 1,000 products a month. We have been growing on an average of 20% every month.

Impact on the lives

We are not doing charity; we are not running any NGO. We are doing business in India but the work we do has a social impact; our products improve the lives of rural people. We want every product we sell to impact the rural households. The stores that work with us also make money as we give a commission of around 10-30%.

Many of those who purchased our products first were small businesses, who were able to work longer hours like roadside vendors, hotel owners, sari weavers and barber shops.

I still remember visiting one of our very early customers, a barber shop owner whose little shop was not connected to the grid. One day, when we called out his name, he came out of his house and opened the shop and turned on the solar lantern. Suddenly, a customer turned up, and he spoke to us while cutting the customer's hair with the solar lantern on. It felt so amazing. I could see the impact our product had on the barber's life.

I also remember visiting a sari weaver's house. He was not sure whether he should purchase the Rs 1,600 solar lantern as it was understandably an expensive investment for him. He had had many bad experiences with bad-quality Chinese products. As we were leaving, he changed his mind to buy the product. Later, he told us how happy he was and how much the solar lantern changed his life.

Expansion plans for Essmart Global

We know our business can be replicated anywhere in the world. Many people ask us whether we have plans to expand in other countries. At present, we are happy in this geography though we see a lot of potential in this model to go other places.

We will have our presence first in the entire south India, then the whole of India and after that, we will consider south Asia and South East Asian countries and Africa.

It is a lot of hard work, not easy. Our work involves long hours and many travels but seeing the impact our products have on people and working with the team, is very satisfying.

Local Solution Gau Gas for the Kitchen

When most youngsters prefer working for multinational companies in urban areas, these 28 year old young men chose an unconventional field to work; the villages of India. To be precise, to produce Biogas from cow dung. They are Koushik Yanamandram, Piyush Sohani and Shankar Ramakrishnan, classmates and roommates in college.

That is because nine out of every 10 households in rural India rely on firewood and other biomass for cooking. LPG gas is difficult to access and also unaffordable to most of the population.

While around 80 million families in rural India own cattle, at least 40 million families have sufficient space and animal manure to generate Biogas as an affordable solution for their cooking needs.

Their motto is to provide eco-friendly fuel for rural households, sustaining earth which they hope to achieve through SustainEarth Energy Solutions.

SustainEarth was launched in September 2013 but in January 2015, Shankar, one of the three had to move out of the enterprise.

While Koushik Yanamandram works as Director-Field Operations, Piyush Sohani is the CEO in charge of finance and technology.

Koushik tells the story of how he, along with his university friends, founded SustainEarth.

Koushik Yanamandram (right) with Piyush Sohani (left), co-founders of SustainEarth that work in the villages to produce Biogas from cow dung

AS MY father was a banker, I grew up in cities. My family had no background in agriculture or farming or rural India, and my initiation into agriculture happened by sheer accident. I got admission for Agricultural Engineering in the Agricultural University in Hyderabad, and the four years spent at the university studying agriculture changed my perspective on the subject.

I realised that agriculture was the most important and essential industry in India but much neglected. That gave me the motivation to work for rural development as I felt there were a lot of problems we had to solve. That was the reason why I decided to specialise in Renewable energy.

At Delhi University to study Renewable Energy

After I joined Delhi University to do MTech in Renewable Energy Engineering and Management, I met Piyush and Shankar there. Unlike me, Piyush who had done his engineering in Biotechnology was from an agricultural family in Madhya Pradesh. Naturally, he knew rural India quite well and wanted to use technology to improve the lives of people living in rural areas.

You can imagine the condition of his village if I were to say there was no power in his village till he finished 10th standard and he had to walk miles to go to school. So he was very motivated to improve the lives of villagers.

Like me, Shankar also was from a city but an ardent environmentalist and was in love with eco-friendly products.

We were not only classmates but roommates too. Naturally, we bonded over the subject all three of us were passionate about; rural development.

So close to Delhi yet so undeveloped

Our first encounter with real rural India was when Shankar and I went for a rural trek organised by an NGO when we were university students. It was a trek to a rural area just outside Delhi for a day, and our first visit was to a village called Sirohi.

To our shock, we found that 90% of the households used chulha to cook food using cow dung and almost 70% of the households did not have any livelihood options. Sirohi was just 35 kms away but the village was so impoverished and without any facilities while Delhi had big roads, electricity, wifi etc. We decided then that whatever knowledge we have gained, we should use it to improve their lives. We also knew technology could alleviate poverty if used properly.

That was the first motivation. Our teacher, Prof VVM Kishore who was in the bio energy field for a long period, helped us find answers to some of the questions we had.

REED initiative

Fresh after the rural trek, we started our first initiative for rural India, REED (Renewable Energy for Rural Development). We used to visit the villages outside Delhi during the weekends and do energy assessment survey. It was a very exhaustive survey in which we went to each household, and asked them about their energy status and power connections.

We then passed on the results of our survey to the CSR wings of the companies near the villages, so that they could utilise the CSR funds to provide power and power appliances to these houses.

We didn't have any knowledge about startups then, and we thought it was better to start an NGO after our studies; but not a private limited company. We were of the impression that only NGOs worked for people's betterment and private companies worked only for profits!

Internship at TERI

Our internship at The Energy and Resources Institute (TERI) was one of the most educating experiences for us. As I was more interested in rural electrification, I went to Bihar. I moved around the villages in and around Patna for about 2-3 months to learn about rural electrification and it was kind of an eye opener for me as even in 2013, energy was a big problem in rural areas.

That was when I met a person who was an inspiration for me; Gyanesh Pandey of Husk Power Systems. He came back from America to bring light to the villages in Bihar using rice husk. Today, HPS supplies eight to 10 hours of power to 18,500 households in some of the off-grid villages, where the state-run electricity board doesn't reach. Over 1.5 lakh rural Indians have benefited from this and around 250 people have got employed.

After the studies, a startup

After our MTech, we were a bit confused about how we should proceed with our idea of serving rural India. Gnanesh Pandeyji, who was more like a mentor to me, advised us to start a social enterprise, the bottom line of which should be social impact. He told us that we could start a private limited company and make products and services that would impact the lives of people.

So we chose a hybrid model where the technology will be developed by a private limited company and the outreach programme will be done in the not-profit model.

Piyush and Shankar had their scholarship money of about Rs 2 lakh and that was the capital we had, to start our idea. This was not enough at all.

Getting connected to Villgro Innovation Foundation

Before we started looking for more capital, the Villgro programme happened. Villgro Innovation Foundation provides incubation funds and mentoring to social entrepreneurs, and is based out of the IIT Madras Research Park.

We went to them with our initial plan for a not-profit NGO model. At the interview for the Villgro Entrepreneur Residents programme, Villgro asked us an important question. They asked us whether we would continue with our idea even if Villgro did not support us. We told them that whether or not we got support from the programme, we planned to continue, even if we had to struggle. Then they understood our commitment and after that, we were selected for a stipend of Rs 25,000 per month and a capital of Rs 3 lakh for product development. The suggestion was that we were to focus on one particular problem and the technology to find a solution to the problem. We chose Biogas as the problem as there were no private players to solve the issue.

Villgro also asked us to go for a for-profit model, which is more effective and efficient.

A cattle-rich country but no use of Biogas

From our research, we found that India has the largest cattle population in the world, which can generate enough animal manure to produce methane as clean cooking gas through biogas technology. Around 80 million families in rural India own cattle and at least 40 million families have sufficient space and animal manure to generate Biogas as an affordable solution for their cooking needs. But about 144 million households do not have access to clean cooking fuel in India. About 86% of the population use Biomass like firewood, crop residue and dung cake as fuel and they emit hazardous smoke. This has resulted in about 1 million lung-illness deaths annually. Burning firewood also leads to deforestation and GHG emmisions.

SustainEarth is born

In September 2013, our startup was born. We wanted to name it as REED Initiative again, but while registering, we found that they would not accept any acronyms. So, we retained it as our action plan and named our startup SustainEarth Energy Solutions; after all, whatever we do is to sustain the earth.

Doing surveys in 10 states

Before developing the technology, we did an extensive survey in villages in 10 states where a large number of cattle population is available. The states we covered were Haryana, Rajasthan, Gujarat, Maharashtra, Karnataka, Andhra, West Bengal, UP, Orissa and MP. The entire survey lasted for about 6-7 months.

Our intention of the study was to engage with all people involved in the Biogas sector, from NGOs to users to government officials so that we could get an idea of what exactly the problem was and how it could be solved. To understand the perception of Biogas by the villagers, we asked many questions to them and had group discussions with them. The results we gathered from the survey formed the basis for product development. Initially we thought we should invent a new technology but soon we found that technology was there, and the problem was in implementation as nobody had indigenised the technology. If we were to solve the problem across India in all the villages, we had to design a product that could be manufactured in mass and could be adopted easily by the people.

The example is the Solar home-lighting system. Today, people can buy it from the store and can easily install it by themselves. Unless we create a technology that can be easily adopted, installed and used, villagers wouldn't go for it. That is why even when you have 25 million households in India which can use Biogas, only less than 1% use it.

The Biogas plant being used today needs the help of masons to install and that means you require brick, mortar, cement etc to construct the system, and it takes a minimum of 10-15 days to complete the work. This is not an easy task by any means. If it fails due to any crack, it is very difficult to rectify too. That is why millions of Biogas plants have failed in India.

Designing the first Biogas plant—Gau Gas

In January 2015, when Shankar had to leave the team, Himanshu Mishra, a designer from IISC, Bangalore joined us.

We designed a pre-fabricated flexible bag-like Biogas plant, which does not need the help of a mason to install it. We wanted to test the prototypes not in a lab but in the villages itself. From the very first prototype onwards, we had been testing it at the farmer's place. So far, we have installed the prototypes at nine farmers' houses; two in Andhra Pradesh and the rest in Karnataka.

From our survey, we had found that customers were willing to pay Rs 12,000 for a Biogas plant but we have not been able to bring the price down to below Rs 25,000.

Our first plant, named GauGas was installed at farmer Krishna Reddy's house in a village near Tirupathi around mid-2015. He had 10-12 cows and because it was our first plant, we asked him to use it for a few months and pay us if he was satisfied. After six months, he paid us Rs15,000 and the plant is working very well.

More than that, he has become our brand ambassador, talking to other villagers about our product and has brought in many others to buy it. We started getting orders from the nearby villages too.

Our modus operandi is to procure most of the small components from Tirupati and a couple of others are imported from China. Our manufacturers are in Chennai and Nashik and it takes just two days to install the plant which we are sure will run for ten years without any problem.

Another advantage is, we have installed a device in each plant, which would send signal to our server in case there is any breakdown, so that we can send a service personnel immediately.

Biogas and Bio-fertiliser too

Now, a family with 2-3 cows can cook every meal of theirs using the Biogas plant. There are 25 million farmers in India with at least 2-3 cows and if all them use Biogas to cook, millions of LPG and firewood can be saved. Above all, it is eco-friendly and will not pollute nature.

Other than biogas, there is an important byproduct from the Biogas plants; bio fertiliser. Our plan is to help the farmer commoditise the bio-fertiliser and make some income from it. We want to form self-help groups of women in villages and give the ownership of the plants to women.

I would say our GauGas plants are reliable, easy to install by the farmer himself and he gets an additional income through bio-fertilisers. A farmer would get enough gas for cooking throughout the year while the old conventional plants will not work during rainy days.

Plans for future

Our target is to install one plant in a week and 100-150 plants in one village. We want to at least install 500 units in the next financial year and 5,000 units in the next 2-3 years. We are contacting the CSR units of many companies that work in villages to help us reach the villagers.

There are 166 million households in rural India, out of which 80 million own cattle. From 80 million households, we can give biogas to 25-30 million households. That is the kind of potential we have in front of us.

We want to popularise Biogas as an eco-friendly product. We do not want villagers also to follow the unsustainable path followed by the urban population. Through Biogas, a village can become self sufficient in energy.

The Startup India initiative

To those who are already in the startup arena, the Startup Initiative by the government has not much to offer but this has helped change the public perception of startups. People now know what a startup is. Two years ago, when I said, 'I am in a startup business', people were clueless, not anymore. Even my parents were aghast initially when I started SustainEarth instead of joining a multinational company but now they realise that what we are doing is also interesting and sustainable.

The Pied Piper from India

The HBO's comedy show, Silicon Valley is about a fictional startup Pied Piper and the lives of its developers who write algorithm to compress files.

Believe it or not, when Pied Piper was being aired, two young programmers of a startup called Skcript from Chennai were also writing codes to compresses files. And they were so short of cash that they couldn't afford even an office space and had to do the coding from inside their car!

When 27-year-old Karthik Kamalakannan founded Skcript with his friend Swathi Kakarla in December 2013, little did he realise that Skcript would become the Pied Piper of India one day.

Karthik and Swaathi had to go through several hardships to realise their dream of starting something of their own. Till a person from Bangladesh came like an angel through a friend to help them with funds to develop their product, Shrink that compresses files.

In such a short span, Skcript has quite a few high-paying clients from the Middle East, US and India, and also a swanky office.

Karthik's story as an entrepreneur is about perseverance, patience, dreams and a little bit of luck.

Karthik Kamalakannan founded Skcript that has scripted the software that compresses files

Skcript

EVEN AS A CHILD, I wanted to do what others were not doing. In school and college, everybody dreamt of working in big companies while my dream was to start a company of my own.

My biggest inspiration even when I was in the fourth standard was Steve Jobs. I was such a huge fan of his that my room was filled with his pictures like many have the posters of cricketers in their rooms!

I grew up in a small place called Tiruvallur where my father Kamalakannan worked for the Oriental Insurance. Though he could not study beyond the 12th standard, he worked really hard. When he did a business of more than Rs 2 crore in one year for his company, they appreciated his efforts by gifting him a computer, a printer and a net connection. In fact, the offer was either cash or the computer, and my father opted for the computer as he thought it would help me.

I was eight years old then, and I still remember the day. It was at night that we went to pick the pack. It was an HCL computer and we gave it a place in the drawing room.

But I had to wait till the next morning for the computer engineers to come, load it and boot it. The first boot was magical. It was a dial up connection and it opened a wide new world for me.

It was through this window that I learned all about computers and a virtual world full of knowledge. I had no interest in games like my friends. Till I finished my 10th standard, I didn't play a single game on my computer unlike other children; I used it initially only to learn English and typing. Growing up in such a small place, the chances of learning good English are quite grim.

From learning English, I moved on to learning about computers and soon computer languages like C and C+.

During the weekends, I used to go to Kanchipuram to learn computer languages from my cousin who was studying at a computer centre with the hope of getting a job. I started learning computer languages as they fascinated me, and I was too young to think about jobs then. By age 10, I started programming in C.

My love story with computers that started at 8 still continues.

Joining the Microsoft Student Partner Programme

Because of my love for computers, I joined an Engineering college near Chennai after school and pursued computer science. I spent all my time after college hours learning more and more about computers.

The first step was joining the Microsoft Student Partner Programme after successfully completing seven rounds of interviews.

Through this programme, another window opened up for me, taking me into the fascinating world of Information Technology. Instead of attending college, I used to go to the office Microsoft had in Chennai and worked there on many projects. I would say, I made the maximum use of the Microsoft Student Partner programme. The biggest learning I had because of the programme was to learn to write good professional code that would help customers.

Also, as a young kid in the office, all the others with 10-15 years of experience helped me learn everything in the proper way.

From the day I touched the computers at the age of 8 till today, not a day has passed without me learning something new.

Starting a company when in college

When I was doing my second year in college, I along with a couple of my friends, Prithviraj and Arulraj, started a company called 20 QBE Solutions. The reason behind starting our own company was because we were quite dissatisfied with the kind of websites that were built in those days. We thought we could do better.

We had a few clients and we used to make Rs 2-3 lakh per assignment but as students, we were so naïve that we hired two people and took a shared office space in the heart of Chennai on rent.

Though we made Rs10 lakh in the one and a half years, when the market crashed, we had no money left with us. It was obvious that we didn't know how to build a company.

So when we passed out in 2010, there was a lot of pressure from our families to work outside and not restart the company.

But running a company when in college was a huge learning experience for me. I understood that you need a good working capital to start with, you shouldn't get into services as there are already a million service-based companies from India who can do much better than you as they have been in the business for years. If you want to make a difference, you should be a product-based company. And if you want to be a product-based company, you need working capital.

At 21, I learnt these lessons.

iOS Engineer at Apple

Though I joined Wipro due to family pressure, after two years, I knew I had to quit. The good thing was I got a chance to first work with a project with Apple as an iOS Engineer.

As a boy who idolized Steve Job, it was a dream come true for me. Working for Apple was one of the highs of my career. All that I did not learn in the 24 years of my life, I learnt in the two years I was with Apple.

During my visits to the US while working for Apple, I used to meet people who were of the opinion that India was for IT coolies and China for hardware. It hurt me. I felt it was high time we came up with products and sold them to the world market.

Starting a Google developers' group in Chennai

Even while in college, I wanted to move in a community that talked technology and not films but in college, I heard most of my classmates talk only about film stars and films.

That was the reason why myself and a friend of mine, Jayanthan who used to organise technology events at college, gathered a few geeks like us in 2010 and started the Google Technology User group informally. There were many geeks in Chennai and as soon it grew to a community of 100-200 we met regularly.

As the numbers grew, Google started supporting us and we rebranded it as Google Developer's group; there are around 500 such groups across the world.

It was at one such event that I met my co-founder Swathi Kakarla. She was the only female developer in our group of 100 people who met almost every month. We had strikingly similar ideas on developing products and running a company. She can write a very good code, and that's how we became friends.

Both of us love programming; we love the idea of creating something by writing code! We want every single code we write to be like Ilayaraja's symphony!

Love for writing codes and starting a company

Because of our love for programming, we always felt it would be great to create a good product.

In December 2013, we decided it was time we started our own company.

We named our company Skcript because we believed that communication was the key whether it was through sign language or written language or spoken language or code language.

The spelling Skcript had the first letters from our names and also the first letters of my parents' names, Shyamala and Kamalakannan. I wanted to tell my mother that the SK stands for their names so that she would be happy!

Shared work space to start with

I had saved just Rs 1 lakh from my job and Swathi was still a student, so we didn't have enough money to have an office at that time. But nothing deterred us from starting our own company and creating a dream product and a dream company.

To start with, we worked in a shared workspace, which meant in a common room where we could rent out chairs. We needed to pay only for the chairs. We sat there with out laptops and wrote our codes.

Swaathi worked after college hours while I worked from morning. The only money I spent was on the workspace.

Days and months passed and there came a time when I didn't have the money to even pay for the shared work space because we hadn't started earning any money.

Car becomes the office

I had my car, a Ford Fiego which I had bought after I started working, and it became our work space when money ran out to rent out even two chairs. So, I used to park the car wherever there was free parking. We sat in the car and wrote codes in our laptop.

There were instances of the police looking at us with suspicion. Luckily, they didn't harass us because we kept the door open and we didn't work after sunset.

For three months, the car was our office. Mind you, we didn't even have a client and we were developing something that we thought would help us eventually.

We somehow believed that a break would come some day, and we waited for that day! I think God was testing our patience and perseverance.

Only Rs 120 in the bank

One day, when we had just Rs120 in the bank which we could not withdraw, and the diesel in the car had reached the empty level, we decided that enough was enough. I decided to go back to Apple and Swathi would join some company, and we would make enough money to continue chasing our dreams.

That day when I was back at home, a cousin of mine came to meet me. His friend in the Middle East wanted a solution to solve the data explosion he was facing, and he was in Chennai at that time.

We had three products in mind and only one of them was on data compression but we didn't take it up initially as we knew that we had to have huge capital to build it.

I spoke to this guy from Bangladesh and fixed up an appointment to meet him the next day. I knew that was the last chance I was going to have and I made the best pitch I had done in my entire life. He was impressed and said he would pay 50% as advance and the rest of the 50% after we build the product.

He gave me advance which was very big money for us.

Developing Shrink with the advance

With the money in hand, we were all charged up and in less than sixty days our product, Shrink was ready, though they gave us three months time. We had a happy client. While we developed the product, at every point we were checking with the client and writing the code as per their wishes and requirements.

In fact, they were so happy with our product that they became our sales agents too. Shrink was officially launched in Dubai at GITEX, a tech event there.

Shrink uses compression algorithms to minimize files to the smallest possible size. Imagine how much data is stored in a 1GB memory card but after you shrink your data, you can store 1.5GB-2GB data in the same memory card. What we do is in the magnitude of 100 gigabytes and 96% smaller in size.

In three months time, we broke even and moved to a good office with seven people working for us. As our product is priced at few thousands to hundreds of thousands dollars per year, within a year, we had a revenue of around $200,000.

Right now, we have 10 customers, mostly from the Middle East, the US and India. Our partners include GSS, Microsoft, Google, iGrid, Amazon Web services.

Pied Piper and Skcript

It was when we were struggling, working from my car that we heard about the HBO show, Silicon Valley and the developers Pied Piper. It was interesting to know that they were also working on compressing files.

Looking back, I feel it was adventurous and fun, but experiencing it was not fun. It was very tough. When all your friends were earning their salaries in thousands, there I was without any money to even pay rent and working from inside the car. Going through those days was psychologically and emotionally a terrible experience.

Now that we have gone beyond those struggling days, today my ambition is to build a world-class company.

The biggest lesson I have learnt so far is, never stop believing in yourself, and that miracles do happen if you are patient.

A Dosa Machine from India!

Here is a young man who read the book, *Simply Fly* by Captain Gopinath when he was in the 12th standard and got fascinated by him. From then on, he had no doubt about who he wanted to be; an entrepreneur. Captain Gopinath's story made him realise that he did not have to be a businessman's son to be an entrepreneur.

The young man is Eshwar K Vikas who, as a final year engineering student at the SRM University in Chennai, started his own enterprise. Though his earlier plan was to be an engineer first, take an MBA degree next and then become an entrepreneur; perhaps he didn't have the patience to wait that long.

With Prince William and Kate spending so much time with Eshwar and William himself making a dosa and tasting it has made the whole world look at the Dosa Machine from India with great interest.

Eshwar K Vikas is the man behind Dosamatic, the world's first automatic table top dosa making machine!

ALTHOUGH MY father was a bank officer in Andhra Pradesh, I always wanted to be on my own and start my own company. Maybe it was in my genes as all the other family members except my father were into some business or the other.

When teachers asked the students in school, 'what do you want to become', I always said, a businessman much to the amusement of my classmates and teacher.

At that time, I did not know the word entrepreneur but by the time I was in my 11th standard, I started reading about entrepreneurship. When I was in my 12th , I got so fascinated by the book *Simply Fly* by Captain Gopinath that from then on, I had no doubt about who I wanted to be; an entrepreneur. Captain Gopinath's story made me realise that I did not have to be a businessman's son to be an entrepreneur.

First influence

What changed my life happened when I was in college in Chennai, studying Electrical Engineering. When I was in the first semester, my college conducted a seminar on entrepreneurship awareness. Raj Shankar, who did consultancy services for small businesses, was one of the guest speakers.

At the end of the presentation, I walked up to him with a business idea. He didn't brush me aside but asked me to meet him at his office. I promptly went to his office with a friend of mine, and he listened to us patiently. We gave an idea about a placement website which companies could use and recruit people. He was fine with the idea and very soon, eight of my friends started working on the idea but after two months, I was the only one left!

That was when I realised that I needed some experience in a company to start something on my own. So, I decided to do an internship with Raj Shankar's company even while studying.

After classes were over at four in the evening, I used to travel two hours to his office and work there. It was a great experience for me as I got involved in numerous events on entrepreneurship the company conducted at many places.

An entrepreneur is born

My first stint as an entrepreneur was starting a food stall selling vada pav and jal jeera at the cultural fest in my college. We didn't have the capital to have a stall. So, six of us pooled in Rs 50 each and printed posters in black and white saying we would sell vada pav at the fest, and if students booked in advance, they could get them for a discounted price of Rs 8.

We went to classes and sold tokens for 1000 vada pav, and collected Rs 8000. Then we told the college authorities that we had already sold tokens and we were in need of a stall. Though they refused first saying, 'no stalls for students', seeing our enthusiasm they gave us a free stall.

We had huge sales for three days, and we made a profit of Rs 20,000!

That was my first entrepreneurial venture, and I was 17 years old then.

Internship to get experience

I was sure then that I would be an entrepreneur after my studies but before I started my own business, I wanted to gain more experience. So even while studying, I decided to work with the Amar Group of industries, again, after college hours. I persuaded my friend Sudeep Sabat also to join the company.

When I told the CEO, I didn't want any salary, he said, 'I will give you a nominal salary; you work as my Executive Assistant'.

His office was at the Industrial Estate at Ambathur, quite far from my college. He used to send us to Hyderabad for marketing during weekends. After that, more travels to many more places happened.

Yes, life was tough for us, after all we were college students and we had to study for the exams. Working after college left with us just 4 to 5 hours of sleep every day. I was not a college topper but I used to score 70-75% which was quite good.

Food sector appeals

One day, I decided that whenever I start my own business, it would be in the food sector. I am a foodie who loves Indian vegetarian food. The success of vada pav made me decide that that was where I was going to work in future.

When we were in the 3rd year, we had to make a trip to Delhi and there we were shocked at the price of a masala dosa. It was Rs130. When we asked the restaurant owner why it cost so much, he said, to get a south Indian cook to make good dosas, he had to pay a lot.

I wondered if we could have a machine that could print dosa like we take print outs. Sudeep also liked the idea.

We conceptualised a small machine that would 'print food like the printer does'.

When I suggested the idea to the CEO of Amar group, he was quite enthusiastic and gave the factory premises at the industrialist estate to experiment on the machine. Sudeep and I started designing.

To design the machine, first I observed how a dosa is made. You disperse batter, spread it, apply oil on it and when crisp, remove it from the tawa. After that, clean the tawa with water. I wanted the machine we design to do all this.

We started work on the machine with Rs 70,000 I had saved while working as an intern with the Amar group. I was naive to think that

I could make the machine in about Rs 50,000 but the budget went up. Then we managed to convince our college to sponsor my work and the college gave us Rs 120,000.

After that, both of us thought and worked only on this project. We went to the factory and worked with the factory workers on the prototype, till the place closed at 7pm. It was not a romantic experience making the machine. We were travelling a lot, and working really hard with very little sleep. Because we worked with the machines in the factory, our dresses used to get dirty and since we stayed in the hostel, we had to wash them ourselves. By the time we came back, the mess would be closed and we had to make our own food. We survived on Maggi noodles.

Those were tough days. We had only two things in our lives; attending college and working on the dosa machine.

First dosa, a disaster

After three months, the machine was ready and all the factory workers at Amar group were eager to see how a machine made dosa. It was a disaster, and the factory workers instead of encouraging us said, "come on, you guys will never make it!"

The workers genuinely believed that the machine would never work and lost interest in the project.

The long hours of travel was also taking a toll on our health. So we decided to shift our project to a place near the college.

Luckily, for us, the redesigned machine soon started making good dosas and it took less than a minute for the machine to make a dosa!

Now, what to do with the machine?

We found a street side vendor selling idlis and made a deal with him; that I and my friend would make dosas with the machine and he would sell them.

The machine made 5 dosas first and all the five dosas got sold in a jiffy. We were very happy. We were not making any money but we were happy when people bought the dosas made from our machine, and appreciated it. The customers didn't know that the dosas were made by a machine. We were not sure how they would react if we told them the truth.

The problem now was, only we knew how to operate the machine. But at least we understood what could be done to make it commercially viable.

That was when I came to know that the Central Food Technological Research Institute (CFTRI), Mysore, has already produced an automated dosa machine. But it was huge and what we had in mind was a small one, like a normal microwave oven.

Getting a prize for innovation

In 2012, the National Institute of Technology (NIT) Trichy had organised an international competition where students from 16 countries participated, and our dosa machine was selected for the first prize in the innovation category.

That led to Indian Angel Networks coming forward to incubate our product. Along with that, we got our first mentor in Hari Balasubramaniam.

Starting a private limited company

After incubation, Sudeep Sabat, Sudarshan Lodha and I started a Private Ltd company, Mukunda Foods Pvt Ltd and registered it in May 2012.

By August, a prototype of the new small machine, which was 10% bigger than the standard microwave oven, was ready. In the meantime, I also patented the dosa machine.

Enthused by the industry response, we charted out plans for the future, that once we got the funds, we would start manufacturing and enter the market. In the first six months, we would make around 200 machines and after that, we would scale up. We were sure that we would be able to sell our dosa machine in thousands.

Those were our dreams before we entered the real market as entrepreneurs.

Passing out of college and the real test starts

We passed out of college with dreams of making it big as entrepreneurs. We were no longer students and were expected to work and make a living.

And the real examination started then.

When we passed out of college, we had the prototype ready but the problem was, only Sudeep or I could operate it. It meant the prototype we had was not commercially viable; we had to fix some of the technical issues so that anybody could operate the machine.

In October when we got money from our investors, we started working in Chennai. But then, Chennai had long hours of power cuts in November 2013. So we moved to Bangalore where the power situation was much better.

Because we did not have lots of investor's money, we knew we had to be very cautious about using it. So we found a small place for our office. Both of us stayed as paying guests and took just Rs 15,000 as our salary. We did so many things to save money; like when we wanted to hire a fabricator for the company to help in welding, instead of finding someone through an agent and pay him a commission, we pasted 'wanted' stickers at many places in Bangalore.

Before setting up a factory, we went to a factory and asked for some space to work, introducing ourselves as college students doing final year projects.

After two months, we got some space for a factory and hired a team of about 8-10 people that included an accountant, fabricators, R&D Engineer, welders etc. Monthly salary for all came to around Rs 3 lakh.

Our initial plan was to get a working prototype ready but it took us 9 months to get it made. Meanwhile, I was giving demonstrations to many hotels and restaurants, and the response from the industry was quite fantastic.

A few people gave us orders for the machine. In the next 6 months, we got 15-20 orders and what we did was collect an advance of Rs 50,000 for the Rs 1 lakh machine so we could streamline the machine.

At that time, we were almost running out of the investor money but we had to do quite a bit of corrections before we started manufacturing the machine. We also knew that it would take three more months to make those changes and by then, we realised we had money for only three months. We were in a Catch 22 situation.

We worked at a factory at night, which had a lathe and machinery as we didn't have the money to own a factory of our own then.

By the end of the third month, we did all the technical corrections and the product was ready for shipment. Were we relieved and happy? Not exactly. For three months, we didn't sleep at all, and were working so hard. At that time, we were so exhausted that we only wanted to sleep.

It was not that the moment the machines were ready, the problems were over. No. The first machine had to go to Uttarakhand and we found that we had to get a form signed from there and send it with the machine! Since we had a good relationship with the client, he got the form filled in and signed and sent to us; normally clients would not do that.

Finally, the first machine was shipped in August 2014. In the next two months, we shipped all the orders one by one, and I personally went and supervised the installation.

We also had a buyer from London for which I had to get another form. Next problem we encountered was, though our factory was in Bangalore, we had first registered it in Chennai. The offices in both the cities made me shuttle between Bangalore and Chennai quite a few times, and the running took so much time that my London order got cancelled.

I realised then that as an entrepreneur, you required a lot of patience to deal with the bureaucracy and the hurdles they create in front of you.

A man from Chattisgarh called me and said, the machine didn't work well and the dosas it made were horrible. He wanted us to take back the machine. I found out that he tried to make dosa batter with just rice and no udad dal. I had to also tell him that the batter had to ferment before making dosa.

I asked him, If you buy a Mercedes car and put water in it, will it run? Likewise, dosa machine makes good dosas only if the batter is properly made. Finally, I had to teach him to make dosa batter. Now, he sells hundreds of dosas everyday but the man who complained twenty times a day never made one call to thank us. That's how most clients are, we learnt slowly.

This experience made us write the conditions to be signed by the buyer before buying the machine!

But it gave us a lot of satisfaction to see something you made being used by people and making money! It was like looking at the baby you created when it starts crawling. For a moment, we forgot all the struggles we went through.

When we got some seed funding in two instalments, we decided to employ more people and delegate work. Otherwise, Sudeep and I were doing all the work. We were constantly working on innovating the product, and in every new batch, we tried to make them better and better. On an average, we were making 5-6 machines every month at that time. Sales were painstakingly slow and this is what happens to all hardware products. In the first year, we made sales of Rs 15-16 lakh. Once the revenue started increasing, we also took some more money as salary.

2015 dawns

When 2015 dawned, it was the second stage of our life as entrepreneurs. In the first stage, an entrepreneur has to prove himself with the product, and the second stage get involved in sustaining it by getting orders continuously and manufacturing without any break.

2015 also witnessed a gold rush for startups and we saw software companies getting millions of dollars as funding. We were doing good but companies with no business plan or proper work got huge amounts of money, while nobody wanted to invest in a hardware company. All these software companies had to just go and pitch an idea to get a cheque.

Those were the moments I regretted in being in the manufacturing sector. We asked ourselves, did we do a mistake by entering the hardware field? We saw software engineers sit and code and make lots of money and fame, and here we were toiling so hard, working late in the factories but the results were not that satisfactory. I stopped reading business newspapers because they affected my morale. We survived because we had customers, although we had no investors.

There were frightening times when we thought we would not last the next month but we survived all the scares slowly. In March 2015, we had almost no money in our bank account. An Expo was happening at that time in Delhi and we got 30 orders there and suddenly there was Rs 25 lakh in the account! We went to Delhi by train and came back by flight!

There were many such instances in our lives as entrepreneurs when we thought the next month would be the end of our life as entrepreneurs, and then some miracle happened to save us. I always told myself, somehow I was going to get over the crisis and take the company forward, and it was that conviction that helped us tide over all the crises.

An entrepreneur needs passion in the beginning but as you move ahead, you need a lot of will power to stay afloat. By end 2015, when we saw all those paperless startups closing down, we were happy that we were in the manufacturing sector and from 1-2 orders in the beginning of 2015, we were getting 15-16 orders a month by the year end.

In 2015, our R&D team started working on a domestic Dosa machine, after we started getting so many enquiries. By the end of 2015, we were ready with a domestic dosa machine too.

Now in mid-2016, we have four offices in India with our manufacturing unit in Bangalore, 55 people work for us, and we sell around 30 machines a month each worth Rs 1.5 lakh.

That way, we are a million dollar revenue company, and 30% of our revenue comes from selling our machine abroad. We have our footprint in 16 countries. We are proud that a 'Made in India' product is being sold in so many countries outside India. It is not that all of them have bought to make our dosas. In Germany, one restaurant bought it to make pancakes.

Meeting Prince William and Kate

We were lucky to be one of the four hardware manufacturers to be invited at the Expo organised for Prince William and Kate by the British High Commission in association with the UK Trade and Investment Council. The brief from Kate and William before coming to India was that they wanted to meet a few product companies and not software companies.

There are very few product companies as startups in India, and we happened to be one of the few. That was how we were invited to have a demonstration for them. We thought it was a great opportunity for us to showcase our machine to the world on such a platform.

I was pleasantly surprised to see both of them taking time with each startup. While they spent five minutes with me, Kate asked me about how dosa was made in the machine and how dosa batter was made. William wanted to know what my future plans were for the startup, whether we had any plans for the UK, whether we had any clients in London etc. They were genuinely interested to know about the machine and it was not just a photo op.

I told them how dosa was made and they themselves made the dosa. I told them, it was so easy to make that even a Prince could make it! The High Commission told me in advance that the Royals would not eat in public. Still I took my chance and said, if you went back from India without tasting the dosa, it would be a shame. Then the Prince took a piece and ate it, and asked Kate whether she would like to have. She said, she was full and didn't want then.

William said, it was a wonderful machine, and then Kate said she wanted one in the Palace but after they left, despite my enquiries, I didn't hear from the palace again. The time spent with William and Kate gave us a lot of visibility internationally and we got lots and lots of calls from all over the world.

Four years

It is easy to describe the difficult times we experienced in the last four years as challenges now, but when you went through them, they were really difficult. There were many times we felt like leaving everything, so that all the struggles would end but we persisted.

The truth is, to build a consumer brand in India is very difficult even now. To meet the expectations of consumers in today's times when they are exposed to the best in the word is also very tough.

But we are sure that we would succeed in our ultimate vision of becoming the complete kitchen robotics company from India. Our R&D department is working towards that vision!

Returning Kuruvai to the Menu

Generally, educated youngsters do not show much interest in carrying on the farming tradition of their forefathers but one 29-year-old chucked his job as a networking professional in Delhi to be a farmer in Kerala. Moreover, he has chosen to farm without the use of pesticides which is organic or natural farming.

His dream, he says, is to attract as many youngsters as possible to farming so that we can save the environment and also assure better living.

This networking professional turned farmer is Tibin Parakal from Thrissur in Kerala.

Tibin Parakal chose to quit networking to be an organic farmer

annakairali

Earth Perma-culture Agro-ecology

THOUGH MY father was a farmer, he discouraged me from being one. In fact, I was forced to study Information Technology and Networking but my heart was in farming. He was of the opinion that there was no life for a farmer in modern times. I disagreed with him totally but, at the time I had no choice.

Even while studying, I was more interested in trekking to the interiors of nature and spending time with animals and trees. Nature always fascinated me and that could be why I was interested in farming.

When I had to go to Delhi to work as a networking professional, I was heartbroken but then my father was happy that I did not become a farmer like him.

From the cradle of nature, I was thrown into the concrete jungle that is Delhi, and from day one, I felt suffocated. I didn't see human beings around me; only machines that worked to earn lots of money.

The mountains I climbed, the butterflies I counted, the streams I swam, the jungles I walked along; all called me back. The urge to go back to nature was very strong. But there was no way I could chuck the job I had and go back at that time.

Coming back to Kerala to start an organic restaurant

When I was a student, I had seen a friend of mine running an organic restaurant in Trivandrum where my friends and I used to hang out. I liked the idea and admired his courage to start something like that, way back in the 1990s. At that time itself, I had this desire at the back of my mind to work on similar lines.

When I got so fed up of my mechanical life in Delhi, I started contacting my friends and began planning an organic restaurant in Trissur. I hid my plans from my parents as I knew they would be horrified if their son quit a well-paying job in Delhi to start a 'hotel' in Trissur. I only discussed the viability of the idea with my friends, one of whom was George K Jose who had just joined Infosys in Bangalore.

After months of planning through mails and phone, finally, George, Aneesh and I decided to plunge in. In 2010, we pooled in one lakh rupees to start our very first venture, an organic restaurant called Pathayam, in Trissur.

Only when I came back, did my parents come to know of what I was going to do. Naturally, they were horrified. They tried their best to dissuade me from my doing something unthinkable and blackmailed me to go back to Delhi.

I also tried blackmail tactics to scare them, saying, 'If you want to see me alive till I am 60, let me do what I want to. But if I continue to work in Delhi, you will see me only till I am 35!'

Finally they had no option but remain silent.

The restaurant, Pathayam opened during Onam.

It was a great day for us; realisation of our dreams. We were so excited and dreamed that we were going to be successful from day one. To cut cost, we employed only the cooks; serving and the rest of the work was done by the three of us, and some of our friends also joined us on the first day. The idea of youngsters resigning their well-paying jobs and starting an organic restaurant attracted a lot of publicity in the media even before we opened.

We chose an evening as our opening day. Because of the publicity, people thronged to our place on the first day. We decided to offer people something unique and served five types of *puttu* like ragi, wheat, vegetable, corn etc.

Hundreds of people came to the restaurant; in fact, they had to wait outside as we didn't have enough space to accommodate all. It was unprecedented, beyond our expectations.

What heartened us that night was that every single person who visited us appreciated our efforts and also the food we served.

In no time, we were making a revenue of Rs 10,000 daily with a profit of around Rs 5000-6000. Unfortunately, the happy days did not last long.

Our dreams were shattered when we had to close down the restaurant because of some construction work in the vicinity. From the time we knew we had to close down, we hunted for a new appropriate place to continue our project. But we couldn't find another place within our budget and finally, we had to abandon the project with a heavy heart. I can only say what started with so much excitement and fanfare ended dramatically.

Choosing to be a farmer

But I was not dejected by the failure of our first venture. I had always wanted to be a farmer, and I thought it was a good opportunity to chase my first dream. In a way, we started in the reverse order; instead of starting with organic food made without any chemicals, our first step should have been natural farming itself.

What George and I did to prepare ourselves for farming was attend a five-day seminar on Zero Budget Natural Farming, by Subhash Palekar from Maharashtra.

The seminar was an eye opener for us; we were bowled over by Palekarji's ideas. Nature lovers like us found that he understood the real vibrations of nature more than us. In those five days, it was not farming that he taught us; he made us understand and feel the pulse of nature. He introduced us to the minutest living beings in nature. We understood that we could do a lot for nature and society.

Coming back from the seminar, we were all geared up to start farming. But the question was, where was the land?

My father had been farming on several acres of land for years but what we wanted to do was organic farming. We had no inclination to do conventional farming; we wanted to experiment with natural farming based on what we had learnt from Palekarji.

My father was shocked to hear about natural farming, and was not at all in favour of such experiments. He asked me, 'Do you think we are fools? I have been cultivating paddy for the last several years and are you saying we don't know anything? Even with pesticides, our yield is only this much, and you want to show us that without pesticides, you can have more yield?'

He was literally laughing at us. I begged him for a small piece of land so that we could do our experiment, just once. Reluctantly, he agreed to give us 10 cents of land (0.1 acre). Perhaps he wanted to see what his 'crazy' son and his friend were going to do!

Natural farming

In 2011, finally we realised our dream of becoming farmers. We first planted paddy in the 10 cents of land using the seeds of an ancient variety of rice called kuruvai, which was cultivated by the adivasis. After a lot of enquiries, we went to an adivasi village and collected the seeds from them. Kuruvai had almost disappeared from Kerala society and nobody even knew about it when we tried to get its seeds.

Once we had the seeds, we tilled the land and did the planting also ourselves.

What we planned to follow was Zero budget natural farming which needed only one kilo of cow dung for 10 cents of land. But we must have the cow dung and urine from the pure breed cows and not cross-breeds. From where to get cow dung and urine from pure breed cows was the next question.

With great difficulty, we found one person in the village who had such cows and I went on my motorbike to collect the cow dung and urine from him.

Instead of pesticides which other farmers used, we had something we call Amrut: the Jeevamrutha solution made of cow dung, cow's urine, jaggery, flour, soil and water, created by Palekarji.

Palekarji's idea of natural farming taught us that one gram of cow dung and urine of pure bred cows contains 300-500 crore micro organisms. But the cow dung of the cross-breed cows contains only 40-50 lakh micro organisms.

The Jeevamrutha solution that is added to the crop acts on the micro-organisms and help them multiply in large numbers.

Crop shocks conventional farmers

When our crop grew, it was a shock to everyone. Our paddy was much healthier, greener and bigger than the one cultivated by my father using chemical pesticides.

Our paddy looked healthy, and when the paddy of the nearby areas got infected, ours remained unaffected. That was when my father and the other farmers realised there was something right in what we did.

My father was indeed shocked when we got more yield than he had ever got in his life!

That was our first success in farming as natural organic farmers.

We decided to keep most of the first yield as seeds for the next season. We also distributed the seeds among other farmers. We are happy to say that today many farmers in Kerala cultivate kuruvai from the seeds we had distributed.

My biggest triumph was converting my father to organic farming. Today my father cultivates Kuruvai on his entire one-acre plot and follows zero budget natural farming!

In a way, we brought back Kuruvai to the people of Kerala from wilderness. Today, fans of Kuruvai include the former Chief Minister of Kerala, VS Achuthanandan, actors Mammootty and Srinivasan. In fact, we inspired the film actors also to start farming and we became their consultants.

Farming in more land

After our first success, we expanded cultivation from the 10 cents of land we had borrowed from my father to another two acres of land taken on lease. We made a profit of Rs 50,000 in the second year.

Successes in the first two yields gave us more confidence and we increased our land holding to 25 acres of land. This time the yield was worth more than Rs 15 lakh.

That's when we realised that we need to have a marketing system also in place and not just farming. Because of faulty marketing, we ended up with a loss of Rs 7 lakh.

But we were not disheartened. We knew the loss was due to marketing failure and not farming.

Focusing on promoting organic farming

By 2015, we knew that just the three of us involved in organic farming would not change the farming scenario; we had to involve many more farmers into the fold. So, we decided to focus on three areas to popularise organic farming; one is farming itself, then promoting through various initiatives and the third is, marketing. One of our initiatives was starting a magazine called *Anna Kairali* through which we want to attract people to organic farming and an alternate lifestyle. We invested around Rs 10-15 lakh for starting the magazine.

2015 has been, in a way, a good year for us as whatever we wanted to do happened 'organically'. Today, we farm paddy in 20 acres of land in Palakkad, in another 7 acres of land in Kattapana in Wayanad, we have cardamom, coffee etc. and near Munnar, we have 8 acres of land where we cultivate around 500kg vegetables every week. We also cultivate vegetables in another 4 acres of land in Muvattupuzha.

Organic farming consultancy service

With the idea of popularising the concept, we have also started a consultancy service on organic farming under the name Anna Kairali in early 2016. The idea came when we realised there was only so much that we could do. So it is our duty to popularise organic farming and attract more and more people into this. Also, we learnt so many things by trial and terror in these six years which we can now pass on to others in a capsule format!

What our consultancy service does is convert land owned by others into an organic farm and hand it back to the person. This is to encourage those who have land to convert it to organic farms so that not only they but the people of the state also benefit from it.

So far, it was those who work in the Middle East, who have shown interest in this endeavour. They want a cultivated land for them to stay when they come back to Kerala for good. In the first few months of us starting the service, at least 15 proposals have come asking us to convert their land as organic farms. There are also many young men who approach us to learn farming. In 2015, people from 15 countries like Canada, France, Brazil, Sweden, South Africa, England etc. came to us to learn about organic farming.

If we want to feed 1,000 families for an entire year, we have to cultivate paddy in at least 350 acres of land. That is why we want as many young men to come into this field as we do not consider anyone as our competition and there cannot be any competition as the need is much, much more.

Now, we are able to make a profit of Rs 1 lakh every month, we put back the rest of our income into farming itself.

Farming today

Unlike in the past, with mechanisation, farming is not a difficult profession these days. One person can easily manage 10 acres of land and he can make at least Rs 3 lakh a month. Not only that, the kind of respect an organic farmer gets from society is tremendous.

What our consultancy service does is, we either develop land and pass it on to the owner, or we manage the land with our labourers. We have all the machines and tools needed for farming and also a labour force of 18 people with us. Our entire work force is from West Bengal and not Kerala.

Award from the government of India

It was an extremely humbling and satisfying moment for us when we won the Environmental award from the Government of India under the Swachch Bharat Mission initiative. The award was in appreciation of our effort in natural farming because in a way, we are protecting nature through natural farming.

Farmer's club

We have formed a Farmers Club of youngsters, and we had a state conference of young farmers in Trissur in 2016 and around 500 young farmers assembled here along with Madhav Gadgil. Perhaps it was for the first time that all of us who had moved from other jobs to farming, had assembled like this.

We had also invited many college students to make them realise that we were also like them before we became farmers. We want to inspire them to look at farming as a good career option. If we need healthy living, more and more youngsters should take up farming as an option.

Our life is dedicated to farming and we know we will survive as farmers but we want others also to do zero budget natural farming. That is why we work as advisers. Our desire is to convert around 10,000 acres of land to organic farming this year. If we can convert all the rubber plantations as vegetable and fruits farms, we can supply vegetables not only to this state but all over India itself.

The Ideas Man

Not many boys dream of becoming social entrepreneurs when in school. Not many say 'no' to well-paying placements in college.

Not many youngsters go around the city collecting food and serving it to the hungry.

Not many travel by bus to lecture school children about the need to not waste food.

Twenty three-year-old AG Padmanabhan is different from most young men his age.

His earliest inspiration was APJ Abdul Kalam.

The former President was in Salem and Padmanabhan, who was in Class VIII then, was one of the few students selected to be part of his audience.

Inspired by Kalam's Vision 2020 speech, Padmanabhan and some of his friends put together 20 ideas that India should follow to become a developed country by 2020.

Apart from Abdul Kalam, his teachers encouraged and inspired Padmanabhan to do something for society.

AG Padmanabhan is known as the Nofoodwaste man but that is just one of the many startups he has built

NO FOOD WASTE

WHEN I was in 8th standard, I was chosen by my school to listen to Abdul Kalam speak in Salem and I was mesmerised by what he said. He spoke about his dreams and what we as students could do to realise his dreams. I was so inspired by Vision 2020 that I wanted to contribute something to society and make India a developed nation by 2020.

That is why I wanted to be a social entrepreneur and make my country a great nation. As a part of my ambition, I started participating in all the community events when I was in school. My teachers and principal encouraged me to be a leader and work for society, and it continued in college too.

I concentrated on my studies, scored very good marks in school and got admission in Coimbatore's prestigious Government College of Technology to study Production Engineering in 2010.

I chose Production Engineering as I felt it could add value to my journey as an entrepreneur. The course taught me innovation, marketing, entrepreneurship and a little bit of management.

Alternate Wood, and an award

My first experiment as an innovator was when I was in my second year in college; I developed an 'alternative wood'. A huge tree plantation drive was taking place in Coimbatore at that time. I knew we had to cut trees for various needs. That was when I thought, why we could not have something that could be used as an alternative to wood?

There were the three of us, Hari Prakash, Dinesh and me and we used to call ourselves PHD (the first letters of their names) in college. We had taken a vow that, every year, we would develop something that would be of some use to the public or college. Maybe because of our enthusiasm, our college principal and teachers gave us permission to go out and explore things on our own. To them also, we were PHD!

In fact, I spent less than 20 days in college every semester. Most days were spent either in some factory or symposium or conference to learn things.

With an idea to develop alternate wood, we sat down to work on it. We made a composite material from banana fibre, coconut shell powder, sugarcane waste etc, bound them together by soya binder, cow dung and resin. Believe it or not, the end product had 90 to 95% of the qualities of wood and, after lamination, could be used exactly like wood. Our lab was our hostel room and our professor also helped us with a lot of inputs.

What people call R&D is nothing but trial and error and we did a lot of trial and finally, after four-five months, we were successful in coming out with a strong product.

This invention got us an invitation from the International Green Campus Conference organised by international universities in collaboration with the Pondicherry University in Pondicherry. There were students from 50 countries and our composite wood, which we named Natural Fibre Wood Composite, won the best innovative natural product award. It was a huge motivation for us.

We are now in the process of fine-tuning the composite wood so that we can produce it on a bigger scale.

The Green Club and Paperless Conferences

The conference in Pondicherry was an eye opener for us in another way. We saw that hundreds of pamphlets were used in conferences but they were not read by most of the attendees. The pamphlets just floated around, a lot of paper being wasted and also that many trees. That is when we decided to start a Green Club and promote paperless conferences.

In 2013, we organised a conference in our campus and named it Prakruti and, in the entire conference that had 1200 participants, not a single sheet of paper was used; everything was digital and online. The banners were made of cloth. The paperless conference was a huge success and inspired many other colleges in Coimbatore to follow suit.

Innovate! Innovate! Innovate!

We also came out with a mission for our Green Club; and it was not just enough to plant trees and that we had started the club to plant trees but produce more 'green engineers'. That is why we decided to start the Student Research Foundation in our campus.

When we were working on composite wood, we lacked proper guidance and funding. SRF plans to help students innovate, network and get funding for their projects.

We want to inspire young engineers to innovate and become entrepreneurs. That is one of our mottos.

A student, and a teacher

While I was an engineering student, I used to teach school children STEM (Science, Technology, Engineering and Mathematics) learning, which is quite popular in the United States. There is another reason for me becoming a teacher. I could use the earnings from this part-time job in my research projects.

I didn't want to disturb my parents' finances for my education. This was the way I funded my studies. I also taught government school children about the need to innovate, save the environment and become entrepreneurs. That was my way of inspiring young children, and it was done for free.

As much as I worked, I talked also!

In fact, when the placements were going on in my college, I was in a government school taking free classes. I had absolutely no plans to take up a fancy job with an MNC but my mother and friends forced me to attend at least one interview, so I did. I got the job. Of course, I didn't join.

Here comes SPICE

I was doing so many things under many different names. So I felt it was necessary to bring all under one umbrella. That was how SPICE (Society Promoting Innovation, Creativity and Entrepreneurship) came into being, bringing Green Club, SRF and other ideas I had under it.

SPICE started functioning two days after I graduated.

Under SPICE, we have created programmes for school curriculum that will encourage innovation and entrepreneurship; two schools have already adopted the curriculum.

Food for eating, not wasting

When I went to teach in schools, I used to spend a lot of time with school students during their lunch break. That was when I noticed that many of them dumped food into dustbins without even a second thought.

One afternoon, after all the students left, I weighed the food they had thrown away; it weighed 18 kilos.

This got me really worried. It always upsets me when people waste food. We have thousands of people in India who go hungry every day.

Then, I happened to be at a wedding and there too a lot of food was wasted.

One day, I asked the waiter to pack half of the biryani I had ordered at a restaurant. I gave that packet of untouched food to an old lady who was sitting outside the restaurant. I still cannot forget the smile on her face.

That very night , I registered Nofoodwaste.in. I also formulated a plan to make children aware of the importance of not wasting food.

On 16 October 2014, International Food Day, I went to many schools and spoke to the children about why they should not waste food. I told them that 15% of India's population go hungry every day, and we are on the top of the global charts when it comes to hunger and malnutrition. At the same time, in a city like Bengaluru, 940 tonnes of good untouched food is wasted annually in marriages alone. Naturally, the children were shocked to hear these statistics.

I started writing to the schools in Coimbatore requesting the students to audit the amount of food wasted in their schools everyday. Initially, 30 schools responded. I trained the student representatives of those schools on how to audit wasted food and how to spread awareness among other students. I also trained them to use the wasted food as compost for the school.

I found that, in a school with less than 1,000 students, the daily food waste was about 10 to 12 kilos. There are 300 schools in and around Coimbatore so you can imagine the amount of food wasted daily! It was 9 lakh kilos a year!

We also encouraged some of the schools to develop compost out of food waste, plant trees and use it as manure.

Collecting food and distributing it

When I came to know that people associated with wedding planning and other functions didn't know whom to contact when they had extra food, I created a helpline number.

It is not enough to just to collect untouched food but it should also go to the needy. I also identified the poor localities in the city where the food could be distributed.

By January 2015, I could put things in place and started getting calls to collect food.

The problem was I was a one-man army.

Those were tough days as our company was going through a crisis. I wondered why I was all alone when I was trying to work for a good cause. There I was, going to various places, packing extra food and carrying them in shopping bags and travelling in public transport to distribute the food. I continued like this till March.

The number of calls multiplied but I didn't have anyone to help me. That was when Dinesh of our PHD came back to join me, and another college mate, Sudhakar M also joined us. We managed to buy a second-hand Honda Activa and named it Foodiva for our food travels. With the scooter at our disposal, travelling became easier.

By 2016, our plan to buy a Maruti van to transport food and link self-help groups working for the poor through a mobile app came true. It was sponsored by the Rotary Club. Now we have a food storage space, two people to take care of it and coordinate and with the van also at our disposal, we are able to feed a minimum of 500 people everyday in Coimbatore.

Along with the nofoodwaste project, we also started waste management. The money we get from selling dry waste comes handy to pay the salaries of the people who work for us in the nofoodwaste project.

This idea can be replicated in any city by organising an awareness drive through rallies, marketing the helpline number and looking for sponsors for a vehicle. We are already working in seven cities.

Ideas, more ideas

It has been a habit with me to write down every new idea in my diary when it strikes me, and then buy a domain for it. This is done with the hope that one day, I will be able to execute the idea.

It is like a hobby for me. I have a ten dimensional approach in social entrepreneurship but I have been able to work only in food, education, and sanitation so far. Besides the nofoodwaste project, I have decided to restrict myself in three areas; educating school children, innovation and solid waste management.

On Swami Vivekanada's birthday in 2016, we started Edudharma, an online platform where people can crowd-fund the education of deserving poor students. We put the details of the students only after a local NGO verifies their credentials and then, anyone can donate and it can even be as low as Rs 50.

The idea to start Edudhrama came from our experience in our college where we have seen many students finding it difficult to pay fees. We used to collect money and pay their fees.

Another project I have started is Toilets First as a part of the Swachch Bharat Mission and we have already constructed 1,500 toilets. I plan to work in solid waste management to create 'zero waste campuses'.

I have so many ideas and I am not able to implement all of them. I feel 24 hours is not enough for me.

My biggest disappointment

My dream is to make India a 'no food waste economy', no open defecation country and promote sustainable ideas.

I want to make my father feel proud of what I am doing but my father, a central government employee, was dead against his son becoming an entrepreneur.

I learnt simplicity, understanding the difference between need and want and doing things properly from him, but the cold war between us is still going on. Though I have been doing this for the last four years, I haven't had a single word of appreciation from my father. In fact, he doesn't even speak to me. I am waiting for the day when he will appreciate my work. I am sure that, one day, he will be proud of me.

I became a social entrepreneur after meeting and hearing Dr Abdul Kalam but one of the disappointments in my life is, I and my team were to meet Dr Kalam on 31 July at 7.30 pm but he died a day before. I felt like an orphan then. I do not know why destiny played such a cruel joke on us. But I will make India a 'no food waste' country by 2020 and fulfil Dr Kalam's Vision 2020.

Promoting Khadi, His Mission in Life

This is the story of a 25-year-old engineer who worships Mahatma Gandhi and Rajaji, not MS Dhoni and Virat Kohli.

He walks around in a khadi kurta and mundu (dhoti), not a pair of jeans and a T-shirt.

His passion is not to be a financially successful entrepreneur, but to be one that promotes and popularises khadi. He wants to do so by selling khadi jeans online to youngsters like him who are otherwise reluctant to buy khadi.

Luxury travel is not for him; he always sits in the unreserved class.

He doesn't have a wardrobe full of clothes; just three sets of kurtas and mundus.

He has also pledged to plant a sapling for every pair of denim jeans he sells. It is his way of conserving the environment.

He is Siddharth Mohan Nair, an engineer from Palakkad who is studying to be a lawyer and preparing to be an IAS officer. He is also the accidental founder of DesiTude, an online platform that sells khadi jeans.

And this is his interesting and unusual story.

Siddharth Mohan Nair of DesiTude

THOUGH MY father was a businessman, I had absolutely no interest in becoming one; my ambition even as a small child was to be an IAS officer. I was a three-year-old when my father moved to Palakkad from Mumbai. On Independence day that year, he took me to the maidan where celebrations were taking place. I was so fascinated to see many men in uniform marching past while saluting a lady. So impressed was I by the exercise that I asked my father who the lady was. He told me she was the District Collector, an IAS officer. Seeing her being saluted by so many members of the armed forces was so inspiring for me that I decided at that moment that I also wanted to be an IAS officer.

And then came my 10th Standard board exams. I performed poorly and was disheartened as I grew ever more convinced I would never become an IAS officer; I felt I didn't have the ability in me to pass the exam.

So I decided to become an engineer and joined the Tamil Nadu Agricultural University in Coimbatore. I chose Energy and Environment as my field because of my ardent interest in nature and agriculture. Unlike the other kids of my generation, I was never into video games or TV; I grew up playing in the mud amidst trees, paddy fields and nature.

Even as a school student, I had this desire to conserve energy and not abuse the environment. So obsessed was I about saving energy that even when Palakkad baked in the summer heat, I refused to switch on the fans. Another obsession of mine was going around switching off lights and fans when nobody was in the room. So, in a way, it was but a natural progression for me to go to college to study Energy and Environment. I am also against heating up water or cooling it down; only natural water for me—again, my small way of saving energy.

The lecture that turned him vegetarian

When I was a student in Coimbatore, I happened to listen to a lecture by Rajendra Pachauri of The Energy and Resources Institute (TERI). It had such an impact on me that I turned vegetarian that day. He told us that the carbon footprint of a meat eater was much higher than that of a vegetarian, and that we had to spend 15 litres of water to get a kilogram of meat on our plates. He said that if we wanted to be more environmentally friendly, it was better to be vegetarian. As a lover of nature and the environment, I could not help but agree and put his suggestion into practice.

Meeting Anna Hazare, working for Kiran Bedi

My plan was to study further on environment and do something more in that field. But it was not to be. When I was in my final year of Engineering, the Anna Hazare movement started in Delhi. I was taken aback and delighted at the sight of all of these people gathering and waving the national flag.

A friend of mine and myself arranged a similar meeting in Coimbatore, but the college authorities rebuked us for organising a movement against the government in a government college. I realised then that if we faced such opposition to arrange such a small gathering, those in Delhi must be dealing with so much more!

I decided to go to Delhi and be a part of the movement, and also do my final year internship at TERI in Delhi. The Anna Hazare movement was at its peak then, and I used to go to the maidan whenever I had the time. I also wrote an e-mail to Kiran Bedi, telling her I was an intern at TERI who would like to volunteer for the movement. To my surprise, I received a reply from her within two minutes, asking me to come along and meet her. And in the end, instead of becoming a volunteer at the movement, I ended up working in her office. Though I refused to accept any money from her for the work I did, she said I should take money for the work I would be doing at her office and that I shouldn't take any money from my parents at this age.

I helped her collect information for the book she was writing on the Lokpal Bill, and consequently learnt a lot about the bill. I sat next to her for months, watching her work with such energy, dedication, sincerity and enthusiasm. Through the course of this period, she became a great influence and inspiration. I never saw her make anyone wait for her; as much as she valued her time, she attached a lot of importance to others' time.

Another major change that happened in my life during this period—due in no small part to my close proximity to her—was that I began to read a lot more. She had a huge library in her office, and encouraged me to read a selection she picked out for me. If I am a voracious reader today, it is all because of Kiran Bedi.

Civil Service Examination and joining AAP

She also encouraged me to attend coaching classes for the Civil Service Examination.

During this period, I also met Arvind Kejriwal with the intention of joining AAP. But he dissuaded me and asked me to focus on my education rather than join politics.

When I didn't get through the Civil Service preliminary examination, I decided to come back to Palakkad. My parents were happy that Kejriwal echoed what they had been telling me all along. He wanted me to be a civil servant, work for sometime and then think about joining a political party. Yet, after coming back to Palakkad, I started working for AAP there. But I gave up after a while when I felt disillusioned with the others in the local party. Anyway, because of all of the party work I was involved in, I didn't prepare well for the exam and did not clear it the second time either.

All of the research I had done for Kiran Bedi had got me interested in the law; as a result, I joined the Madras Law College in 2014. I supported myself through the course by writing articles for *The News Minute*, an online publication.

Influence of Gandhiji and Rajaji and getting interested in Khadi

During my time with Kiran Bedi and the Anna Hazare movement four years ago, I participated in a few fasts with them. Before each fast, we would all go to Rajghat to pray. Soon, I found myself going there every Sunday to pray. Some of Mahatma Gandhi's principles influenced me so much that I became a swadeshi and started dressing exclusively in khadi. I also took a vow that I would only tell the truth.

But when I got a chance to read about Rajaji, I became so fascinated by the man that I decided to change my attire to a kurta and mundu (dhoti). If he could pull off wearing traditional South Indian attire with dignity, why couldn't I? What attracted me about Rajaji's personality was, of course his intellect and strength of character; he could stand like a rock in front of a towering personality like the Mahatma even when he disagreed with the great man.

My family and friends were aghast to see me in a mundu. I was the subject of much ridicule, but nothing and nobody could change my decision. In fact, my attire created a variety of reactions wherever I travelled. Once, when I was on the Delhi metro, some small kids started singing lungi dance upon seeing me. But instead of feeling angry or embarrassed, I explained to them that I was not wearing a lungi but a mundu—a dhoti in their language.

So enthralled was I of Rajaji's life that my present to myself on my 23rd birthday was to visit the Tiruchengodu Gandhi Ashram he had established. He had stayed there in a hut for 4-5 years.

Though I had been wearing khadi for a couple of years at this point, this was the first time I got the opportunity to see khadi woven.

The village was starved of water, and many of the villagers had migrated to the cities for work. Those who were too old and weak to travel worked in the ashram. It was when I saw a very old man who could hardly see in spite of his thick glasses carry cotton fibre in to the ashram that I felt it was the duty of people like us to promote cloth people like him help weave.

I tried influencing people of my generation to use khadi but they were not impressed or influenced by my talk. I was nonplussed as to how I'd promote it, until I made a trip to Mumbai.

As I wore only khadi, in one of my travels to Mumbai, I went to the Khadi Bhandar to buy kurtas and to my surprise, I saw rolls of denim material made from Khadi. When I found out that it was only woven by the Rajkot Sarvodaya Sangh, I made a trip to Rajkot to see how the weavers worked.

What attracted me to khadi denim was the possibility that it could be used to make khadi popular among the young, thus making them move towards swadeshi clothing.

An entrepreneur is born

That is when I decided to become an entrepreneur and run a startup of my own.

I asked some of my friends to design a logo and create a Facebook page but I needed money to buy material initially. Luckily, a fixed deposit in my name matured at that time, and I then took a loan of Rs 30,000 from my mother.

And thus it came to be that I started my venture on the 22nd of March 2016. I bought material from Ahmedabad for Rs 20,000 and kept aside Rs10,000 for stitching it into jeans.

Later when I needed money to register the company and order labels, two of my friends came forward to invest Rs 10,000 each in the venture. They did it purely as friends and not as business partners.

I named my venture DesiTude. In April, I supplied 12 jeans; the initial orders came from my friends and cousins. But the articles in the *Kochi Post* and *Manorama Online* after Independence Day gave us a big boost. After that, strangers started enquiring and some began to place orders too.

Though some people are put off by us asking for measurements, I insist on that. As I have seen how people toil hard to make khadi material, I want as much human involvement when stitching the jeans too. That's why I insist on personal measurement so that the person who wears it gets the feeling that it was custom-made for him or her.

My plan is to expand the number of khadi items under the name DesiTude and not limit myself to Denim jeans alone. Only then will I be truly promoting khadi.

Though there were two designers selling khadi jeans at the time I started my venture, each pair were priced in the five figures; the sort of price that only a select few can afford to pay. If I want to promote and popularise khadi among the ordinary young Indians, it has to be within their reach. That's why I decided to price a pair of khad jeans at Rs 3,500.

Just three sets of dress

People ask me, isn't khadi expensive? As I have only three sets of clothes, I don't find it as expensive as people think. I chose three sets because of the influence Mother Teresa has had on me. I had read in her biography that she had only three sets of clothes, and I then decided to limit my number of dresses also to three. All of my mundus are white with a black border. That way, nobody could ask me if I had just worn the same clothes the previous day!

But when I travel, I wear a saffron khadi mundu because white is a colour that is difficult to maintain when travelling. Yes, there were instances of people mistaking me for a coolie because of my attire and they get flabbergasted to know that I am an engineer by profession!

Maybe I look odd selling denim khadi jeans while wearing a mundu. But my counter-argument is that my intention is to popularise the khadi material and not jeans. I can make khadi popular among those of my generation only by giving them what they want, jeans.

My dressing is a part of the swadeshi idealism I believe in. I believe in khadi; I also believe in our traditional attire, the mundu, which is vanishing completely from society. I don't believe that wearing western clothing is a requirement for modernity.

Life as an entrepreneur

Creating a Facebook page for DesiTude was easy but I had no idea how to promote my venture; even now, I do not know how to go about it in a professional manner. The truth is, though it's a startup, I do not look at DesiTude as a business venture.

This will never be my profession, my livelihood or a commercial venture. That is because I plan to become a lawyer if I do not clear the Civil Service Examination.

Through this venture, if I can help at least 2-3 villages, I will be extremely satisfied and happy. Khadi is my passion. The only idea behind this startup is to promote and popularise khadi; it's my mission in life, my passion, and a part of the ideals that drive me.